FINDING CLAIRE

FINDING CLAIRE

PAMELA HUMPHREY

For Mike

CHAPTER ONE

January 8, 2016 – 9:27pm

The night I woke up in the back of a van with my hands bound, my whole world changed. It was a Friday.

I opened my eyes and fought to remember how I ended up in a dark, moving vehicle. As if rising from the depths of a deep lake, I struggled, desperate for a glimpse of the familiar. Rope burned my wrists. I didn't have the presence of mind or the courage to formulate an escape. Panic rendered me useless as someone drove me to the middle of nowhere.

The kidnappers' most helpful accomplice, my own fear, held me prisoner. The worst part of it all, my mind hid memories from me. I didn't even know my own name.

A greasy, foul-smelling man marched me into a dark house. Images of how I'd be killed flashed through my mind when he shoved me into a putrid closet. Another man did his bidding, and talked incessantly. More than a day, being fed nothing but bologna sandwiches, I wallowed in that tiny space.

CHAPTER TWO

January 10, 2016 – 12:48am

I stumbled through the brush, ever conscious of the darkness pressing in on me. The flashlight did little to hold it off. With my hands tied together, I slugged through the night, fighting to stay on my feet.

The circle of light jostled as I moved. I tripped on fallen limbs as noises spurred me on faster. I tumbled, and my knees connected with a large rock, half-buried in the ground. My hands in front of me, I caught my fall. But my palm oozed blood where something sharp tore through my flesh.

Exhausted, I pulled cold, wet air into my lungs and struggled to my feet. The heavy mist plastered my clothes to my skin. But the wet ground absorbed the pounding of my footsteps, keeping the sound from echoing through the night.

Progress was impossible to measure in the grey haze. Everything my light touched looked the same. I prayed I wouldn't circle back to the house I'd left.

I pushed between juniper bushes, wincing as the evergreen branches scratched at my cheeks. As I cleared the trees, breath caught in my throat.

A house.

I approached it slowly, making sure it wasn't the same one I'd just left.

I picked my steps through the underbrush, then hurried up the three porch steps. I knocked, over and over, louder and louder. All my pleading accomplished nothing. I walked around the outside hoping for a glimmer of light in a window. But silence and darkness encased the house.

Tears stung my scratches as I continued my search for help.

Drips ran down my hand, leaving a trail of blood as I stumbled through the trees. The clouds above still clung to their rain. The smell of moist earth permeated the air. I glanced up and wished for a just a glimpse of the moon or stars. The darkness taunted me, mocking the fact that I was alone.

I clung to the flashlight as I zigzagged around a prickly pear cactus. The ones I didn't see left their marks on my legs. Tears filled my eyes, blurring my surroundings. I yelped as I snagged a barbed wire fence. The echo cackled as it scurried through the trees.

Leaves rustled nearby. I froze. The sense of something closing in tightened in my chest.

Eeeeeeeeeeee.

The screech of the owl sent terror pulsing through me. I pulled away from the wires, and my clothes tore. The whimper of an animal faded into the distance. I tried to forget that the blood and shreds would be easily visible in the daylight. I stared at the fence, desperately pleading for a way through. I tamped down the bottom wires with my foot and tried ducking under the other wires, but it didn't work. Finally, I dropped face first to the ground and slithered under the bottom wire. I swallowed my cry as the barbs scraped my back.

I pushed forward, my heart wanting to run, my feet hindered by limbs and rocks. I glanced behind me into the darkness, sure the men were in pursuit, following the sound of my pain.

Shivering, I stopped to catch my breath. Wisps of white appeared in front of me each time I released my hot breath into the night.

Something near me hit the ground. I whipped around, bumping the switch on the flashlight. I was plunged into a vat of ink.

A snapping sound carried through the air. I looked back expecting lights bouncing through the trees. Feeling around the flashlight, I found the switch. When the light clicked on, the shadows returned, my welcome companions.

The underbrush slowed my progress as I hiked away from captivity. Somewhere in the night safety called to me, like Heathcliff on the moors. *I'm hearing things.*

I walked a bit farther and stopped. I heard it again. Laughter. I turned my head and waited for the sound to return. Pushed down by the damp air, it couldn't have carried far. I tightened my grip on the flashlight and turned it off. Suffocated by the darkness, I scanned around me for light, any glimmer.

The wind blew, and for a moment, light appeared far off somewhere ahead. I hit the switch and surveyed to see what shielded the glow I'd seen. More juniper bushes. Their scent, pleasant only in small doses, clung to my clothes and hair like cheap cologne on an urban cowboy.

I shoved my way through the bushes, unsure of what lay on the other side, the light beckoning me forward. A house. My next step sent me skidding down. I bounced down the rocky incline on my hip, my tied hands useless to stop me. When I hit the bottom, my hip burned, and my head ached.

I crawled to a nearby boulder and used it to help me up. My legs were gelatin. When I stood, blood trickled down my face.

I limped toward the house, anticipating freedom from the rope and safety from the kidnappers. The sounds from before, clearer now, raucous laughter and men's voices, rang out from the haven in front of me. I hurried my pace.

Closer, I smelled food. My mouth salivated.

A crunching sound beneath my foot stopped me cold.

I pointed the flashlight down. Beer cans carpeted the ground.

I darted, still limping, toward the trees before my legs gave out. The hope of safety torn away left a gaping hole in my chest. The light and sounds, so welcoming at first, mocked my fear. The front door opened, illuminating me. Not yet to the trees, I kept moving but switched off the flashlight.

A man stepped out the door. His pee splashed on the leaves, and I prayed he wouldn't see me.

As I neared bushes, he shrieked, but I didn't stop until I was hidden.

"What's wrong, Gil?" A man called from inside the house. The *s* sliding into the word beside it.

"I saw someone."

Cackles and snorts erupted from inside. "He saw Bigfoot."

"Shut up! I know I saw someone. A woman, I think."

"Gil's little wife is sneaking out to check up on him."

Their conversation devolved into yelling, and then someone threw a punch. What wasn't safe before became outright dangerous. I pressed on, disappointment pouring out of my eyes. Blood, clothing, and now an eyewitness. *So much for leave no trace.* If I didn't find help before the sun crested the horizon, I'd be eating a bologna and mayo sandwich for breakfast again. My stomach wretched at the thought.

My hair snagged on a mangled branch, and I ducked to keep my eyes from being punctured. The circle of light just ahead of me, fear nipped at my heels. I had to keep moving. Beyond the beam, a shroud of darkness made it impossible to see if I'd walked in circles.

Desperation disguised as hope propelled me forward, trusting that the lack of familiar sights meant I'd pushed farther away from the closet.

I skirted around yet another stand of juniper bushes. My sobs escaped into the night before I could catch them. The whoosh of fluttering birds, disrupted from their roosting, echoed around me.

A solid rock wall blocked my path, the side of a hill sheared off, leaving the white rocky insides exposed. It was too steep to climb. I stumbled to a large rock and crumpled into a heap. Blood dripped from my gashes and scratches, dotting the limestone, leaving yet another marker along my trail.

I pointed the flashlight to the right. The stone continued farther than the light could reach. The other direction, the rock sloped into weeds and bushes several yards away.

Mustering the last remnants of strength from my tired muscles, I pushed myself off the rock and trudged to the left. I inched my way up a small incline. Exhausted, I sprawled on the damp ground. Cold and sore, I ached to be inside somewhere, to be safe and protected.

The chill of the wet earth permeated the skin on my cheek. My eyelids begged to close, the temptation to sleep growing stronger every second I spent on the ground. The sky opened up and thundering raindrops pounded me. The rain urged me to continue, promising to wash away my tracks.

I lifted my head. A cabin. Just a few paces ahead, a cabin sat nestled in the trees. Firelight flickered in the windows. Adrenaline coursed through me. I struggled to my feet.

The lure of safety pulled me forward, my footsteps nearly silent on the soggy ground. A cat jumped onto the window sill. My heart raced. I dragged my tired body to the door.

April 21, 1987

My Sweet Little Claire,

Your daddy suggested I write to you. He thought it might help me. This afternoon, he found me still in my pajamas, crying into my pillow. He slipped into the nursery without turning on the overhead light or opening the curtains. And after picking up the tissue wads scattered around the bed, he perched on the edge and rubbed my back.

It tortured him to see me so upset, but he understood. He pleaded in his soft, soothing voice for me to get up. (But that voice, that tender, I'll-take-care-of-you voice always makes me cry.) I managed to shift to a sitting position and lean against him to cry. He wrapped his arms around me and rocked gently, trying to say what he could to give me comfort. His shaking shoulders reminded me of how much he misses you, too.

He left work early and bought a birthday cake, a beautiful round cake with lots of layers. On the top was a 3. No names. No message. Just the number three. Circling the top and bottom edges of the cake were tiny blue flowers made of icing.

That cake remained in the middle of the table all day without either of us cutting it. I watched the back door and prayed that you would push it open, arms spread wide, happy to see us.

Do you still have your floppy rabbit? Do you still snuggle him to go to sleep? Your daddy still talks about the day he gave you that rabbit.

There is a story you need to know, but I hope you're home before you're old enough to read it. I wrote it out in the weeks just after you left so no matter when you returned, it would be ready.

Wherever you are, know your daddy and I both love you. We 'll never stop looking for you.

Love & Birthday Wishes,

Mommy & Daddy

April 21, 1988

My Dear Claire,

The sun didn't show up this morning. Raindrops pattered out a sad song on the porch.

How can you be four already?

Your daddy didn't go to work today. He suggested we shop for you. We spent hours at the toy store, but I didn't know if you liked dolls or kittens or blocks or hair bows. How can a mommy not know what her baby girl likes?

We bought you a cake. It was a big yellow flower. I cried while we sang happy birthday.

What we wouldn't give to see your big brown eyes again.

I wish you were never taken from me, from us.

Love always,

Mommy & Daddy

April 21, 1989

Happy Birthday, Claire.

I marked another X on the calendar. Like every other morning, I did it before breakfast. I'd rather mark days without food than days without you.

Your daddy suggested I write to you. He thought giving you updates of our life might hurry the time, draw you back somehow, and help me, too.

For this birthday, I had a special cake made for you. It looked like a princess with a frilly blue gown.

I miss you, princess.

Have you ever heard a story where the princess is snatched away and knights search and try to rescue her? You were the little princess, and you were taken from us by a beast. (You love him, not knowing what he's capable of. But I can't be anything other than honest with you. He's a beast.)

Where is he hiding you?

Your daddy, the brave knight, searched and searched. He promised not to give up until his last breath.

I moved into Grandma Betty's house. Daddy and I fixed up a bedroom for you. No matter when you come back, there will be a room for you here.

Your daddy and I send big Texas wishes for the happiest of birthdays. We miss you.

Love forever,

Mommy & Daddy

CHAPTER THREE

January 10, 2016 – 2:54am

Thud. Thud.

Alex winced as Bureau leaped onto his diaphragm and meowed in his face. "What do you want?" He moved the cat to the floor and shifted in the chair.

Bang, bang, bang.

He jumped up. His book landed in a wad of gnarled pages. "Who's there?" he called as he stumbled to the door. His foot caught the edge of the quilt, and it dragged behind him. He opened the door just enough to see her.

Muddy brown eyes pleaded for help. Blood streaked her forehead and clothes. She was soaking wet. Several strands of her brown curls lay matted against her tear-stained cheeks. *What the hell?* She shivered as raindrops pelted her. Her lips parted, but he didn't wait for her to speak. She needed help, his help.

He yanked open the door. "Who tied you up?" He reached to pull her inside, and she shrank back, her eyes wide with fear. He put his hands up and stepped back from the door. "I won't touch you. Come on in." His mind raced trying to figure out what kind of craziness had showed up at his door. He scanned the darkness behind her. *Are you being set up? This can't be real.* One glance at the woman in front of him left no doubt she was in real trouble.

She took one step inside and warily looked around the dimly lit room, her chest heaving.

"What happened to you?" He used a soft voice, trying to calm her and get answers.

She glanced toward the kitchen, then to the bedroom and office. *What's she looking for?* "I'm the only one here. Just me and the cat."

Her gaze finally settled on him. "Help me, please."

Without question, he planned to help her. "Of course. I'll get you to a hospital. What's your name?" *What happened to her? How long has she been outside?*

She shuddered and stared at the quilt on the floor. Tears welled up in her eyes, but her voice remained even. "I don't know who I am."

"We need to get you thawed out. You're freezing." He rubbed the cleft in his chin. "We need to call the police. My friend is an investigator with the local sheriff's office. I'll call him."

She nodded without looking at him.

Alex pointed to the fireplace, then slipped around her, careful not to brush against her. "And let's get that rope off you. Warm up by the fire while I grab the scissors." He ran to the kitchen and yanked a pair from the drawer. Before he was out of the kitchen, he stopped at the pantry. *You need to save the rope. DJ will need the evidence.* He snatched a baggie out of its box.

As he walked back to her, he saw gashes on her back through her torn shirt. *Rope? Gashes? What was she involved with?* He stepped in front of her and looked her in the eye. "I'm going to cut off the rope now." He slid the steel between her hands and freed her with one snap of the blades.

She gripped the rope, her wrists raw and bloody, then dropped it into the baggie he held open. Her hands free, she tucked them into her jean pockets and whimpered as the fabric scraped her wounds. She was a grown woman, but she looked like a scared child. Part of him wanted to wrap his arms around her to warm her and assure her she was safe, but touching her only frightened her more. He didn't want to be the reason for her fear. Firelight reflected in her dark eyes, her pupils still wide. He resisted the urge to barrage her with questions. He picked up his phone. "We need to report this."

Before he dialed, she spoke, her gaze fixed on the dancing flames. "I was kidnapped." She kicked at the pattern in the rug. "But I escaped."

His neck muscles tightened, and he clenched his fists. His earlobes burned as anger bubbled inside him. Painful memories stabbed at him. "There is blood all over you. Did they do that to you?" The softness was gone from his voice. His question sounded sharp, infuriation evident in every word.

"No." She turned and pointed at his grandmother's quilt that still lay near the door. When she pulled her hand out of her pocket, pictures fell to the floor. "Can I use that?"

Alex grabbed the quilt and handed it to her before he picked up the photos. "What are these?"

"I found them at the kidnappers' house. I want to use them to figure out who I am."

"You have to give these to the police."

She shook her head. "I need them."

"I'll scan them." He hated to take the extra time, but if it meant she'd give the pictures to police, the few minutes were worth it. "Do you want to sit down?"

She shook her head and stared into the fire.

He stepped into the office and laid a photo on the scanner. "This one of you looks recent, and it's printed on copy paper."

She stared at the hearth. "I only saw my face."

"The other one has names and a year on the back. It says Emma and Claire 1986."

"The kidnappers mentioned the name Claire."

"Are you Claire?"

She shrugged and shook her head helplessly. "I don't know."

"I'll be right back." Before retreating to the bedroom, he bolted the front door and thought through what she might need at the hospital. A small overnight bag toppled off the closet shelf when he yanked the strap. He dialed DJ and held the phone to his ear with his shoulder as he dug through his bureau. He tried to find something suitable for her to change into. She was a foot shorter than he was and a smaller build. He'd gotten rid of his wife's clothes, but they wouldn't have fit anyway. He piled a pair of drawstring pants, an extra-large sweatshirt, and a pair of tube socks in the bag.

A groggy DJ answered. "What's wrong, Alex? Do you know what time it is?"

"Yes. It's after three. I'm calling to report a kidnapping." Alex could hear Becca asking if everything was okay.

Instantly DJ was awake and all business. "Tell me what happened."

"A woman showed up at my door. She escaped from the kidnappers, but she's hurt. I'm taking her to the hospital to get checked out."

"What's her name?"

"She doesn't remember."

"Try to preserve as much evidence as you can. I'll meet you there." DJ was in full investigative mode.

"I haven't touched her." Alex ended the call. He returned to the office and tucked the photos in his pocket. "I would offer you a shower and a change of clothes, but I think it's best if you go as you are, and maybe shower when you come back." He hesitated. "I mean you don't have to come back here, but you can if you want. Anyway, I'm taking along some clothes, in case they need yours as evidence." *Why are you inviting her back here?*

She covered her face with the quilt, and he winced wishing he hadn't said anything about evidence. He felt like a heel for making her cry again.

Alex laced up his tennis shoes, then snatched up the bag. He glanced down at his flannel pants and too tight tee shirt. He didn't want to delay any longer, but he looked ridiculous. He pulled on his jacket and ignored his attire. "Ready to go?"

She pulled the quilt around her and shuffled to the door.

The rain had subsided, and only a light drizzle fell. Alex walked out and scanned the tree line, making sure they were alone. He held the door open for her.

One foot outside, she slipped and stopped her fall by grabbing the doorframe. She stifled a cry as her injured hand clung to the rough wood.

He reached out to grab her, but stopped when he saw her eyes. Fear stared back at him. He kept his hand out so she could grab it if she needed it. "Need help?"

She shook her head and wrapped the quilt around her a second time. He stayed close behind her as she limped to the truck, praying she wouldn't fall again. It wasn't as if she gave him the option of helping her when she did. He clicked a button on his key fob, and the lights in the truck switched on, casting light on their path.

In the distance, an engine rumbled. She stopped and turned to face him. "They're coming." She fell against his chest, her body quaking as she silently sobbed.

He froze, completely unprepared for the sudden change. *She didn't want you to touch her.* He held his arms out to his side, not wanting to make her feel trapped. "Please don't cry."

She clutched his tee shirt and sobbed even harder.

Wind rustled through the trees, and large raindrops flung themselves to earth. Alex pulled the quilt up and used it to cover her head, then wrapped his arms around her. *So much for not touching her.*

Her shoulders stop shaking, but she didn't move.

"Let's get out of the rain." He guided her to the passenger side and opened the door. He tossed the bag in the backseat while she attempted to climb into her seat.

Her foot slipped, but he caught her before she hit the ground. She steadied herself, then recoiled from him. Gritting her teeth, she pulled herself into the truck.

"I'm only trying to help you, to protect you." He closed her door and ran around to the driver's side.

As he started the engine, she began to cry, and he flipped on the interior light.

She stared through the windshield, as if looking back in time. "I remember a van." The color left her face, and she started to mumble.

~

Turpentine. The smell of turpentine and paint stung my nose. My stomach churned. Even with my eyes wide open, I could make out very little around me. I twisted my wrists, trying to free my hands. The rope tore at my skin. It hurt.

Splotches of light moved along beside me intermittently. The swooshing in my ears warned me to slow my breathing before I passed out. I could barely hear anything over my heart pounding in my ears.

As light bounced by, I saw bags, duffel bags, in front of me. The white metal chamber met at double doors not far from my feet. A cargo van.

~

Fear and pain clouded her expression.

He gripped the steering wheel, wanting to hurt whoever did this to her. "Are you okay?" He hesitated to touch her, afraid it would startle her.

She nodded. Her finger traced the circles on the wedding ring quilt. "I'm sorry I got you all wet. Now there's blood on your tee shirt and on this." She patted the quilt. "Please forgive me." Sobs escaped, and she buried her face in her hands.

"It's okay, really." Alex started the engine. "We need to go." *You have a chance to make up for the past. It fell in your lap, no, actually, in your arms.*

"I'm scared." She focused on him silently pleading for something he couldn't do, begging him to make it all go away.

He cringed as her knuckles went white clutching the quilt. He reached out to pat her hand but withdrew before touching her. "Let me get you to the hospital." Mud splattered as he tore away from the cabin.

With each mile, her breathing slowed and her shoulders relaxed a little more. She stared out the window. "Where are we?"

"Outside Kerrville."

"Where?"

"...in Texas."

"I don't even..." She shook her head. "I wonder if those men are after me."

Alex kept his eyes glued to the dark road. Windshield wipers swiped back and forth in a never-ending battle with the rain, beating out a rhythm that echoed his heartbeat.

"They won't get you a second time. I'll be sure of it." He glanced in his rearview mirror and checked for headlights.

CHAPTER FOUR

January 10, 2016 – 3:11am

In the dark, I watched him navigate the wet roads, concern etched in his brow, his jaw set in anger. *Should I trust him?* "What's your name?"

"Alex Ramirez." He took one hand off the wheel and rubbed his thumb on his chin.

Raindrops trailed down the window. "I don't remember anything before waking up in the back of the van." *What will I tell the police? I don't even know for sure how long I was captive?*

"How long ago?" He glanced my direction.

The truck hit a pothole, and I dug my mud-caked nails into the armrests. Every muscle in my body complained.

He heard my sharp inhale. "Sorry, missed it in the dark."

"Last night, I think. There was a basketball game, and the kidnappers watched the news late. But I don't remember them grabbing me."

"My friend is meeting us at the hospital. We'll figure it out." He slowed the truck and turned off the narrow road.

Us. We. I clung to those words as a promise of help. I wanted to trust him. "I measured my time in the closet by the number of sandwiches. Every meal was a bologna and mayo sandwich."

"Yuck."

"I ate four of them. I never want to see another one."

"DJ's a good investigator."

"I don't even know their names. What if they...?" Not remembering stirred my fears about what they did to me. I balled up the quilt and hugged it to my chest like a shield. *I can't talk to him about that.*

"Whatever happened, we'll find a way to fix it." He hadn't absorbed the meaning of my question.

In the glow of the dash lights, I peered at him. *I do trust him, but why?* I didn't have a logical answer, only a feeling. As much as the kidnappers made my skin want to crawl off my body, Alex had the opposite effect. Everything about him, his arms, his eyes, his smile, conveyed a sense of safety and protection. He stirred memories of someplace I'd never been.

"I crawled under a barbed wire fence."

"Your back?"

"Uh huh, and tumbled down a rocky incline." I touched my head, but he couldn't see my gash in the dark. "That's how I hurt my head and hip."

"What about your hand?"

"When I tried to run, I fell. I'm not sure what cut it."

In town, the street lights illuminated his face. When he stopped at a light, he looked at me. "We're almost there. You okay?"

I shrugged. "If you hadn't opened the door..."

"But I did."

Unless his friend, the investigator, warned against it, I planned to go back to the cabin.

"The hospital will get you checked out to make sure nothing is broken."

I pulled the quilt to my chin. "What if something broke that can't be fixed?"

Chapter Five

January 10, 2016 – 3:25am

As Alex neared the hospital, his passenger tensed. She clenched the quilt and held it near her chin.

He stopped in the loading zone near the emergency room doors. "I'll get you inside and then come back out and move the truck."

Her face went pale, and she chewed her lip. "Please stay with me."

"Of course. Whatever you want." He turned off the engine and ran around to the passenger side.

She didn't wait for his help. When her wet tennis shoe landed on the slick door frame, she toppled out of the truck. "Ack. Ouch."

A lot of good you are. She's fallen twice. He reached out his hand but waited to let her take it. "Please let me help you."

Sitting on pavement, big tears streaked down her face. "I hurt. Everything hurts." She slipped her hand into his.

He helped her back to her feet and wrapped an arm around her waist. "Lean on me."

She rested against him. "My hip hurts most."

He shoved the door closed. "Think you can make it inside?"

"Yeah, maybe." She tried to hide a wince as she took another step.

"Wait, um. If it's okay, why don't I carry you?"

She nodded without looking up.

"Wrap your arms around my neck." As her feet left the ground, a wash of memories flooded over Alex. Visions of his wife, Ellie, tossing her head back in laughter danced in his mind. The pulse in his neck was surely visible. Wind gusted, sending a spray of rain at them pulling him out of the memory. He gripped the woman tighter and carried her through the double doors.

DJ stood just inside the emergency room. He shook his head and shot Alex a curious glance before tipping his cowboy hat. "Howdy, ma'am, my name is DJ Crawford." It was the middle of the night, but he wore khakis and a dress shirt, his badge prominently displayed on his pocket. He motioned to the security guard standing near the reception desk.

Alex hoped his tall, lanky friend's casual manner would help her relax. Even in his arms, she felt rigid and tense.

She studied DJ. "Hi."

All but two chairs in the small emergency waiting room sat empty. An older gentleman dozed in his chair. Another man, next to him, maybe a son, was busy on his cellphone.

"Are they expecting her?" Alex headed to a group of chairs, away from the two men but near the doors leading to the back.

DJ bobbed his head slowly, eyeing the woman Alex carried.

Alex put her down in front of the chairs. Gingerly, she lowered herself into an armchair and gathered the quilt into her lap. With the bag at his feet, he stood next to her.

DJ whispered, "What happened to 'I haven't touched her.'?"

Alex ran his fingers through his hair. "She wanted my help." He glanced at her, but she only stared into the distance. "Do you want me to tell you what happened?"

"Yeah. I won't get her statement until after they check her out."

In a lowered voice, Alex recounted to DJ what happened and the things she'd said.

"Didn't catch even a first name?" DJ scribbled in his notebook.

A nurse dressed in pale pink scrubs stepped through the double doors. "Is this our Jane Doe?"

Alex helped his brown-eyed friend out of the chair and started to ask about a wheelchair, but stopped when she pointed at him.

"I'd like for him to stay with me." She looked at the nurse for approval.

"Of course, ma'am." The nurse looked up from the chart and smiled. "Right down this way."

Alex handed DJ the overnight bag and quilt without making eye contact and lifted the stranger back into his arms.

The nurse stopped. "Need me to grab her a wheelchair?"

"I got her." Alex started toward the double doors.

The nurse glanced at DJ, who shrugged. "It's not far." She led the three of them back to a private room.

Alex headed straight for the bed and put the injured stranger on the crisp white sheets. She'd gone from flinching each time he almost touched her to burying her face in his chest. This was twice she'd asked him not to leave. The requests surprised him. She wanted him to protect her. *You're the last person who should be protecting someone.*

"We'll need to get you out of those clothes." The nurse opened a cabinet just outside the door and pulled out a folded gown. "If you guys don't mind stepping outside. She needs to change."

"I'm sorry," DJ gestured to the bag he laid on the bed. "...but we're going to need to take your clothes for evidence." He followed Alex out the door, the nurse right behind him.

In the hall, DJ ribbed Alex about his fashionable late-night attire. "Let me guess. You have on that ratty, old tee shirt under your coat? I can't believe you still have it after all these years. You got it in what? Our junior year?" DJ read the tension on Alex's face and tried to ease it with humor. He ran his fingers through his light brown hair.

"We don't all have fancy uniforms and cowboy hats to wear." Alex opened his coat revealing the bloody tee shirt.

At the sight of the stain, DJ's tone changed, and he lowered his voice. "How did you...?"

"From the gash on her head."

"You said she doesn't know any names. Hell, we don't even have a first name for our victim. I wish we had more to go on."

"He can't get away with it this time."

"Alex? I'm not sure you being involved with this is a great idea."

"I meant to say, those guys need to be caught."

"We'll catch 'em. Listen, I need to include her description in the report."

They stepped aside as the doctor and nurse entered the room.

"Oh." Alex slipped the photos out of his pocket. "She grabbed these before she escaped. And here's the rope I cut off her hands."

DJ slipped the baggie in his pocket and studied the recent photo. "She was targeted. It wasn't random." Then he looked over the older one. "Emma and Claire?"

"She said the kidnappers mentioned Claire."

"I'll hang on to these, but the first priority is to catch those guys."

Alex leaned back against the wall. "You need a description?"

"Yeah. I saw her, but I'll need some help. Female. Brown Hair. Brown Eyes. Height?" DJ eyed Alex. "I've hardly seen her on her feet."

Alex held his hand horizontal just below his chin. "She came to about here. I'd guess five foot."

DJ continued to scribble notes. "How old do you think she is?"

"I'm horrible at guessing women's ages."

"Late twenties?"

"Maybe. I suppose she could be thirty."

"Okay." DJ continued talking to himself as he wrote. "Found wearing jeans, a long-sleeve red shirt, and blue tennis shoes. Her shoes were blue, right?"

"I think so. I need to get sizes off her clothes to get her some replacements."

Another nurse with a clipboard walked into the room, and moments later the doctor stepped out and hurried away.

Alex rubbed his face. "It's taking a long time."

"That's probably the SANE nurse."

"SANE? What's that?"

"A Sexual Assault Nurse Examiner. They're trained to ask questions and conduct an exam to determine if there was a sexual assault."

Alex clenched his fists.

"As I said before, you don't have to stay involved. I can find her a safe place at a women's shelter until we figure out who she is." DJ tucked the notebook in his pocket.

Shaking his head, Alex set his jaw. "Unless she feels otherwise, she stays with me." She'd asked for his help.

"I imagine this has dredged up some unpleasant memories for you."

Alex tilted his head back to the wall. "Ellie's parents emailed again. Once a year, same note as always. 'Thinking of our sweet girl today.' As if I needed the reminder."

"I didn't realize it was her birthday. You aren't still buying a cupcake each year, are you?"

"Fancy cupcakes were Ellie's favorite."

"What if this woman isn't what she appears to be? You don't need—."

"She needs me."

"Who needs you, Alex? Who? Ellie's gone. I don't want you getting wrapped up in something that makes you relive the past over and over."

Alex pointed to the door and tried to keep his voice down. "That bleeding, scared woman wants my help. I'm going to protect her."

"It won't make up for what happened to Ellie, which wasn't your fault."

"I should've been there, but I wasn't. Tonight I was. I was there when she knocked, and she needs me."

DJ paced. "I think you're making a mistake."

Alex closed his eyes and rubbed the side of his thumb up and down the cleft in his chin. He'd had the habit as long as he could remember. But he didn't do it often, only when something bothered him.

DJ tucked his hands in his pockets. "I think maybe you wore the cleft in your chin rubbing it that way."

"Ellie used to say that." Alex pinched the bridge of his nose. "My truck. Would you mind moving it? I left it parked outside the door."

"I'm not moving your truck. I'm waiting until I can interview the victim." DJ glanced toward her door. "I already got your statement."

Alex cursed under his breath and hurried out to the truck. The lot was mostly empty, and finding a parking space proved easy. But, it was a hike back to the emergency room. *Hopefully, she only has scratches and bruises, things that can heal.*

The hall outside her room empty, Alex assumed DJ had already started asking questions and knocked gently at the door.

"Come in." DJ's voice dripped with irritation.

Poking his head in before stepping in all the way, Alex ignored the glare from DJ and smiled at the woman. "You okay?"

"You said you'd stay with me." She sat on the bed in the hospital gown, the quilt balled in her lap with her arms wrapped around herself.

Alex reprimanded DJ with a scowl.

She whimpered when she shifted. "You brought some clothes?" There were scrapes and gashes on her legs. Faint bruises circled her upper right arm.

The nurse returned holding two syringes. "This is something for the pain. Don't drive after this one. The other is a tetanus shot. The doctor ordered it since you ran into that barbed-wire fence."

Alex's injured friend lifted up her sleeve and flinched as the nurse pricked her with the tetanus shot.

"Rub that in really well to avoid a knot. Sometimes people get one in the muscle, and that doesn't feel good. This one I can't give in your arm." The nurse glanced over her shoulder at Alex and DJ. "Mind stepping outside for a second, gentlemen?"

They obediently exited the room and waited. "What has she told you?" Alex paced outside the door.

"She wouldn't answer my questions until you returned."

Alex thought he misheard. "She what?"

"You realize I have to put that in my report. Please tell me what's going on. Do you know her? Is she someone from your past? I don't remember her from college."

"Honest, DJ. I'm as floored as you are. I think she's just scared, mostly because she doesn't know who she is."

DJ pointed his pen at Alex, but the nurse pulled open the door before he said anything else.

"All clear. You can come back in." Flipping through the chart, the nurse gave Alex's new houseguest instructions for follow-up care. "After you shower, bandage the wounds again. The pain killer will last you awhile, and as I said, don't drive. I recommend you take something over-the-counter for the next few days. You were pretty banged up."

"All right." The brown-eyed woman rubbed the injection site on her arm.

"Normally we'd send you home with a prescription for something a little stronger, but without ID, that won't work." She tossed the needles in the red sharps container mounted on the wall by the door and hurried out of the room.

DJ stepped up to the bed. "I really need you to answer my questions."

The injured woman stared at the quilt in her lap. "I know."

"Did the two men hurt you?"

Alex sucked in a deep breath. *Please, God, no.*

The woman rubbed her upper arms and hugged herself. In almost a whisper, she said, "The nurse said there was no sign of that."

Alex breathed an audible sigh of relief and set the clothes at the foot of the bed. She slid her hand toward him and caught his hand. He froze. His chest pounded, but he didn't pull away; although, he'd have been less uncomfortable if she'd bitten him.

DJ's focus went straight to their connected hands. In the last three years, Alex had never even taken a woman to dinner, let alone held her hand. But besides a slightly raised eyebrow, DJ kept further questions to himself.

He pulled the small black notebook out of his shirt pocket and turned to Alex. "Now that you're here, maybe I can find out what happened."

"Do you trust him?" She focused on DJ but nodded toward Alex, her voice soft.

DJ nodded slowly. "I do."

"He's safe?" She looked down, but didn't let go of Alex's hand.

DJ pulled a chair closer to the bed and sat down. "He won't hurt you."

"I only waited because ... I was scared." She looked at Alex. "Please, stay."

Without pulling out of her grasp, Alex dropped into the armchair beside the bed. "Of course."

DJ cleared his throat. "I need to snap a few pictures." He clicked his phone and made sure he captured images of her face, wrists, and other injuries. "Your jeans and shirt are torn."

"It happened during my escape."

"Start at the beginning. Tell me what you remember."

She let go of Alex's hand and hugged the quilt to her chest, toying with a loose thread. She started telling DJ about the van, then her eyes glazed. She lay down on her side, half-folded, speaking softly, almost to herself.

~

Shopping bags crinkled behind me. The van slowed and rounded a sharp corner. My face planted into grimy duffel bags. The grocery bags spilled their contents, and cans slammed into the back of my head. They sloshed when they moved. Maybe they were canned vegetables or possibly cans of soup.

~

She winced as if they'd just collided with her head. DJ jotted notes as she mumbled.

Alex reached for her hand, recognizing the expression he'd seen earlier. "You okay?"

"Sorry." She blinked several times but made no move to sit up. "I keep seeing it."

"Tell him what you remember."

"They drove to where there weren't any lights. And..."

~

The van stopped. There was no place for me to hide. I drew my knees up to my chest. Doors slammed. Footsteps.

A man yanked open the doors. "Get out!" He spat a wad of chew into the darkness.

I couldn't budge. He grabbed my ankles. I didn't want him to touch me.

~

She curled into a ball, and, speaking to a memory, whimpered, "Don't touch me."

DJ shook his head when Alex reached out to touch her, hoping to pull her out of the terrifying reverie. He drew his hand back and stared at her, wishing he could chase away her fear.

~

He jerked me out of the back. I landed in the dirt, not on my feet. I scrambled to get up but fell back down when a wave of nausea crawled like an army of ants from my intestines to my throat, my stomach contents in hot pursuit.

The man spewed a string of profanities. I'd splattered his boots.

~

"Was there only one man?" DJ glanced up from his notebook.

"No. Two." She sat up and took a deep breath. "The other man was younger." She wiped her face with the quilt. "Gum. He was always smacking gum."

Alex leaned closer to the bed.

"He ran to my side. He pulled my hair out of my face and squatted next to me until I finished being sick. I don't know why he was being nice. The older one never was."

Her distant look returned, and Alex stomach tightened.

~

My arm screamed as the older man's fingers tightened around it. The grip on my arm kept me upright as he dragged me through the dark. The interior light in the van reflected off a window pane in front of me. I could just make out the outline of a house.

There was only a tiny sliver of a moon.

The angry man barked orders at the other man. "Park the van in the brush. Use the tarp to cover it."

"Yes, sir." The younger guy acted like a green recruit, following orders like it earned him rank. He prattled on about whatever crossed his mind. "Sure is dark tonight. There's hardly any moon."

The angry man huffed. "And don't forget to unload the stuff."

We stepped up to the back door, and he opened it. His grip was so tight, there was no chance of escape. My heart pounded in my ears as he pushed me up the three steps and into the house. Walking into a dark house far from everywhere was too much like the beginning of a murder mystery. I didn't want to be murdered, or anything else. The anything else scared me the most.

~

"I don't want to die. I want to wear my new sundress. It's in the trunk." She dropped her head into her hands and sobbed.

Alex watched helplessly as she relived her nightmare. He leaned forward wanting to sooth her, but DJ grabbed his arm.

He shook his head and put a finger to his lips. "Let her talk."

~

Flipping a switch next to me, he released my arm but hovered behind me. The foul smell of wet tobacco clung to him.

~

She shuddered and scrunched up her nose. The haze disappeared from her eyes, and she looked at DJ. "We were in a kitchen. Drab avocado curtains hung from a bent rod above the sink. A grimy, vinyl tablecloth covered a square table against a wainscoted wall. The house smelled musty and sour. The floors hadn't met a mop, maybe ever."

He scribbled notes.

"Sorry, you probably don't care about the kitchen."

"I want to know everything you remember." DJ's easygoing manner gave him an edge handling difficult situations. "I'm sorry I'm making you relive it, but I need to know what happened."

"The living room was a long rectangle. I'll spare you the description, but someone in the 70's had groovy taste." The hint of a smile disappeared before her cheeks even twitched.

Alex chuckled nervously, then watched her drift away again, mumbling.

~

He flung open the little door, and the imprisoned stench of musty blankets, stale cigarettes, and dirty socks tried to make an escape. He shoved me into a closet. I'd barely cleared the doorway when he slammed the door. The doorknob rattled then clicked.

I sank to the floor wondering what they would do to me.

~

She squeezed her eyes closed, and swiped at them like she was trying to wipe away whatever she remembered.

Alex glanced at DJ, who shook his head.

~

A hundred possible scenarios, none of them good, flipped like flashcards in my head. Monster tears stampeded down my cheeks, splashing and puddling on the floor below.

I tried to remember how it happened, how I ended up in the back of the van. But my memory was like a dark room, and I couldn't find the light switch. I couldn't remember anything before the fly.

~

She bit her lip, and tears ran down her cheeks.

The panic in her eyes gripped Alex. He leaned in close ignoring DJ. "You're not in the closet, anymore. You're with me."

She looked at him, desperation circling her pupils. "I still don't know who I am."

DJ watched her closely. "I'll figure out who you are." His determined tone sounded almost cold.

"And you might remember on your own, now that you're away from those men." Alex gave her what he hoped was a reassuring smile.

"What was that about a fly?" DJ looked over his notes.

"What fly?"

"Never mind. Continue." DJ readied his pen.

Her eyes glazed. She pulled her knees to her chest and covered her ears, rocking as she murmured.

~

"What did she say when you told her we got the girl? I bet she was happy."

"She said she would call us in the morning with the plan." Angry impatience was evident in the foul-smelling man's tone.

I almost felt sorry for the younger guy. Almost.

"How do you think she'll convince her she's Claire?" The younger guy's penchant for asking questions annoyed me. Always talking, he acted as if we were enjoying a weekend away. I hated that he made light of my situation.

But I wanted to know who Claire was.

"I'm confused, though. The picture I saw was a baby. Was Claire the baby from 1986?" The younger guy never quit talking.

"Go make some dinner." The older guy turned on the television.

"What do you want? A potpie, a frozen dinner, or tomato soup?"

"Frozen dinner."

"You sure? It's cold out, the soup might warm you up." The younger guy yelped in pain. "I'll make you a frozen dinner."

~

She flinched as she talked about the yelp, her large tears landing on the quilt. Alex reached out, ignoring DJ as he shook his head. She was clearly terrified, but calmed at Alex's touch.

DJ leaned close. "Leave her alone or get out. I need to get her account."

Alex pulled his hand back.

~

"The news is late tonight. Because of the basketball game, right?" The younger guy really liked to talk.

"Shut up." The angry guy's voice sounded like sandpaper rubbed on tree bark.

"Do you think she'll die?" He didn't sound happy this time, and I wondered if he was talking about me.

"Enough talking! Go get her some food. We don't want the golden ticket to starve."

Footsteps retreated from the room.

Minutes later, the door swung open. I blinked trying to get my eyes to adjust to the lamplight that filled the room.

~

She put her hands to her eyes, warding off the light.

~

The talkative guy—he wasn't that young; he had wrinkles—stood there smacking his gum and holding out half a sandwich. "Here."

I sniffed it.

"There ain't nothing wrong with it. We just bought the stuff."

He held it out, and I took a small bite. Bologna and mayo. A combination I hadn't had since I was a kid. It tasted awful, but I choked it down. The angry guy wanted me to eat, and I wasn't about to cross him. After giving me a few sips of water, the other one locked the closet again.

I listened to the drone of the television. My head fell onto my knees, my battle against sleep lost.

~

She dropped her head to the quilt and sat silent and motionless for nearly a minute. Alex held his breath. DJ rubbed his brow. They nearly jumped when her head popped up, her eyes wide with fright.

~

"Please don't kill me." I woke myself talking in my sleep. I fought the desperate need to close my eyes, only to wake up in a cold sweat, terrified.

~

Alex couldn't stand the fear in her eyes and touched her arm again. "Want me to go get you something to drink?"

She crawled away from him and cowered on the other side of the bed, blinking, then shook her head. "Please don't leave me." She inched back toward him and grasped his hand.

DJ waited a minute before asking questions. "How long did they keep you in the closet?"

"I ate four sandwiches."

"How often did they feed you?"

She shrugged. "That's what he gave me the first night, then hours later, when the sun was so bright even squinting was painful, he gave me another one. I figured it must be morning. And two more later that day. I think it was the same day."

"The sun was bright? Were you near a window?"

"I couldn't see it from the closet, but the living room was bright during the day."

"Is there anything else you remember?"

"The younger guy said he didn't like the plan. He didn't tell me what it was, but when I overheard the two of them later, the older guy told the younger guy to quit talking to me. The angry guy also said something about buying a lot more food. It made me think they planned to keep me for a long time."

She closed her eyes. "I don't know how I ended up in the van."

The color drained from her face, and she began to mumble again, still gripping Alex's hand.

~

Incessant tickling brought me out of my sluggish haze. My eyelids resisted as I tried to open them. A fly perched on the tip of my nose, and I focused on trying to get the beastly little insect to leave. I shook my head, and it lifted off but didn't go far. When I tried to swipe at it with my hands, rope burned at my wrists. My hands were tied behind my back.

~

Alex stared at her wrist, stuffing his anger.

"Behind you?" DJ wrote as fast as she talked.

She wiped her face and nodded. "Yeah, they were that way almost the whole time."

"But when you got to my door, they were tied in front." Alex looked at DJ and shrugged.

"The younger guy was stupid."

DJ ran a finger down his page of notes. "You spent the night in the closet with your hands tied behind your back?"

"It hurt." She tugged Alex's hand to the quilt and pulled them both to her chest.

Alex felt the sharpness of DJ's glare but didn't look at him.

~

Even the lamplight seemed bright after hours in the dark. The angry guy sat in front of the television across the room as I was given my half sandwich for dinner. I thought death would taste like bologna and mayo.

My bladder ached. The door was halfway closed when I stuck out my foot. "Please, I need to pee." I shoved my knees together and squirmed.

The younger guy nodded and stuck out his hand. He wasn't very bright. I wriggled my way back up, pushing off from the wall with my hands, which were still tied behind my back. I followed him to the hall. After opening the door, he leaned into the bathroom, flipped on the light, and spat his gum into the trash can near the door.

"Untie me."

~

The fear in her voice faded slightly, replaced with what sounded like determination.

~

"Oh, sorry." He fiddled with the rope only a minute before it fell loose.

I rubbed my wrists. They were red and burned where the rope scraped against my skin, I shuddered at the thought of him tying my hands again. That was the worst part of bathroom trips.

~

Alex squeezed her hand. "So they let you out of the closet. Is that how you escaped?"

She didn't seem to hear his question, the faraway look still focused on the far wall.

DJ shot him a look and pointed to the door. Alex pointed to his hand, still clutched to her chest. He wasn't about to pull away.

~

The walls were a blur of green tiles and olive paint, with one tiny window that mocked my less-than-narrow-hips. I emptied my bladder. Whatever the plan was, I was pretty sure I didn't like it either. I needed my own plan. That's when I remembered the gum.

~

She grinned, an actual smile that pushed out her cheeks.

~

I palmed it and formed my own plan.

When I opened the door, I worried he'd see it in my hand. He didn't mention tying my hands so I didn't bring it up. I shuffled back toward the closet and glanced down as I passed the desk. I saw my own face. A picture of me lay on the desk.

When we reached the closet, I...

~

She grinned again, her eyes clear. "...*stumbled*..." She emphasized her meaning with air quotes, then the glaze and mumbles returned.

~

...and grabbed the door frame. I wasn't ready to go back in the closet. With my heart racing, I glanced at the angry guy. He was watching the sportscaster discussing game highlights.

Looking back over my shoulder, I asked in a voice low enough the angry guy couldn't hear, "Why did you kidnap me?"

The talkative one stared at the floor silently and drew circles with the tip of his shoe. After a couple seconds, he muttered an unintelligible reply. I hadn't expected an answer but got what I needed. Time.

"I need to tie your hands again."

"Okay." I held my fists together in front of me, and he tied my hands. I'm not sure if he was being kind or inept, but whatever the case, my shoulders appreciated the reprieve.

The door closed, and the lock clicked.

I suffered through more late night television, but this time sleep didn't tempt me. I waited while they lulled into a stupor.

~

She sat bolt upright and stared at DJ, her eyes wide with fright. "Where is she?"

Alex stayed silent, unwilling to cross DJ at the moment.

"Who?" The worry in DJ's voice startled Alex.

Was there more than one woman kidnapped? Alex worried that another woman was roaming somewhere in the dark or hovering in a small closet.

"I don't know." She whimpered and faded back to her memories.

~

I leaned against the closet doorframe and gingerly placed my ear to the door. They were moving around. The light seeping under the door disappeared. Footsteps faded as the two of them plodded farther away from me. I leaned down, face to the floor, and peered through the gap. Everything was dark and quiet. Nothing moved. That was my chance to make an escape.

Quiet as a wallflower at a school dance, I felt around the floor. I needed something to free my hands. A pile of scratchy blankets were stacked near my feet. Tattered and mildewed, they stank up the closet. Next to my hip were several pairs of boots. There was nothing helpful in that nasty closet. I slumped back, discouraged. Escaping with my hands tied together would be difficult.

Ear to the door, I listened again. Snorts and snuffles wafted from the direction of the hall. Conveniently, the kidnappers snored. I needed them to be louder than my footsteps and door creaks.

I twisted the doorknob. It was locked, so—hoping the gum trick worked—I pushed gently on the door. It didn't open. I took a deep breath and shoved with a little more force. The door swung partway open. I pulled the gum out of the doorjamb and stuck it to the wall inside the closet. It had kept the door from latching just as I'd hoped.

~

Alex and DJ exchanged a look.

~

I closed the door, careful not to let it bang on the frame. Then I locked it. I hoped if they saw it locked, they would assume I was still inside.

Before I left, I remembered the photo. I glanced at the desk across the room. I thought the photo might shine light on my identity so I risked grabbing it. Tiptoeing across the room, I picked up the picture. Below it was another photo. I couldn't make it out in the dark, but I slipped them both in my pocket. Before stepping away, I glimpsed a flashlight laying on the desk. After stuffing it in my pocket, I froze when the floor creaked in the kitchen. A faint light poured from the arched doorway near the coat closet. Someone was awake.

~

DJ and Alex inched forward in their seats, waiting for her to continue.

Tap. Tap. The nurse pushed open the door. Alex's brown-eyed friend shrieked and shielded herself with the quilt.

The nurse grimaced. "Sorry." She quickly backed out of the room.

Alex kept his mouth shut and let DJ handle the interview.

"Someone was awake?" DJ asked quietly.

~

Flattening myself against the wall next to the desk, I focused on taking shallow, inaudible breaths. I waited and listened. Footsteps moved closer to the living room, so I crouched down. A figure stepped into the room and lumbered over to the closet. Thankfully, the locked door fooled him.

"I hope I'm not waking you. They aren't treating you very well. I didn't know it would be this way. And I'm sorry about your friend." He sounded as though he might cry.

~

DJ wrote *They?* and *Friend?* in his notebook and circled both words.

~

I peered around the edge of the desk. The younger guy reached for the doorknob. He unlocked the lock. I tried to formulate a plan. His hand was almost on the doorknob when he hesitated. He shook his head. My lungs started to hurt from holding my breath.

"Goodnight. It is probably not comfortable in there, but I can't let you out. Sorry. He would have my hide. I'm not even supposed to be talking to you." He relocked the door, tapped the doorframe, and slipped back out of the room. The light in the kitchen went out.

Relieved, I let out my breath. Still crouched beside the desk, my leg muscles screamed at me. Bedsprings creaked on the other end of the house.

My knees popped as I stood up. I tiptoed through the room to the front door. Only that door stood between me and freedom. I turned the bolt ever so slowly. No one stirred. I breathed in deep and prayed the door wouldn't squeak. I gripped the knob and twisted. Cold air slapped against my face. I slipped outside and pulled the door closed behind me.

~

Alex handed her a tissue, and she wiped her eyes.

"Then I ran. Well, I couldn't run, really. Every time I ran, I fell. That's how I hurt my hand. I tried to find help, but it was so empty and so dark."

"A new moon." Alex was glad she'd finished most of the retelling and hoped she could leave the events in the past. "It's a good thing you found the flashlight."

"He mentioned a friend? Is there anything else you remember about that? Do you have any idea who he meant?" DJ glanced at Alex nervously.

"No." Heartbreaking anguish filled her voice. "I can't remember."

"When you talked about the younger kidnapper, you mentioned he said 'they.' I'm confused because I thought there were only two kidnappers. Who was he referring to?"

"Both of them talked about a woman. Never used her name. She wanted me to think I was Claire."

"How long were you outside? Any idea how far you walked?" DJ filled the last page of the notebook as she talked.

"I don't know. They watched late night shows. I slipped out after that. Outside, it felt like forever. I walked and walked. Then there was a wall of rock. I had to go around it and crawl up a small hill. I almost gave up then. If it hadn't started raining, I might still be laying out there in the dirt. But…"

She regarded Alex with a worn and tired smile.

"… I saw the cabin. I banged on the door, and Alex let me in."

DJ tucked the notebook in his shirt pocket. "Thank you. I know that wasn't easy."

"Let's get sizes off these clothes before DJ takes them." Alex handed her the bag.

She nodded and called them out while he recorded them in a note on his phone.

When they were finished, DJ picked up the bag. "Thank you."

"What about this?" She pointed at the quilt lying in her lap.

"Did you get it from the house?"

"No. From Alex." She hugged it tighter as she said it.

"Keep it." DJ walked to the door and stopped. "When you're done here, I need you to come by the station."

She stiffened.

"We'll get your prints and try to figure out who you are. And I want to have you sit down with a sketch artist."

"To describe the kidnappers?"

"Exactly. I'll be in the waiting room. I'm happy to give you a ride. And I can find you a place to stay where you'll be safe."

"Alex said I could stay at his cabin."

DJ rolled his shoulders and looked from Alex to her. "Is that what you want?"

She looked at Alex. "Is it really okay?"

"Absolutely." He patted the bed, then tucked his hand in his pocket. With her close, he could protect her.

"That's what I want. Can Alex take me to the station?"

DJ nodded.

"Why don't we give you some privacy so you can change?" Alex pointed to the pile of clothes sitting on the bed. "The clothes won't win any fashion awards, but they're dry and clean."

"I'll see y'all at the station." DJ tipped his hat and disappeared down the hallway.

Alex stood with his back to the door. Every muscle in his body ached from the hours of being tense. He closed his eyes, rubbed his temples, and shoved aside emotions that were inconvenient reminders of his past.

The door opened behind him. When he turned around, he stifled a laugh. The pants were cuffed multiple times. The sweatshirt almost swallowed his new friend. She shuffled back across the room and climbed onto the bed.

"Alex, if you'd rather I not ..."

"Stay." His voice was taut.

"The cabin feels safe."

"Please let me help you." He met her gaze hoping she understood he needed to protect her.

The doctor walked in after a quick rap on the door. "Well, your injuries will all heal, but you'll be sore for the next day or two."

"What about my memory?" She reached for Alex's hand. At least this time, he didn't freeze when she clasped it.

"You have what used to be called Psychogenic Amnesia. They don't call it that anymore, but I'll spare you any more of the technical names. I fully expect your memory to return."

"So I can go?"

"I could keep you overnight, but you show no signs of head trauma, and there is nothing I can do to bring your memory back. You have to give it time to return on its own."

"How long will that take?" Even hidden under the sweatshirt, her shoulders were tense.

"I can't say. But the best situation for recalling memories is to be somewhere you feel safe. Do you have a place like that?"

She nodded and squeezed Alex's hand. He prayed he wouldn't let her down.

"Good. Rest. Give it a few days, maybe a week. If your memory doesn't return, call the hospital. They'll give you the name of a specialist you can see. Have any questions?"

"Is there anything I can do?" She looked at the doctor clearly wanting him to give her the steps to get her memory back.

"Memories can be triggered by sight, smell, taste… but feeling safe is what's most important for you right now." He shook her hand, and then turned to Alex and stuck out his hand. "Just call if y'all have questions."

Alex opened the passenger side door and chuckled as she pulled up her tube socks for the third time.

"They keep sliding down." She grabbed his arm and slid out of the truck. "What if I did something horrid and they arrest me?" She danced her eyebrows and giggled.

"I guess we'll have to wait and see." He decided her pain medication had taken effect. Alex pressed a buzzer, and a dispatcher let them into the sheriff's office.

"I'll let Captain Crawford know you're here. Have a seat. He should be out in a minute." He tucked in behind the desk and picked up the phone.

"Thanks." Alex steered his friend toward a chair.

"Does he know who I am?" she whispered loud enough anyone near the front desk could hear.

"I doubt it. You want to ask him?" He glanced back over his shoulder and saw the dispatcher grin.

The brown-eyed woman stared at Alex, an admiring smile plastered on her face. "You're really strong."

"Hey, DJ." Alex jumped up seconds after he'd perched on the edge of a chair.

DJ raised an eyebrow. "I'm only going to get prints right now. This won't take long. I'll have her come back later for the sketch artist."

"That's probably good because they gave her something for the pain." Alex smirked.

"Gotcha." DJ chuckled. "Just wait here. I'll have her back out in a few minutes."

She fluttered her fingers at Alex as she followed DJ to the back.

In Alex's near reclusive life, there were two people he saw consistently, DJ and Becca. He'd known DJ in college, but only crossed paths with him again three years ago. That was when he met Becca. They were friends he could count on in any situation. Alex texted her: *Please call when you're up. I have a favor to ask.*

His phone rang moments after he hit send.

"Alex, is everything okay? I've been worried since DJ left."

"I wondered if you'd be awake. The woman is going to be fine. We are at the station now. She's getting fingerprinted to try and figure out who she is."

"Are you okay?"

"Yeah. Listen, can you do me a huge favor? Her clothes were collected as evidence. Right now she is wearing a pair of my drawstring pants, a sweatshirt, and tube socks. She's swimming in them. Could you get her something to wear?"

"Do you have her sizes?"

"Yeah." Alex rattled off sizes between glances at the note. "Thanks. I can drop off my credit card to you or give you cash after the fact."

"You can pay me whenever. She's staying with you?" Clearly, she hadn't yet spoken with DJ.

"Yeah. We'll be back in town later. I'll get them from you then."

"Okay, text me."

"Oh, and maybe get something for her hair."

"Something like what?"

"Whatever y'all use to pull it up. I don't know. Her hair is kinda long."

My Big Girl Claire,

Happy Birthday! You're six years old!

Last night I dreamt of the day the beast stole you away. To the rest of the world, he looked like anyone else. Your daddy and I learned the truth too late.

I almost didn't buy you a cake. It seemed like too much to hope that you'd return. Your daddy said I couldn't think that way, that hope was the only thing we had left. So, we went to the bakery, and I picked out the happiest cake they had. It had bright pink frosting and a plastic puppy perched on top.

I don't know if you look like me or Daddy. I don't know if your hair is long or short. I don't know you, and it breaks my heart.

Love from Texas,

Mommy & Daddy

Dear Claire,

Forgive the spots on this letter. My tears make the paper wrinkly.

I had such dreams about how our life would be. I've missed the little things like combing your hair, letting you stir the pot when I'm cooking, or licking the batter from the spatula. I imagined we would go out and shop for dresses or blue jeans or books. I'd dreamt life would be a fairy tale with you in it, but the beast rewrote that story.

I hope this is the year you come home. Please come home.

This year's birthday cake was decorated to look like a forest. A blue lake filled the center and around it were trees made of chocolate. Walking alone through the forest was Little Red Riding Hood.

My brave, little Claire, I miss you. Can I trust the beast to keep you safe? I know he's frightening when he stomps and roars. I hope the beast never scares you the way he scared me.

My tears are smearing the ink, so I'll close this letter. We love you, Claire.

Hugs and Kisses,

Mommy & Daddy

April 21, 1992

Dear Claire,

I asked a little girl at the bakery which cake I should choose for you. She told me that lots of girls like Polly Pockets and pointed to a cake decorated to look like a case with real dolls on it. I bought that cake.

(This is your daddy. We are still searching. Love you.)

Love always,

Mommy & Daddy

CHAPTER SIX

January 10, 2016 – 5:46am

"They didn't turn my fingers black." I wrapped my arms around Alex's neck and giggled as he lifted me into the truck.

He was so strong and warm. I smiled at him, and eyes the color of juniper bushes and rimmed with the fiery gold of the last rays before sunset smiled back. He would never grace the cover of a GQ magazine, but there was something comfortable about him. He was good-looking in a boyish sense. His eyes, though, were fabulous but cloudy. Set against his brown skin, they were like gems. I swooned.

"They used a fingerprint scanner?" He smelled like mountain air, with the slightest hint of mud. The mud was probably my fault.

"I don't remember what DJ called it. I guess I didn't do anything bad. They didn't arrest me." *What was in the injection the nurse gave me?* The pain meds had definitely kicked in. I wasn't swooning. I was loopy. The nurse advised me not to drive, but she should have warned me not to talk. The meds loosened my muscles making it easier to move without flinching. Unfortunately, they affected my tongue too. "But the computer didn't give him my name."

"I'm not too surprised." He climbed into the driver's seat and started the engine.

"Why are you single?" Through the haze of whatever the nurse gave me, I saw all of Alex's positive attributes. A feeling of safety replaced my fear, and I credited Alex and his willingness to protect me.

He glanced to the left before pulling out of the lot but didn't answer my question.

I grinned at him stupidly until a horrifying thought popped in my head, then promptly escaped my mouth. "I wonder if I'm single." If I couldn't remember anything about myself, maybe I was married or involved in a long-term relationship. "Maybe I have a husband worried about me or a boyfriend." I looked at Alex to see a reaction, but he never took his eyes off the road. "I don't feel married. Do you think people feel married?"

"Yeah." He still wouldn't look at me.

"Then I'm not married. When you hug me and hold my hand, I don't feel guilty so I must not have a husband." Instinctively, I glanced down at my hand. "See, no ring. I'm single." And unless the street lights were playing tricks on me, there was no pale line where a ring used to be.

"Are you married?" I leaned over the console to be close to him.

He finally glanced at me. "No."

"Do you have a girlfriend?" My mouth would not quit spewing words.

He shook his head and patted my hand. Or maybe he wanted me to move it. I'd laid it on his leg.

When he tapped me, heat radiated off his hand. I welcomed his touch on such a cold night. "You're warm."

"If you're cold, snuggle up under the quilt." He suggested I move in a nice way, at least.

I clutched the quilt and tried to shake my pain med saturated haze. *Stop talking.* If I was quiet and observed my surroundings, maybe I'd remember something helpful. But he hadn't even made it to the highway when I opened my mouth again.

"I have questions." I shifted to face him.

"Okay?" He seemed nervous.

"Please don't laugh. These are serious questions."

He shot me a curious look. A smirk played at the corners of his mouth.

"What day is it?" I wanted to reach for his hand. *Don't grab his hand.* I obeyed the words in my head.

"Saturday, January ninth. No, it is Sunday now, so January tenth."

"And we are in Texas?" I tried to focus on his answers while simultaneously bemoaning the fact his truck didn't have a bench seat in front. It would've been warmer if I was in the middle.

"We are in the Texas Hill Country. My cabin's in Kerr County, west of Kerrville." He sounded so smart. "It must be frustrating not to remember anything."

"You have no idea." My voice quivered. *Happy to tears in half a second.* Those were powerful drugs.

"You're safe with me until things get sorted out. Your memory will come back."

"You'll be my bodyguard?" I liked the sound of that.

"Something like that." His voice was like hot cocoa on a cold night, smooth and soothing.

"What's your cat's name?" I was glad he couldn't hear my thoughts. My words were embarrassing enough.

"Bureau."

"He's the reason I knocked on your door. He jumped into the window. It was like he was inviting me in."

"I'll be sure and thank him." He cracked a slight smile.

Alex clicked on his high beams. The rain had stopped, but the road glistened as his headlights danced along the pavement. I managed to keep myself quiet for a few miles by studying him. He was fairly tall, six foot or taller, I'd guess. But seeing the world from my viewpoint, lots of people seemed tall. His dark wavy hair was cut short, and except for a five o'clock shadow, there was no facial hair. But for the record, I was a big fan of his five o'clock shadow. He was broad shouldered and filled out his tee shirt quite nicely. There was a little extra fluff around his middle. He wasn't starving, at least. Murky green ponds aren't exactly pretty, but that color looked great in his eyes. I stared, taking in the curve of his neck, the shape of his arms, and the scale of his hands. *Do not reach for his hand!*

He shot me several sideways glances. He was like fine art in a gallery. I couldn't help but stare.

"Are you always so quiet?" I squinted my eyes and tried to imagine what he'd look like with a beard.

"Are you always so inquisitive?" The hesitation in his voice tickled me.

I giggled like he'd said the funniest punchline ever. "I don't know." I shrugged and slid my hand to where his rested on the center console but stopped when our pinkies touched. "You didn't answer my question."

"Most of the time." He pulled his hand off the console and clutched the wheel.

"How old are you?"

"Thirty-five."

Grey light hovered near the horizon. The cabin looked like a fortress and trees surrounded it like sentries. Alex parked not far from the door. "Stay put, and let me help you out, please."

I listened, mostly because I was tired of falling, but helping me out of the truck meant he'd touch me. I liked that part. When he opened the door, I slid my arms around his neck. He didn't carry me, just put me down and offered his arm for support. At the door, he pressed his hand into the small of my back and ushered me into the cabin. "You need to sleep off those meds."

When he switched on the lamp, a wash of golden light filled the living room. Bureau lay curled up on the rug near the fireplace. I dropped to my knees by the cat. "Hello, kitty."

Stroking the soft black fur, I tucked my legs next to me and leaned against the plush recliner, the only chair in the room. The limestone fireplace cradled its ashes waiting to give off warmth. The paint on the walls reminded me of perfectly baked bread, fresh out of the oven. Dark-stained, wooden doors surrounded me. I was in the heart of the cabin.

Alex sat on the hearth. "You should really get some rest."

"I'm hungry, and I want to take a shower."

"I'll warm you some food. The bathroom is through that door, next to the bedroom." He walked across the room.

"Where are you going?" I trailed behind him.

"You'll sleep in here." A king sized, unmade bed took up most of the bedroom. Opposite the bed was a dresser. On the far wall was a closet with sliding doors. He rushed around the room scooping laundry off the floor, then tossed the pile in the closet.

I stared at the large bed and shook my head.

"Please, take the bed. I can throw clean sheets on really quick."

"Don't worry about the sheets." I stepped into the bathroom and swung the door closed. When the latch clicked, I crumpled to the floor in tears. It was like being in the closet all over again.

"What's wrong? Are you okay?" His voice was a little muffled by the door, but he sounded worried.

"Please open the door. I don't want it closed." I huddled on the floor.

"Are you dressed?"

"Uh-huh."

The door swung partway open. "What's wrong?"

"I don't want to be alone in the closet." I sounded silly even to myself, but fear consumed me. "Can I leave it open?"

"I'll be in the kitchen." My bodyguard escaped to the only room without a sightline to the bathroom.

Catching sight of myself in the mirror, I cried yet again. This time, he didn't come and ask about the tears. A dirty, blood-streaked face stared back at me. Even through my happy, drugged up fog, the terror of my ordeal bubbled back to the surface. I yanked off the tube socks and glanced out the door. Undressing with it open, knowing a stranger was around the corner prompted more tears. After slipping out of Alex's over-sized clothes, I stepped into the stream of hot water and let it cascade over my body. The navy shower curtain separated me from the real world. As the water cleaned off the dirt and blood, tears washed away the fear and stress of the last several hours.

I stepped out of the shower and wrapped the towel around me. I stared at the clothes in a heap on the floor. Both the sweatshirt and pants were stained with blood. I couldn't put those back on. Tears threatened as I tried to figure out what to do.

Knock, knock.

Alex stood at the door facing away from me. "I dug out some clean clothes." Arm extended behind him, he handed them in. "I'm going back to the kitchen."

"Wait."

He stopped without saying a word.

"I need fresh bandages."

"In the cabinet," he said before disappearing around the corner.

I pulled on a pair of flannel pants that thankfully had a drawstring to hold them up and slipped a Texas Aggie sweatshirt over my head. It wasn't any smaller than the other one I wore. I padded into the kitchen. "What's a Texas Aggie?"

"What are you talking about?" He left a pot simmering on the stove and stepped toward me.

I pointed at the front of the sweatshirt.

"I went to college there."

I held out the ointment and bandages. "I can't reach the scratches on my back."

He paled, and for a moment, I worried he'd be sick.

"Never mind." I hobbled out toward the fireplace.

"I'll help you." He held out his hand.

When I whipped around, he focused those green eyes on me for the first since we'd been back at the cabin. In that moment, complete awareness that we were alone settled on me like a hooded cloak. I dropped the stuff in his hand and looked away from him.

He pointed to the living room. "If you sit sideways in the recliner..." The tube of ointment hit the floor, and he cursed under his breath.

I started toward the chair, made it almost all the way there, then, only three steps away, tripped on nothing, toppling face-first toward the chair. He caught me before I collided with anything. My heart was pounding too fast for my breath to keep up. In the truck, I wanted him to touch me, but now it scared me. Fear must've showed on my face because he let go of me like I was the handle of a hot cast iron pan.

I climbed into the chair. Perched sideways, I crossed my arms over my chest and leaned forward.

"The sweatshirt's in the way."

I lifted it a little.

"Not high enough."

"I ... you lift it." I hugged my arms to my chest, terrified the sweatshirt would ride too high.

He lifted the back of it. I braced, anticipating the cold ointment. Bandages fluttered to the ground next to me followed by the cap of the ointment.

I looked toward the kitchen. *Just breathe.* Stubble grazed my side, and I inhaled sharply, catching a scream before it left my lips.

"Crap. Sorry." He knelt down on the floor and gathered things up. "I leaned down. I didn't mean to..."

When I sensed him behind me again, I closed my eyes waiting for the sting.

After several seconds of shuffling, I felt the warmth of his finger, the chill of the cream and flinched.

"Sorry."

I wanted to say, "It's okay." But I had sobs trapped in my throat, and if I opened my mouth, it wasn't going to be pretty.

He pulled my shirt back into place. "You can sit back now."

I shifted, then tensed as he lifted my pant leg. "What are you doing?" I pulled my knees up to my chest.

He backed away. "The gashes on your legs."

"Oh." I let my legs fall in front of the chair, but he only stared at me. I slowly lifted the flannel fabric, stopping when the wounds were visible.

He applied the ointment and bandages, then pulled the pant legs down as he finished. I stuck out my hand. My fear subsided, replaced with... I'm not exactly sure what.

He wrapped up my hand after treating the gash. "Close your eyes." It sounded as smooth as cocoa until he cleared his throat after the last word.

I did as I was asked, knowing he wanted to bandage the gash above my eyebrow. But I wasn't prepared to feel his breath on my cheek. *All aboard the painkiller roller coaster.* Short and frequent, his breaths betrayed his nervousness. When the bandage touched my head, I opened my eyes.

Inches from me, he froze when he saw me watching. "Done."

There was no thank you from me, no expression of gratitude. In that moment, I didn't trust my tongue in the least. I kept my mouth shut, eyeing his every move.

"I warmed food. Let me get it." He headed for the kitchen. A minute or two later, he handed me a bowl of chili. "Want a cup of tea?"

I nodded.

Off he went again. I sniffed the bowl. Spices filled my senses, but my stomach took its time deciding if it was allowing food. Hunger and nausea couldn't both be appeased. I took a small bite and nearly tossed my cookies. After a deep breath, the food stayed down. *Don't eat too fast.* I shoveled down the chili.

He set a mug of tea on the table next to me. "I made Vanilla Chai Caramel. I wasn't sure what you liked."

"Do you always save people?"

His expression twisted in pain as if I'd stuck a dagger in his chest. "No." He turned to the fireplace and piled logs in the grate.

I sipped my tea in silence. He continued poking at the logs. With the mug still half-full, I set it on the table. "Goodnight."

He turned and followed me to the bedroom door. "If you need anything…"

As I slid under the covers, Bureau jumped up and twirled in circles near my feet. Alex switched off the light as he exited the room. The darkness taunted me, reviving memories of the putrid closet.

"Please don't leave me."

He stopped and slowly turned around. "I'm not going to be far away." He pointed toward the living room.

"Please." My eyes stung as I tried to blink away the evidence of my fear.

He trudged across the room and sat on the bed. He stiffened when I laid my head in his lap. "Uh. Let me shift a little." He stretched out on top of the covers, and I laid my head on his chest.

I appreciated the pounding of his heart, a constant, thumping reminder I wasn't alone. "Do you think they'll come after me?"

"Shh." He patted my shoulder, then pulled his hand away. His heart raced as if he'd taken a jaunt through the trees.

Clouds rained down a lullaby. Snuggled against Alex's warm body, sleep didn't hide from me. I glanced up before I closed my eyes. With his arms tucked behind his head and eyes wide open, he bored holes into the ceiling. Too relaxed to wonder at his stiffness, I drifted off to sleep.

Flashes of my confinement and escape disturbed my rest, and I woke in a sweat. The sunlight pouring through the gap in the curtains served as a cheery reminder I wasn't in a closet. I glanced around the room, and memories of the last few hours flooded back. Alex stirred and snuggled into my back, his head buried under a pillow.

I dared not move. Birds prattled on with each other complaining about the cold. Having him in bed next to me was a lot less weird when I fell asleep. My brain restarted the torturous loop of the kidnapping, escape, and hospital visit that had played in my head all through the night. Images of the nurse and the exam brought tears to my eyes. I shifted away from Alex. The pain meds had made it easy to ramble about other things and forget. I'd said things to him, and asked things of him that embarrassed me now. But the drugs had worn off, and I lay in bed with a man I'd only just met.

My chest heaved. *I have to get out of this bed.* I slipped out from under the covers. As my feet hit the floor, I stifled a yelp. One hip still ached from the fall. How I hiked so far after taking that tumble mystified me.

"I'll be up in a bit, Ellie." He rolled onto his stomach, sprawled in the middle of the bed.

Who's Ellie?

I limped gingerly into the kitchen. Really, some unknown force pulled me into the kitchen. I needed to cook. I poked around the cabinets until I found where he stored the pans. Careful not to bang them, I pulled out two pans: one large skillet and a smaller non-stick pan. Despite the awkwardness of waking up next to him, I appreciated all Alex had done. And nothing says "I'm sorry for running my mouth" and "thank you for…"—probably just "thank you" was best—like a hot breakfast.

The window above the sink welcomed the daylight. I wasn't sure what I expected in a bachelor's kitchen, but his was tidy. Dishes rested in the drying rack. Two chairs kept a small round table company. A cabinet nestled in the corner near the pantry housed plates, silverware, and serving pieces.

After rummaging through the refrigerator, I set to work. I didn't know my name, but I knew what I wanted for breakfast. I smiled at the package of bacon and half-dozen eggs in the refrigerator. And coffee. I wanted coffee, several cups.

My muscles protested as I shuffled around the kitchen. I dropped the skillet and thought for sure Alex would come running, but he slept right through it. Given the number of times I woke up crying, he likely hadn't slept much.

Finally, after dropping pans and nearly falling on my face a couple of times, bacon sizzled in the pan. The sound served as a balm for my soul, and it smelled good, too. The coffee maker sputtered to life when I flipped the switch, and I dug through his cabinet looking for my Sherlock mug. *Maybe I already packed it. Duh, that's in my apartment, not here.* I really did need my morning mug, or noon mug in this case.

Bureau trotted into the kitchen. He planted himself next to his bowls and stared at me. Answering his silent request, I filled his water bowl and after a quick search found his cat food. He brushed against my legs as I dumped a scoop into his bowl.

I lifted the bacon out onto a platter and laid more bacon strips in the pan. While the second batch cooked, I set plates and silverware on the table and sipped a second cup of coffee.

Breakfast was almost ready. I glanced at the heaps of food and shook my head. *I hope he likes bacon as much as I do.* I wanted Alex to wake up.

CHAPTER SEVEN

January 10, 2016 – 12:38pm

The smell of bacon wafted in from the kitchen. Alex startled awake. Alone in the bed, he remembered the long night of nightmares and soothing. Plates clinked in the kitchen. He tumbled out of bed and tried to smooth down his hair.

In the kitchen, he found her standing at the stove scrambling eggs. It was like a Saturday morning breakfast all over again, but with a different woman in a different kitchen. He rubbed his face trying to push back the memory.

"Good morning." She lifted bacon slices out of the pan and laid them on a towel-covered platter.

"You didn't have to cook." He brewed himself a mug of coffee.

"I needed bacon. And to apologize for last night."

He waved off her apology.

Her face colored a warm pink. "No, I do. I'm embarrassed even thinking about it." She carried a pan to the table, still limping, and dished eggs onto each plate.

"It was kinda funny." He took the pan from her. "Please sit. Let me do that. What happened to your hand?"

She lowered herself into the seat and smiled to cover her wince. "Grease splattered. Bandage caught the worst of it."

After setting the pan on the stove, he returned with the platter of bacon and snatched a slice as he set it down. "Let me get you a clean one."

"After we eat. Please eat. I made too much food. You don't have any eggs or bacon left in the fridge." She'd clearly slept off the pain meds.

Despite how nervous it made him, it amused him to listen to her ramble last night. And the way she'd looked at him with a faraway stare, he'd found rather cute. "Last night—" He snapped a slice of bacon in half and took a bite.

"Please, can we forget about that? Or at least not talk about it?"

He wasn't sure he wanted to forget. He picked up another slice. "I can't resist bacon."

"I know. I love the stuff." She reached for another slice.

Alex ran to the office and picked up a notepad and pen. When he got back to the table, he handed them to her. "You remembered something. You should write it down."

"I also remembered my favorite mug. Think they can figure out my identity based on that?"

"We can search The Backstreet Boys fan club and see if any names trigger a memory." He hoped the comment would earn him a laugh.

She rolled her eyes. "What time am I supposed to meet with the sketch artist to describe Corey and the other guy?"

"Corey?"

"Yeah. He was the guy that wouldn't quit talking. The other one told him to shut up in the van."

"DJ said to let him know when you were up."

Alex tapped out a quick message: *She remembered a first name. Corey. What time today?*

DJ replied: *2 pm. Thanks for the name.*

Once the plates were cleared off the table and the dishes washed up, Alex sat down across from her at the table. "I asked DJ's wife, Becca, to get you some clothes. Not that those lounge pants and massive sweatshirt don't look just amazing on you."

Melodic laughter burst out of her like popcorn from an air popper.

Alex struggled to remember what he was saying. "We'll stop by her house on the way to the station."

"Thanks. It'll be nice to not run around in tube socks." She leaned back in her chair, and Bureau jumped into her lap. "Your cat's name is funny. Did you work for the FBI?"

"No." He chuckled.

"You have that quiet presence. It made me wonder. So how did Bureau get his name?" She stroked the shiny black fur.

"Well, when I moved in here, I needed furniture."

The cat jumped down, and she leaned forward on the table, her chin resting on a fist.

"I stopped by a yard sale and bought my recliner, this table, and the bureau that's in the bedroom. I wrangled DJ into helping me unload it all."

Her eyes twinkled when she smiled. He hopped up and dropped another pod into the single-serve coffee maker. As his coffee brewed, he continued his story.

"Anyway, much later that night, I woke to a horrible yowling. It was coming from the bureau. A little, black kitten had hitched a ride. In the middle of the night, his empty tummy overcame his fear, and he made his presence known. I fished him out the drawer and fed him leftover chicken. After that, he was my best friend."

"That's adorable."

"He spent the rest of the night curled up near my feet. The next morning I took him back to the house where I'd purchased the furniture, but the people were gone. Moved. According to the neighbor, they had several cats and left them all behind. So I brought the little hitchhiker home and named him..."

"Bureau," she said at the same moment he said the name.

"Seemed like an appropriate name." Alex half smiled. "Speaking of names. I've been thinking about what I can call you until we figure out who you really are."

"If it's a reference to anything I said after the shot, I'll die of embarrassment."

"I wouldn't do that. Bureau got his name from where I found him."

"Please don't call me Door or Outside."

"What about Rainy Night?"

She raised both eyebrows. "I can't tell if you're serious or not."

"Just Rainy for short."

"Okay." She almost giggled.

Before they left the cabin, Alex glanced around. *If one of those thugs looked in, would they know she was staying here?* He ran to the bedroom and gathered the bloody quilt and clothes. He tossed them into the washer and started it before meeting Rainy back in the living room. "I'm ready now."

He unlocked the truck remotely and ushered Rainy out the door. He scanned the trees as he helped her into the passenger seat, then grabbed a ball cap from the backseat. "Put this on."

She tucked her curls up inside and pulled it low over her eyes.

On the way into town, he checked his mirror every few minutes. Keeping her safe was his priority. It was as if he had another chance. It wouldn't make up for what happened to Ellie, but maybe somewhere it would balance the scales.

Alex helped Rainy out of the truck. As they walked up the sidewalk, he slowed his steps and matched her pace.

Becca answered the door, smiling. "Come on in."

"Becca, this is my friend Rainy. That's what I'm calling her until someone tells me otherwise. Rainy, this is Becca."

"Let me guess, Alex chose the name?" Becca shook her head.

"It was raining when I showed up."

Becca rolled her eyes. "Alex sent me your sizes. I hope the stuff I got fits." She led them into the living room. Spread out on the couch were several outfits, undergarments, and a pair of tennis shoes. On the coffee table lay beauty products, hair ties, and deodorant. "I washed all the clothes."

Rainy wiped her cheeks. "This is overwhelming. It's too much."

"Becca, pack it all back up." Alex stared at Rainy stone-faced for several seconds. "She prefers my tube socks." He winked at her, hoping to hear that laugh again.

She rewarded him and blinked away the tears. "Okay, you made your point." She hugged Becca. "Thank you."

"I put a tote bag there on the couch. Choose what you want to wear, and we can stow the rest in the bag. You can change in the bathroom, that way."

Rainy gathered an outfit and padded off to change.

"Alex, are you sure this is a good idea? You seem invested. This isn't like taking in a lost kitten." Becca kept her voice low.

"Good idea or not, she's staying with me until the kidnappers are caught or she wants to leave."

"I'm worried about you. DJ said you were carrying her and holding her hand. You don't know anything about her. Protecting her won't change the past."

Alex glared at her. "I am painfully aware that *nothing* will change the past."

"Alex, don't." Becca sounded near tears, and he immediately regretted his tone.

"How much do I owe you for all this?" He slid his wallet out of his back pocket.

"Don't worry about it." Becca dabbed the corners of her eyes.

"I insist. Please." He had a debt to pay, and he couldn't allow her to forgive it.

She handed him the receipt. "I got some groceries also. I wasn't sure if you needed extra now that you had a houseguest."

He rifled through his wallet, pulling out cash. "Thank you. I'm sorry I got mad."

"Promise me you'll talk to DJ—" She clapped her hands. "Yay. They fit."

Alex spun around. Rainy's hair was pulled back into a ponytail, but rebel curls hung loose near her face. *Why do you find her so captivating?* She looked nothing like Ellie. Rainy's hair was brown, and she was several inches shorter.

Dressed in jeans and a fitted blouse, she ran her hands down the sides of her waist. "Thank you, Becca. They're perfect." She laid her hand on Alex's arm. "I know you arranged for all this."

"Do y'all have time for coffee?" Becca pointed to the kitchen.

Alex checked his phone. "Unfortunately not. I need to have her at the station in ten minutes. Raincheck?"

"I wish we had more time. I really appreciate all this." Rainy tied the laces on her new shoes.

"I'll stop back by and pick up the groceries and clothes when we're finished at the station." He held out his hand to help Rainy up.

"Sure." Becca followed them out to the porch and waved as they climbed into the truck.

"Alex, you're very lucky to have friends like Becca and DJ. They don't even know me."

"DJ has to help. That's his job." Alex chuckled. "But, yeah."

When they walked into the station, DJ was standing near the front desk. "Speak of the devil. You're right on time."

"DJ, meet Rainy."

"You let him give you a name? Did you get to hear the cat story first?"

She laughed. "I did, but I kinda owe him so I let him choose. I kinda like it."

"It's really Rainy Night, but I shortened it." Alex flashed a boyish grin.

"Well, Rainy, follow me back and I'll get you set up with Sally, our sketch artist."

DJ handed Alex a cup of coffee. "Not sure how long it'll take."

"Any leads?"

"Nothing yet. I put out a BOLO on the van. Her prints didn't match any in AFIS."

"BOLO?"

"Be on the lookout." DJ ran his fingers through his hair. "It may take a few days, but we'll get 'em."

"Think they'll come after her?"

"Without knowing more, I can't say. It's possible, but they could've skipped town after she escaped."

"She's more relaxed now, but she was pretty scared last night."

"That's not surprising."

"During the night, she woke nearly every hour in tears."

"You *slept* with her?"

"Keep your voice down!" Alex felt his face grow warm. DJ's implication made him mad. "Not like that."

"Alex, as your friend, I have to say..." He drank down the rest of his coffee. "That was a really bad idea."

"Was I supposed to let her sob the whole night?"

"What did she mean when she said she owes you?"

"I had Becca buy her clothes."

DJ shook his head.

Alex stifled his irritation. "You know me."

"I thought I did. This you is not the same guy I've known for the last three years."

"You've known me longer than that."

"Yeah, well, a lot has happened."

Alex stewed on the way back to the cabin, still irritated with DJ.

Rainy turned to face him. "The sketch artist did a good job. Her drawings looked like those two guys."

"Hopefully that helps catch 'em."

"We forgot to get the stuff from Becca."

"Crap. I did. We'll drive back in a bit." Alex chided himself for forgetting. He'd let his irritation with DJ occupy his thoughts.

He turned down the narrow road to the cabin. When he rounded the bend in the driveway, he rattled off a few colorful words. The cabin door hung open. He sure hadn't left it that way. Anger raced through his veins and pounded in his neck. *Just like that night.* He reached for Rainy's hand. "Stay in the truck." He half-expected his chest to explode at any moment.

She slouched down and squeezed his hand. "Please don't get out."

Wheel treads left deep grooves in the mud. The doorjamb was splintered.

"I won't." He called DJ. "Someone broke into the cabin while we were in town."

"Don't go inside. I'm on my way," DJ said.

Alex fumed. Rubbing his thumb in the cleft of his chin, he silently cursed the kidnappers.

"They were looking for me, weren't they?" She watched for his reaction.

He stroked her hand with his thumb. "I'm not sure. We'll see if anything is missing. Maybe it was a random break-in." His gut told him she was right.

"What about Bureau?" Her eyes puddled.

"Don't cry. I'll check on him when DJ gets here." He wiped a tear off her cheek. "As soon as I get a chance, I'll run you back to Becca's. You can stay with her while DJ writes up his report and the door gets fixed."

"If you think it's safer."

"Until the door is fixed, I think it is." Keeping his fingers entwined with hers, he called to arrange for a handyman. He called three different businesses before he found one that could fix the door on a Sunday afternoon.

Her cool fingers had a calming effect on him. They pulled his mind away from painful memories. He'd reached for her hand to make her feel safe. He wanted her to know she was not alone.

Her fingers tightened around his hand when the Chevy Tahoe pulled up.

"It's DJ." He gave her hand a gentle squeeze. "Once he gives the all clear, we'll go in."

DJ parked next to Alex's blue GMC truck and started talking before his feet hit the dirt. "Wait here. I'll be back out in a few." Minutes later, he returned. "It's clear. There's no one in there. Let's do a walkthrough. I need to know if anything is missing."

Alex slid out of the truck. "Wait a sec."

She tensed until she saw he'd walked around to her door. He pulled it open and stuck out his hand. She gripped it, but after sliding out of the truck, she didn't let go.

DJ tipped his hat. "Sorry about all this."

At the front door, Rainy pointed. "It's my fault. They knew I came here. Look."

DJ and Alex saw the blood on the door frame, protected from the rain by the overhang of the roof.

"When I fell, I left blood on the door. They know I'm here."

Alex silently berated himself for not noticing. *What if she'd been here when they showed up?*

DJ snapped pictures. "They know you *were* here. I doubt they expect you to return."

In the cabin, they surveyed each room, careful not to touch anything. Alex expected to find the cabin in shambles, but it wasn't. The recliner was shifted to one side. His book no longer rested on the side table but lay open on the floor. Papers on his desk were a jumbled pile rather than the stacks he'd left. The computer was on, but at the login screen.

"They'll assume you've gone to the police, I'd guess. So they'll either lay low or leave town," DJ said as he scribbled in his notebook.

"Where's Bureau?" Rainy looked around.

Alex darted from room to room calling for the black cat. When Bureau didn't come, he trotted into the kitchen and dumped a scoop of kibble into the food bowl. "This usually brings him running." But the cat didn't come. After walking through the entire cabin a second time, Alex ran his fingers through his hair. "Think Becca is up for some company?"

"I'll let her know you're on your way." DJ already had the phone to his ear.

Alex caught Rainy's hand as they walked out to the truck. "I found a guy that can come out today and fix the door."

"Poor Bureau. I'm worried about him."

"I'll go out and look for him later. First, I want to get you out of here."

"I'm sorry."

He turned to face her. "None of this is your fault."

Twenty minutes later, Becca waved from her porch as Alex pulled up along the curb. He followed Rainy inside.

"I'm back for that cup of coffee." She tried to hide her fear.

Becca nodded toward the kitchen. "I've got sandwiches made, and a pot of coffee brewing."

Alex stopped. "They aren't bologna, are they?"

"Eww. No." Becca scrunched up her nose. "Chicken salad and ham salad."

He nabbed a sandwich off the tray and leaned against the wall next to his brown-eyed friend. "I'll be back after a while." He squeezed her hand. "You okay?"

She nodded.

He grabbed another sandwich. "Rainy?"

When she met his gaze, he saw her misty eyelashes.

"I'll be back as soon as I can. I wouldn't leave you here if I didn't think it was safe." He brushed his knuckles along her hand. "Becca has my number if you need anything."

"I'll be fine." She laid her hand on his chest. "Hurry back, though. Please."

"I will." He squeezed her hand against his chest ignoring the questioning stare from Becca. "Lock the door behind me."

April 21, 1993

Dear Claire,

A cake smothered with blue and yellow flowers is disappearing off the cake stand piece by piece. Maybe a sugar coma will help numb my pain.

This year, I am mad. I hate the beast. Once upon a time, he said he loved me, but he lied. Stealing away my little girl was hateful and mean.

Daddy and I moved to a house in San Antonio, but we spent your birthday in Schatzenburg.

Hurry home to me, Claire.

Happy Birthday,

Mommy & Daddy

April 21, 1994

Dear Claire,

Double digits! I want to smother you with hugs and kisses, but that probably isn't what a ten-year-old wants from her mom. Oh, the page is getting wet. I promised myself I wouldn't cry. You don't need to read about my weeping and wailing, but a few teardrops can't be helped.

I am so proud of you. I know that wherever you are, you're a remarkable young lady.

This year I baked cupcakes. Sometimes when I'm upset I cook or bake. Normally I cook lots and lots of food, but as your tenth birthday approached, I baked. I baked ten dozen cupcakes! Your dad laughed when he came into the kitchen. (His laughter is such a wonderful sound.)

He sat at the table and helped me frost all ten dozen. After that, we shopped for your gift.

I miss you, Claire. I miss the sound of your laughter.

Do you mind if I share your cupcakes with the neighbors in Schatzenburg? I try to spend every one of your birthdays at The Castle. That's what I call Grandma Betty's house.

We love you, Claire!

Best Birthday Wishes,

Mom & Dad

Chapter Eight
January 10, 2016 – 3:16pm

I stood at the window a little too long and watched Alex. He stopped to speak with another gentleman and motioned toward the house a time or two. Then the two of them shook hands, and Alex climbed into the truck. He glanced toward the house and saw me at the window. He waved before he pulled away from the curb. I stared until the truck was out of sight.

Becca tilted her head. There was a hint of something in her eyes, something I didn't understand. "That was Brady, my neighbor. Alex probably asked him to keep an eye out while he's gone."

I followed her into the kitchen.

"I don't think I've ever seen Alex so talkative." Becca held out the plate of sandwiches. "Help yourself." There was no hint of sarcasm in her expression.

"You're joking, right?" I took a sandwich from the tray.

"Yes. Alex is more inclined to let other people talk most of the time." She pulled a jug of sweet tea out of the refrigerator and poured us each a glass.

"Makes me wonder what's not being said." The more I was around him, the more I wondered how a guy like him was single.

We settled at the table and munched on chips and sandwiches. Becca didn't share anything else about Alex.

"How are you? Really. And I don't want the 'I'll be fine' answer you gave Alex." Becca wrapped up the remaining sandwiches.

"I've never been more scared than I was last night. When I stumbled on Alex's place, I wasn't sure if it was safe to knock. Then Bureau jumped in the window."

"That cat is the best thing that's happened to him in a while."

I drew circles in the condensation on my glass and worried that the best thing that ever happened to Alex was injured somewhere in the woods. "The fear is never far away. Out of nowhere, it wraps itself around me like vines. He makes me feel protected." I locked eyes with Becca. "Tell me he's a good guy and that it's okay to stay there. I don't want to take advantage of him, but I really need a safe place right now." My voice wavered, but I maintained my composure.

"He'll protect you." She focused on the table, corralling crumbs with her finger. Her interest in the table and her clipped words didn't make it hard to guess there was more to Alex's story, some reason she felt protective of him, some reason she didn't like the idea of me staying at the cabin.

"There is something you aren't saying. Is it a bad thing for him to have me there?"

She stared at the crumbs before finally looking up. "I don't know. Only Alex knows the answer to that, and he asked you to stay." Her brown eyes didn't betray any deeper thoughts.

"Should I go to the women's shelter? Would that be better for him?" My hands shook, and I set down my glass so the tea wouldn't spill.

"You'll have to ask Alex." She carried the sandwiches to the kitchen.

I dropped my head onto my arms. Now I was afraid, not only

that kidnappers were after me, but that in letting Alex protect me, I was hurting him.

Becca sighed when she walked up to the table. "Listen, I shouldn't have said anything. It's just..." She put a hand on my shoulder. "Follow me. Let's go into the craft room."

"Okay." As I stood up, my hip protested the movement. I rubbed it, wishing I'd remembered to take something for the pain.

The bedroom turned craft room had one wall covered in shelves. Bead trays filled over half of them. Under the window, on a standing height counter, black velvet boards displayed ornate necklaces. The table in the middle of the room was covered with old brooches and strands of beads.

"Wow. You made all those?"

"I repurpose old jewelry. Brooches become pendants and focal components. Old strands of beads get restrung."

"Do you have a shop?"

"No. Mostly special orders and occasionally a booth in a local show."

"These are amazing."

Becca became animated as she told me how she started creating jewelry. That topic spawned a new subject and then another, and we conversed easily for over an hour. I liked her. She was interesting and easy to talk to.

"How long have you and DJ been married?" I lined up the bead strands in even rows.

"Four years." Becca held up a wire and let beads slide to the far end.

I grouped the loose beads into piles by color. "How did you meet?"

Becca laughed. "You want my version or DJ's?"

"Yours, of course."

She laid down the wire strung with beads, and her smile hung like a necklace from ear to ear. "He lived here in town and worked for the sheriff's department. I was on a road trip with a girl from church, but it was one of the shortest road trips ever, for me at least. We left San Antonio, and we were almost out of Kerrville when we saw lights flashing behind us."

"Oops. Who was driving?"

"She was. I didn't think it was a big deal, but my friend was in hysterics, crying about how she was going to jail. I thought she was just being dramatic."

"Uh oh."

"She asked me to climb into the driver's seat, and I refused."

"Like that ever works anyway."

"Well, when DJ sauntered up to the window and asked for her license and insurance, she handed them to him. They were both expired. So he told us to sit tight and went back to the patrol car. Meanwhile, my friend acted all weird, and I wondered what she was hiding."

"So what happened?"

"DJ walked back up to the window and handed her tickets. She was free to go."

"Sounds like she was lucky."

"She was mean, is what she was. She told me to get out of the car. As soon as I stepped out, she threw my bag out the window."

I stared at Becca in disbelief. "But DJ was still there?"

"Oh, yeah. He gave me a ride to the sheriff's office."

"So you were stranded?"

"Yep. I texted every friend I could think of to give me a ride. Everyone was busy. My parents were out of town. DJ checked on me every little while. It was downright embarrassing. I probably sat out there two hours before DJ asked if he could take me to dinner."

"And I guess that went well."

Becca scrunched up her nose. "Parts of it went well. He drove me home to San Antonio, but I forgot my bag in his truck. The next morning, he showed up at my door with it. We spent the day together. Six months later, we married." Becca beamed.

"What a great story! What happened to your friend?"

"I never heard from her again," she said as she slid her finger across the screen of her cell phone to answer it. "Hello." She nodded several times as she listened. "Love you. See you later." She ended the call and picked up the necklace she'd been stringing. "DJ said the handyman is on his way to the cabin now."

CHAPTER NINE

January 10, 2016 – 3:40pm

"Peter?" Alex waved as a hefty man in overalls climbed out of a blue van. *Peter O Tool* was painted in large, white letters on the side. The man moseyed to the door, a janitor-size key ring jingling with each step.

"Yep, that's me." He stared at the door and shook his head. "Wow, someone doesn't like you."

"They wanted in but didn't have a key. You can fix it today, right?" Alex shoved his hands deep into his pockets afraid he wouldn't like the answer.

"Yep, yep. No problem." His toothpick bounced up and down as he talked. "Picked up a door and frame on the way out here. I can have a new one installed in no time."

"Thanks so much. Holler if you need something." Alex didn't even ask about the price.

"Will do." Peter sauntered to the van, seemingly unhurried, and swung open the back doors. He struggled to lift the new door, and Alex offered to help.

"Much appreciated. Seems odd having a break-in way out here. Usually not much crime in these parts."

"They didn't even take anything. The only thing missing is my cat."

"Uh oh. We have cat-nappers on the loose." Peter jiggled as he laughed.

Together they hoisted the door out of the back and hauled it to the cabin. Peter wasted no time getting to work. He started by yanking out the broken frame covered in fingerprint dust.

Inside, two officers continued their hunt for prints.

DJ met Alex near the front door. "Let's step outside for a bit. We can search for Bureau."

"What's up?" Alex followed him away from the cabin.

DJ was quiet until they were far enough away to have a private conversation. "Is there anything you aren't telling me?"

"What are you talking about?"

"This all seems a bit crazy, Alex. A woman shows up at your door in the middle of the night. You, Mr. Personal Space, carry her into the hospital, hold hands with her, then sleep with her. She insists on staying with you. And then someone breaks into your house but takes nothing. All of that within the last twelve hours? What gives?"

"I've told you everything." Alex turned his back and stepped away, trying to calm his temper. "And quit saying I slept with her."

"Just be careful." DJ sighed.

"Do you think she's lying about something?"

"I wouldn't have let her go to Becca's if I thought she was dangerous."

"You know what I mean."

"Nothing she's said would make me think she's lied, but I'll feel better when I can confirm any part of her story." DJ lifted his hat and ran his fingers through his hair. "I'm worried about you."

"Listen. When I invited her into my cabin, I took on the responsibility of keeping her safe. I know it sounds stupid, like I'm trying to make up for the past, and maybe I am." Alex inhaled deeply then slowly let the breath escape. "If anything were to happen to her, I couldn't live with myself."

"Don't talk that way."

Alex glanced up into the trees and hoped to spot yellow eyes staring back. "They still working in the office?"

"Yeah. Your desk will be a mess, but they're hoping to pull prints off the keyboard. Maybe they tried to log into the computer."

"If they need to take it, I've got a spare."

An hour later, a new door stood in place of the broken one, fingerprint dust covered surfaces throughout the cabin, and DJ and the other two officers had returned to the station. Alex paid Peter, surprised at how reasonable the charge was.

As soon as the blue van pulled away, Alex snatched his keys off the table. Bureau wouldn't fare well outside after dark, and the black cat would be harder to spot then. After locking the cabin, Alex traversed the surrounding area calling the cat. He plodded a serpentine route through the trees, calling and looking up into the branches. After a discouraging half-hour, there was a faint meow from somewhere in the trees around him.

He spun around, his eyes darting from tree to tree. "Come on down, Bureau. Where are you?" He turned to his right. A small chunk of bark skittered down the tree next to him. Bureau stretched his lean frame trying to work his way down the tree. When the cat was within arm's reach, Alex gathered him up and held him close. "Hello, Bureau Cat."

As soon as Alex stepped into the cabin, the cat jumped from his arms. "I'm glad you came home. Our new friend would never have forgiven herself if you'd stayed gone."

After checking that all the windows were locked and that the front door was secure, Alex climbed into the truck and headed to Becca's house. His foot rested heavy on the accelerator as he zipped toward the highway. Forking his fingers through his hair, he glanced at the time. *Maybe her safety has nothing to do with why you want to be near her.* The thought surprised him. He wasn't ready to admit that. His first priority was to keep her safe until the kidnappers were behind bars.

CHAPTER TEN

January 10, 2016 – 5:15pm

I smiled as a message popped up on Becca's phone. Apparently, my talents extended to reading upside down with ease.

Alex texted: *Tell Rainy I'm on my way.*

"I hope you remember who you are soon." Becca added a crimp bead to the end of the strand and looped the wire through a clasp. "That way he'll quit calling you Rainy."

"I think it's funny."

"Don't encourage him." She snipped the end of the wire. "By the way, you're more than welcome to stay here if you'd like."

I didn't know how to respond.

She smiled at my hesitation. "I understand that sometimes safety isn't about where you are so much as who you're with." She didn't look up from her strand of beads.

"Thanks."

I followed her into the kitchen and helped her gather the groceries. When Alex's truck pulled up to the curb, I watched from the kitchen doorway as she opened the front door.

"Door's fixed. Everything okay here?" He looked past her, focused solely on me.

"Yep." Becca pointed to the kitchen. "Want to take sandwiches with you?"

"Sure." He crossed the room and stopped in front of me. All the tension from earlier had melted away, and he seemed almost relaxed. "I found him. He'd taken refuge in a tree, but he was back inside happily eating when I left."

Thankful the fuzzy little greeter was safe at home, I breathed a little easier. "Oh, good. I'm so glad." I turned to Becca. "Thanks for letting me hang out here."

"Anytime. It was fun, despite the circumstances. You're welcome to come back whenever."

Alex loaded his arms with bags and headed to the truck.

Becca touched my arm as I stepped out the door. "I don't want to leave you with the wrong impression. I do think you landed at his door for a reason. He'll do everything he can to keep you safe, and I think you're helping him, too."

"Wha—?"

She held up her hand warding off any other questions. "That's all I'll say for now."

As soon as Alex opened the cabin door, I scooped up Bureau and smothered him with a hug. If the purring was any indication, he was happy to be home. Alex carried the groceries into the kitchen. "After I get these put away, let's look at those pictures you found."

"Sure." I carried a bag of flour to the pantry. "You planning to do a lot of baking? You have two bags of flour."

"Becca bought the groceries. I guess she thought I'd need flour. Eggs, too." He stacked two cartons of eggs in the refrigerator.

The office stood out in contrast to the other rooms in the cabin. It was crowded. Alex held a rag in each hand. "Give me a few minutes to clean up this mess and fish out my other keyboard."

"I'll start in the kitchen."

"You don't have to."

"I know." I wandered into the bedroom and dug through the bag from Becca for something more suited to scrubbing the kitchen. God bless her. She bought me yoga pants. I pulled on the Texas Aggie sweatshirt, which was draped across the quilt at the foot of the bed. It smelled fresh. *When did he have time for laundry?*

The kitchen didn't have too many areas covered in powder and, within twenty minutes, I had most of it cleaned up.

Alex called out from the office. "All done."

"Looks like you stay busy in here." I gathered my hair back into a ponytail and twisted a hair band around it.

Alex turned to answer me, but he was quiet as a smile spread across his face and twinkled in his green eyes. My cheeks warmed slightly as he stared. It was times like these that I wished thought bubbles showed up above his head. But only his, not mine, especially if I took any more painkillers.

"You changed into my sweatshirt."

"Is that okay?"

"Uh huh. Anyway, I'm a computer guy of sorts, a programmer. I do all kinds of contract jobs that I can work remotely." A rack of computers lined one wall. An L-shaped desk cluttered with papers, monitors, a keyboard, and a mouse covered another two walls. He emptied papers out of his extra chair. "Have a seat. Let me print those pictures." He opened the scanned photos and sent them to the printer.

Alex picked up a photo. He looked at it, then at me. "Have you seen this?"

"No."

He stuck it in my hand. It was of a lady standing on a street corner with a child on her hip. The child was reaching toward the ground. I resembled the lady holding the little girl. Resembled was too mild a word. I looked a lot like her. Her hair was even the same shade of brown and fell to just below the shoulder, like mine.

"That was the one labeled *Emma and Claire 1986.*"

"Nothing about it seems familiar."

He looked at the other photo. "It looks like someone snapped this picture without you knowing." He tilted it so I could see it.

I was standing near a car, a grey Ford Focus. As he handed me the older photograph, his fingertips brushed the edge of my hand.

Pulling my gaze away from his hand, I focused on the photo dated 1986 while he studied the newer picture. "Look at this. There are street signs. One says Main I think, but I can't quite make out the other one."

Alex rummaged through the desk drawers until he found a magnifying glass. "Try this."

I moved the glass up and down until the words were magnified enough to read. "Fourth." The magnifying glass brought out my inner Sherlock. "Do you mind if I use your computer?"

"Not at all." He logged in and opened a browser. I pulled up a map site and searched for the intersection. *Fourth and Main.* They were popular street names. Those two streets crossed in many cities and towns across the United States.

"I need to narrow it down."

"You seem to know what you're doing. Trigger any memories?"

"Yeah, but it doesn't make sense."

"Tell me anyway."

"A tree without branches. When I sat down to search, I thought of a tree, not one with leafless branches, but a tree whose branches were missing. Told you it didn't make sense." I handed him the photo and pointed at the trees. "Speaking of, do you know what kind those are?"

He switched on a desk light and stared at the photo. "Pecan, I think. And what's this here on the ground?"

I copied the entire result list and pasted it into a spreadsheet. That made it easier to delete the results that didn't fit what we knew. I eliminated all the locations where pecan trees aren't found.

Squinting through the magnifying glass to make out the tiny letters, Alex laughed out loud. "Can I use the computer for a second?"

I leaned back in the chair, and he reached in front of me. He smelled like citrus and musk. The combination of scents, subtle and masculine, lingered in the air.

The older photo popped onto the screen, and Alex used the zoom tool to focus in on the street signs. "I guess we really didn't need the magnifying glass. They're both streets." That eliminated all the avenues, boulevards, circles, and roads. The list of possibilities shrunk.

For the next couple hours, I sat in front of the computer. He held the picture, and together we eliminated possibilities.

"The list is still too long. I have no idea where this picture was taken." I pushed back from the desk, frustrated.

Alex rested his hand on my shoulder. "It's a start. We'll chip away at it."

"Slowly. I hate slowly."

He patted me on the shoulder. "Let's shut this down. I'll make dinner."

I looked back at the screen.

"Please." He held out his hand.

In the kitchen, Alex buzzed around, while I pulled dishes out of the cabinet. "I've got rib eye steaks and asparagus. You like asparagus?"

"Who knows?" I shrugged. "I guess I'll find out."

I set two plates on the table along with silverware and napkins. Everything smelled delicious. The asparagus roasted in the oven, the steaks sizzled in a searing hot pan, and the rice steamed in a pot on the back burner. I scored extra points for being rescued by a tall, handsome guy that could cook.

I fished the steak knives out of the drawer. "I keep replaying the things I heard those guys say when I was in that closet." I fiddled with them which put my fingers at great risk. "And what Corey said as I was trying to escape."

He pulled the asparagus out of the oven and turned to face me. "DJ'll figure it out."

"I know. But I keep thinking about what he said. He mentioned my friend. It sounded like they hurt her." I stared at the knives in my hand and dropped them on the table. "And now I've gotten you mixed up in all this. I'm sorry." I had a lot of guilt about his splintered door and runaway cat. At least the cat was home. Unwelcome tears sprang up.

"Please, please don't cry." Alex wiped his hands on a dishtowel and stepped toward me. He opened his arms as if he was going to hug me but hesitated.

I closed the gap and leaned into his chest. He wrapped his arms around me.

"We'll watch the news at ten. Maybe someone is looking for you." He released me and pointed to the table. "Have a seat. Everything is ready."

April 21, 1995

Dear Claire,

Happy Birthday! This year's birthday cake is decorated to look like a big yellow happy face. Is it too much to hope that even living with the beast you're somehow happy?

I finally broke down and hired someone to help me at the house we bought in San Antonio. She is a very nice lady. She keeps the house clean and cooks some of our meals.

There are so many things I want you to know, but, so often when I sit down to write, I forget most of them. Here's an important truth I can never forget. Sometimes people make bad choices, but good things happen anyway. The most amazing things can grow from the worst possible circumstances.

My eyes are full of tears. I love you, Claire.

Love Always,

Mom & Dad

Chapter Eleven

January 10, 2016 – 9:42pm

Alex set a plate in the dish drain and turned to Rainy. "Want to study the pictures a bit more?"

"Yeah." She leaned on the counter next to him while he hung the towel. "I was thinking. Maybe if I find out about Claire, I'll learn something that explains why I was kidnapped."

"Do you think you're Claire?"

"I don't know. I know I look like the mom in that photo, but I'd expect the name Emma or Claire to trigger a memory. It doesn't. Not even a little."

He brushed his hand against hers. "Let's pull up the list of those intersections and sort it by state."

They walked into the office, and after a few clicks of the mouse, she'd reordered the list. "Done."

Alex rested one hand on her shoulder as he reached around her and ran a finger down the screen. "I wonder where Schatzenburg is."

"I'll map it."

A little dot popped up on the map between Kerrville and San Antonio.

"That's pretty close to here, right by Comfort, maybe thirty minutes away."

"Comfort?"

"Great name for a town, isn't it?"

She pulled up the street view. "Alex, you're a genius. That's it." The trees were bigger, and the grass wasn't as green, but it was unmistakably the same place.

"Tomorrow morning we'll drive over there." He let his hand linger on her shoulder. "It's a few minutes after ten. Want to watch the news?"

"Maybe they'll show something about me."

He followed Rainy into the bedroom and tapped the power button on the television before picking up the remote off the nightstand. She sat on the bed, then crawled toward the center, leaving ample room to sit without touching her. He perched at the edge of the bed. As he clicked through the channels, his thoughts replayed the last 24 hours.

"Look! The car." She grabbed his arm.

A picture of a grey Ford Focus filled the screen, then the young reporter, wearing a power tie, asked for anyone with information to call the San Antonio Police Department. They'd missed all the important details of the segment.

"Can you rewind it?"

"I can't. I changed the channel. That car looks the same as the one in the picture." He glanced down at her hand wrapped around his forearm.

"Should we tell DJ or something?" She focused those dark eyes on him, and the room seemed to grow smaller.

"Yeah. I'll let him know." Alex jumped off the bed. "Want some coffee?" He hurried out of the room.

She followed him to the kitchen.

"Or I have cocoa."

"Hot cocoa, please."

He shot off a quick text to DJ while the water boiled and the coffee brewed: *Grey Ford Focus on news. Connection?*

Alex handed her a mug and nodded toward the living room. "Let's sit by the fire."

She burrowed into the recliner, and he used the hearth as a seat. She blew into the mug, sending steam dancing upward. "I've only seen you drink coffee. Why do you have fancy teas and hot cocoa?"

"DJ and Becca. Mostly Becca, I'm sure. They gave me a basket of cookies, tea, and hot chocolate at Christmas."

She sipped on her cocoa, watching over the rim of the cup. "What made you move way out here? Kind of lonely, isn't it?"

The question knocked the air out of his lungs. He stared at the rug, hoping for a coherent explanation to pop into his head.

She waited.

He rested his elbows on his knees and took a deep breath. "I got tired of too many well-intentioned clichés." He sipped his coffee, then ran his thumb through the cleft in his chin.

She slid out of the recliner and sat near him on the floor.

"I heard so many. I'm not sure which I disliked most." He watched her trace the pattern in the rug. "Time heals all wounds. That was a common one. I always wanted to ask 'How much? Does it take years? Decades? Lifetimes…?', but I knew no one would have an answer." He stared into his mug before taking a few more sips.

"Or then there's…" He shifted the coffee cup and wrapped his hands around it. "Every cloud has a silver lining. I hated that one the most because the only silver lining I remember was in her casket."

Rainy's shock came out in a whimper.

He swallowed down the last of his coffee. "And last but not least…" He glared into his empty mug before smashing it against the fireplace. "When God closes a door, he opens a window." He kicked at the pieces on the floor. "She wasn't a door. She was my wife."

Rainy flinched and wiped at tears that wouldn't stop. "What happened to her?"

Straightening, he shook his head slightly and locked eyes with her. "I moved out here to be alone. To never hear those words again." He jumped up, grabbed the bag for wood, and bolted out the front door.

Near the woodpile, he leaned against the shed. Tears stored deep under the surface bubbled up, and he cried, something he hadn't allowed himself to do since they put Ellie in the ground. After a few minutes, he rubbed his face and piled logs in the canvas bag. *You've made a mess of things.* With the wood slung over his shoulder, he headed back toward the cabin. At the window, he stopped.

Rainy's hands shook as she picked up the broken pieces. Over and over, she dragged the back of her empty hand across her face. He stepped back when she walked past. He rested his head on the outside of the door. *You made her cry.*

When he stepped back inside, she wasn't in the living room. Bureau rubbed against his legs and then trotted to the bedroom flicking his tail.

Alex added logs to the fire and listened as she cried softly in the other room. *Great job sharing your feelings.*

Hours later, Bureau wrested Alex from a deep sleep pawing at his face. "What, Bur—" Quiets sobs emanated from the bedroom. Throwing off the quilt, he jumped out of the chair without lowering the footrest. He hesitated. *Has she been crying this whole time?* He stood outside the bedroom and peeked in. Rainy sat on the bed hugging her knees, her brown curls covering her face.

"Rainy?"

She shook her head and continued to sob.

"What can I do?" Helpless, he dropped to his knees next to the bed. *This is your fault.*

She peered at him from under her curls. "There's nothing you can do."

"Please. I'm sorry. I shouldn't have smashed the mug." He reached his hand toward her, but she made no move to hold it.

"The car. I dreamt about the car." She wiped her eyes with her sleeve.

He sat down on the bed. "I know I messed up."

She reached toward him and nodded. "I'm not crying because of you right now."

He sat next to her, and she nestled into his arms. Holding her close, he brushed the hair out of her face. "Shhh. It's okay." He stroked her hair as she sobbed into his tee shirt, clenched in her fist. "Don't cry."

Encircling her with both arms, he pulled her into his lap. With his chin on her head, he rocked gently. Bureau paced, his ears tucked back, unsettled by the crying.

She buried her face in his chest, her words muffled. "My sister. I know that's her car. I know it is."

"Do you ..." He hesitated not wanting to upset her more. "... remember what happened?"

"No," She stifled a whimper and, looking up at him, she whispered, "I'm afraid to." She rubbed her face on the soft cotton of his shirt. "I hate this." She jumped off the bed and paced, flailing her arms as she cried. "It was only a flash. I need to remember even if it scares me. Why did they hurt her? Why did they kidnap me?" She stopped momentarily and stared at him. "Do they want to hurt us both?" She looked at the floor as her feet carried her back at forth. "Will they try to get me again?"

Her cotton nightshirt moved along her curves with every step and turn. Holding her, he hadn't realized how short it was. He let his eyes drift to the gashes on her legs and thought maybe she needed clean bandages and more ointment. He wanted to touch her, to hold her, to chase away the nightmare.

She stopped again, and eyes filled with worry peered at him from under dark, wet lashes. "Something terrible happened to my sister."

He reached out his hand, but she continued pacing, chewing her nails.

"I was the only one in the van. What if they killed her?"

He clenched his jaw, and his breaths grew shallow and frequent. The question transported him to a night three years ago. "He killed Ellie." The memory flooded over him. Words he never intended to utter tumbled out. "My whole body shook. The policeman—his badge said Gomez—held me back while men put her in a body bag." Nausea stirred his insides. "They put her in the back of a van, and she left me."

The bed shifted. Rainy sat next to him and laid her hand on his back. She offered no words, only tears that ran down his arm when she leaned against him.

His own cries from that night echoed in his head. He leaned forward and buried his head in his hands, trying to hold back tears.

If the dam broke now, he'd be in no shape to protect Rainy from anything. After a few deep breaths, pressing down the emotions that threatened to explode, he felt her stand up.

She moved in front of him, the cotton of her nightshirt brushing the top of his head. "I'm sorry. I didn't think about what I saw saying."

He nodded without lifting his head. She combed her cool fingers through short hairs near the nape of his neck. All thoughts of that horrid night disappeared, but her touch released other feelings long-caged. He closed his eyes and tried to corral the emotions, herding them back into confinement. But when he breathed in deep, the scent of chamomile and lavender filled his senses. He lifted his head, and glistening brown eyes stared back. *You gotta walk away.*

Peering into those chocolate pools didn't motivate him to move. He wanted to pull her close and taste her lips. *You can't.* He pulled his gaze away from her face and looked down, catching sight of the hem of her nightshirt. He closed his eyes and sighed. "Let's go in the office. Maybe we can find out more from those pictures."

She stepped back and tugged at the bottom of her nightshirt. "Okay. I'll meet you there in a minute."

He walked to the office. In the doorway, he glanced back toward the bedroom. The urge to run back, to hold her tugged at him. He shook his head and flipped the switch on the computer.

She padded into the office, her hair swept into a ponytail. Yoga pants covered her legs.

He picked up the recent photo and tried to focus. "There has got to be something in this photo that can give us a clue about who you are." He handed it to her. "What do you see?"

She picked up the magnifying glass and studied the photo. "I'm wearing the clothes that I handed over to DJ."

He looked over her shoulder.

"Do you recognize where this picture was taken? It looks like a house number there." She pointed at a number on a brick wall. She slid into the office chair after Alex logged into the computer.

"Was it taken the same day they grabbed you?"

She continued to peer at the photo. "I'm standing by a car in what looks like a neighborhood. I feel like this house number should mean something to me."

"I don't recognize the neighborhood."

"It's like the memory is just out of reach, but I can't make it out because of a heavy fog."

"You'll remember." He rubbed her back. "Can you make out the license plate on the car?"

"Unfortunately, no. I'm standing in front of it." She picked up the older photo. "I remember Corey asking how that woman was going to convince me I was Claire. I understood that to mean I wasn't Claire. They wanted me to think I was, though. I need to find out about her. But it won't tell me who I am. And I wish I knew what that was on the ground."

"Looks like the kid is reaching for it."

"The grass is too high. It covers most of it."

"Okay, so how would you find out more about this Claire? We don't even know her last name."

Rainy opened a new browser window and typed in the URL of a genealogy search site. "I can search for babies named Claire with a mom named Emma. I'll start by searching here in Texas. Maybe we'll find something in the county where this photo was taken."

"Great idea. That would be Kendall County. Check Bexar County, also. That's the county San Antonio is in."

"How do you spell it?"

"K E N-"

"Not that one." She choked out a hint of a laugh.

He smiled at the sound. "B E X A R."

"Not at all like it sounds. How do you get 'bear' out of that?" She busied herself typing and scanning results on the screen. "How old do you think the little girl is in that photo? It's dated 1986. You think 1984 would be a good year to start searching for a birth record?"

He looked at the little girl in the photo again. "I have no idea."

"I'll start with that." She revised the search criteria and narrowed it to births in 1984. That shortened the list. "Do you have a notepad or spiral I could use?"

Alex pulled a yellow pad off his shelves. He shifted the extra chair right next to her and watched as she danced her fingers across the keyboard. "How do you decide which of those is the right Claire?"

"I'm starting with the first one and finding out whatever I can."

She clicked on a newspaper article. "So this first one married in 2004. Her parents' names are listed in the wedding announcement so I know it's the same person, but now I have a married name."

"How does that help you?"

"I search for Claire Petersen. Oh, look. She's on social media. I can see where she lives. She doesn't have her maiden name listed, but she lists her hometown and high school. And her parents are listed here under family."

He pointed at the name Rainy had written on the yellow pad. "So that Claire grew up to be her?"

"Yep. And I doubt they wanted me to think I was this Claire who now resides in Washington State with her husband and three lovely children."

"That's a long list to have to go through one at a time."

"I try to shorten it first. In this case, I'm focusing on the ones born in the counties near here. That girl was born in San Antonio."

He crossed out what she'd written. "So it's not her." He looked over her shoulder. "Who's next?"

She rattled off parents' names and a birth date, and he jotted it down. He hovered next to her as they eliminated possibilities from the list.

"We've been at this over an hour. How about we take a break?"

She was so absorbed in her search that she didn't respond until he touched her shoulder. "I'm good."

"I'll be right back." He grabbed a Coke from the refrigerator and then dropped back into the chair. Her ponytail swung side to side as she looked from the notepad to the screen. He hovered near her shoulder watching as she searched. One curl escaped the hair tie and danced along her shoulder. He wished his lips could trace the same path.

She turned her head, and they were nose to nose. Color rose in her cheeks. Her lips parted, and he breathed harder. Without breaking eye contact, she pointed at the screen and said, "Claire Bentley. I think they wanted me to be Claire Bentley."

He held her gaze. "What makes you think that?" His heart raced.

She trailed her fingers up and down the top of her chest, right above the neckline of her nightshirt. "Where the picture was taken."

"The picture?" He let his gaze fell to her lips.

She licked them, then chewed her bottom lip. "She was, uh, born there."

"Where?" He stared into her brown eyes. The magnetism danced like static electricity between them.

"Kendall County. Her mother's name is Emma." Her hand stopped moving, her fingertips where he wished his were.

"So she's the one?"

Rainy inhaled sharply. "Maybe. The address on her birth certificate is in the same tiny town as where the photo was taken."

"Really?" What she'd said finally penetrated his distracted state. He looked at the screen, and heard her sigh. "Can you pull up the map of Schatzenburg?" He felt her gaze even after he asked the question. When he didn't get an answer, he glanced at her.

Her cheeks flushed and she nodded. "Um, yeah, I can." She rubbed the back of her neck, before her nimble fingers tapped the keys. "The intersection shown in the photo is here."

"And the address of the birth certificate?"

"One block away. Here." She leaned back into the chair, her face right next to him again. "Seems too good to be true." Her words sounded breathy and hopeful.

"So they want you to be Claire Bentley. The million dollar question is why?"

"I don't know."

He jumped up and loaded the paper tray. "Print it."

The printer spat out the birth record. She yawned and stretched. "I should go back to bed before I fall into a black hole of research."

He touched her arm. "I'm sorry about earlier."

"You don't have to explain. I've completely intruded on your solitude."

He trailed his fingers up her arm and looked down at her. "No. That's not it at all. I'm glad you knocked at my door." The guilt of unfaithfulness punched him in the gut. There was no thought of it when he cradled her, trying to chase away her nightmare. But now the guilt landed on him. "You haven't intruded." He withdrew his hand and backed out of the room.

In the living room, Alex pushed his chair into a reclining position and stared at the fire. The glow of the embers chased shadows to the corners of the room. He'd spent the last three years shutting people out. After Ellie's death, it hurt too much to feel so he quit his lucrative programming job, sold most of what he owned, and moved away from people. He ran into DJ, who pushed and prodded until a friendship grew. He and Becca were the only two people Alex counted as friends. He hardly even spoke to his siblings. He quit watching movies because it wasn't any fun alone but continued to cook because he needed to eat. He just did it as little as possible, warming leftovers whenever possible. Since he moved out here, he'd lived with Bureau, who required little conversation and only the occasional scratch. In the cabin, tucked out here in the middle of nowhere, he wasn't required to feel. He handled business via email when he could and earned enough to cover bills and food. But now, an unnamed spark had crashed through the walls of his quiet life. It made him uncomfortable yet excited.

He drifted off to sleep but awoke in a panic. Rainy's descriptions of the kidnapping became flash card images and blurred with memories of Ellie. Doors closed at the back of a van. Rainy's body lay among paint cans in the back next to a large, black body bag. Large hands with dirt under the nails gripped her arm. Ellie waved as she pulled out of the parking lot. The still images morphed into actions scenes. Rainy crouched behind a desk in a dark room, then stumbled over rocks, ducked branches, looked back over her shoulder, and Ellie fell to the carpet in a pool of blood. Alex bolted out of the chair. No sleep was better than watching his subconscious retell nightmares.

April 21, 1996

Dear Claire,

I'd give anything to see you today. Happy 12th Birthday. I tried something different this year. Instead of a cake, I bought a large chocolate chip cookie. Happy Birthday is written in white frosting across the top.

If you were next to me, I'd talk your ear off, but no matter how hard I tried, words wouldn't slide out of the end of my pen. Your dad is pacing next to me as I cry onto the nearly blank page. Count the spots and multiply by a thousand. That is how much we love and miss you.

Love beyond hope,

Mom & Dad

CHAPTER TWELVE

January 11, 2016 – 5:53am

Alex closed his eyes and rested his head on the desk. *You aren't being unfaithful.* Holding Rainy, feeling the softness of her touch had drilled holes in his levee. Staring at his wedding photo, letting tears fall onto Ellie's face, did nothing to plug the leak.

Picking up his phone, he read the time. *6 am.* He hoped DJ was awake.

Becca answered after the third ring. "Hey, Alex."

"Hey. DJ around?"

"He's in the shower. I only answered because I saw it was you."

"I, uh, want to... Have him call me."

"How's Rainy? I can't imagine how awful it must be."

"Staying at my cabin?"

"You know what I mean. Is she there next to you?"

"No, she's not up yet."

"Have her call me when she gets up."

"Sure, okay." Alex hung up the phone wondering why Becca

wanted to talk to Rainy. He stretched, and his stomach growled its demand for breakfast.

When Rainy shuffled out of the bedroom, Alex stood at the stove stirring a pot of oatmeal.

"Good morning. Sleep well?" He brewed himself a cup of coffee. The oatmeal bubbled and sputtered, and he turned off the burner.

"Yep, you?" She wore his sweatshirt and yoga pants.

"Nah, weird dreams." He pointed at his mug. "This is my third cup." He spooned oatmeal into a bowl. "Want some oatmeal? Coffee?" He added brown sugar to the top.

"Coffee, yes. Oatmeal, no." She poured herself a mug of black coffee and added three teaspoons of sugar. "I'd like to search a bit more."

Alex told her the password and encouraged her to help herself to the computer whenever she needed. "Also, Becca asked for you to call her." He slipped the phone out of his pocket.

Rainy's eyes widened in surprise. "She did? You don't mind?"

He handed her the phone. "Of course, I don't mind."

She dialed as she hurried to the bedroom. He wondered what Rainy would tell Becca about last night, or if she'd mention it at all. It wasn't as if they knew each other well.

Rainy glanced down at the magnifying glass still lying on the desk. Alex stood silently in the doorway watching her read the inscription.

She glanced over her shoulder and smiled. "*Find the bugs?* Were you an entomologist is another life?" she asked, grinning.

"It was a gift, a joke from my wife since I had to find bugs in code."

She opened a browser window and googled Claire Bentley. Pages and pages of results filled the screen. A barrel rider with the same name populated most of the first several pages. "Want to help me search?"

He picked up the yellow pad and pulled the extra chair next to her. "I'm ready."

One by one she clicked the links, and they assessed the significance. Many possibilities were easily dismissed because the age wasn't right. Others proved harder to eliminate at first glance. As she clicked to the third page of links, Alex's cell phone jingled.

"Hey." DJ sounded like he was on the job. "I got a hit off the missing person search."

"I called to tell you there was a news report out of San Antonio about a grey Ford Focus. We only saw the tail end of the clip, but she dreamt about that car. It belongs to her sister. I know it's not much to go on, but maybe the incidents are related."

"She fits the description of a person of interest in a San Antonio case. I'm waiting on a call from the detectives. Stay close to the phone."

"Keep us posted." Alex hung up and set his empty mug on the filing cabinet. He watched his houseguest shake her head in frustration.

Her elbows on the desk, she dropped her head into her palms and rubbed her face.

"Everything okay?" He stepped up behind her and massaged her shoulders, then let his fingers wander along the curve of her neck.

"Yeah. None of these links seem to relate to our Claire. It's as if she disappeared. After her birth, there's no mention of her that I can find in the records." She laid her hand on his and tilted her head back, looking up at him.

He fought the urge to lean down and kiss her. "So, search for someone else related to her, like her mom or dad. Maybe you can find information that way." The pit in his stomach grew as a wave of guilt washed over him. He pulled his hands away and stuck them in his pockets.

She sighed and turned back to the computer. "Do you have an Ancestry.com account?"

"Yes. I tried discovering my roots a while back but never had much luck. You seem pretty good at it, though." He opened another tab and logged into his account.

She shrugged. "The mom's name. Is it Carsen with an e or Carson with an o?" She wiggled her fingers above the keys waiting for the name.

"Emma C A R S O N." Alex stepped back from the desk, putting a few feet between them. "I assume that's her maiden name."

She nodded as she typed *Emma Carson* on the search page and narrowed the search to Texas. Pages and pages of results popped onto the screen. There were several women with that name in Texas. He watched as she evaluated each result to assess its relevance to Claire. A marriage record caught Rainy's attention, and she opened the record. "Emma Carson married Scott Bentley in Bexar County, Texas, in 1981."

"Print it."

"The name of the father on the birth certificate is different than the name listed here. I wonder if one of those names was a middle name."

Alex kept his distance and let her talk out her thoughts without interrupting. She searched for Travis Scott Bentley and found a newspaper article about brothers who played high school football in Kendall County, Texas.

"This is weird. She was married to a Scott Bentley, but Claire's father is listed as Travis Bentley. They were brothers. That sounds a bit scandalous."

He stepped up behind her and leaned over her shoulder looking at the screen. "Brothers?"

"Yep." She touched his arm, her face lit by a bright smile. "Want to drive over to that intersection?"

Alex glanced at hope-filled eyes. "We can go whenever."

His truck rumbled along a narrow county road. And just as he started to wonder if the map had steered them wrong, Rainy spotted a house. It was set far off the road next to fenced pastures, which housed a horse and a few goats. A half mile farther down, they passed a green rectangular sign with *Schatzenburg* printed in white letters. There was no risk of getting lost in this town. Four streets ran perpendicular to the road they were on, and two ran parallel to it.

She leaned forward in her seat. "Is this the only road into town?"

"Don't think so. If you look at the map…" He glanced down at his phone. "There are other roads that lead out of here."

"What road are we on?"

He pointed at a sign as they passed it. "Flat Rock Road. At Fourth, we'll turn and head to Main Street." He crept along, both of them commenting on houses and watching for Fourth.

"It's a quaint little town. In a place this small, surely someone knows something about Claire." She peered out the window as if she was committing each house to memory.

At Fourth Street, Alex hung a left. Main Street was the next cross street. After pulling the truck partway into the grass, he threw it in park, and they both jumped out. An arts and crafts bungalow fronted with a porch sat nestled among trees on the corner. A white picket fence marked the property line.

"This is the only house at this corner. Think it has anything to do with Claire?" Rainy twisted a hair tie around her ponytail.

The slate blue house with white trim was well-kept but seemed vacant. There were no cars in the driveway, no plants on the porch, and no lights on inside. But the yard appeared freshly mowed.

Alex studied the house as he hung back by the truck and watched his companion wander closer. She ambled along the fence, her hand hovering over the top of the pickets.

After staring at the house for several minutes, she turned back toward him. "It's a cute house. It appears small from the front, but look how far back it goes."

"Does it spark any memories?"

She walked back to the truck. "No."

"Well, it was worth a try."

They climbed back in the truck, turned left onto Main Street, and drove only a block before she asked him to stop.

"Do you remember the address on the birth certificate? I think this was where Claire lived." She pointed at a small bungalow set back from the street. "I think this was the address."

"The printouts are in the backseat."

She stretched trying to reach them, but her arms weren't quite long enough. "I need another three inches."

He smiled at the sight of her stretched out. He liked her just the way she was. "You don't need 'em." He pointed at the notepad on the center console. "Write down the address. Did you get the one from the house on the corner? You can search property records and find out who owns them."

"Good idea!"

The intersection of Main and First Street was Schatzenburg's downtown. A small post office sat on one corner. A white clapboard church and a bed and breakfast occupied two other corners.

"How does something from the soda fountain sound?" Alex pulled into one of the angled spaces in front of the limestone building across from the church. "Maybe we'll learn a little about this town."

"Sounds great."

He jumped out and walked around to open her door. He offered his arm, and she held it for balance getting out of the truck.

"Still sore?" He closed the door but didn't bother to lock it.

"Yeah, but it's getting better."

When he opened a door, which had *The Drugstore* emblazoned on it in gold lettering, Rainy lit up with a smile. The ornate counter with a real soda fountain was a pleasant discovery. She climbed onto a barstool, and Alex sat down next to her. From the back, they heard a woman call out, "Libby will be right there to help you."

Rainy picked up a menu lying on the counter.

Alex looked at the tin ceiling tiles and plastered walls. "I wonder how long this building has been around."

"Since Schatzenburg was founded in 1883. It was originally the general store." Rainy pointed to the story of the building on the back of the menu.

A minute later, a girl of maybe eighteen, bounced out from the back and smiled when she saw them sharing a menu. "Howdy. I can get y'all another menu."

Alex quickly responded, "Oh no. This is fine."

"Can I get drinks started for y'all?" Libby cocked her head toward the wall of syrups.

"A peppermint vanilla cream soda." Rainy ordered without hesitation.

"A vanilla Dr Pepper for me. Thanks." Alex leaned close and bumped Rainy with his shoulder. "You always order that drink?"

She stared at him several seconds before she slowly bobbed her head up and down. "I do. It's my favorite. I think it tastes like winter in a glass."

"So I'm safe, and you're remembering. I'll have to add that to the list."

She laid a hand on his arm. "Thank you."

After Libby handed them their drinks, he and Rainy focused on deciding what to order.

She pointed at the chalkboard. "They have a Daily Special."

"Did y'all have a chance to decide?" Libby skipped over, her ponytail swinging in rhythm to her steps.

"I'll have the meatloaf." Rainy closed the menu and slid it across the counter.

"One special. That comes with green beans and mashed potatoes. And for you?" Libby looked at Alex.

"The same. And a cup of coffee."

Libby disappeared into the back.

Rainy whispered even though they were the only two in the seating area. "I'm remembering bits. I like researching genealogy."

"And you're good at it."

"And I remember a blue sundress, but I don't know from where."

"It's in the trunk."

Rainy hopped off the barstool and stepped away from Alex. The same fearful eyes from when she shivered outside his door stared at him.

He stood up. "What's wrong?"

"How did you know that?" She inched back farther.

"About the dress?" Confusion muddled his brain. *Why is she upset?*

"How do you know that?" She shook her head when he stepped toward her. "Do you … know … who I am?"

He reached out his hand. "Rainy, you told us at the hospital. You mentioned the dress in your statement to DJ."

She looked at his hand without touching it and climbed back on the barstool. Tears rimmed her eyes. "For a minute, I thought…"

At the sound of footsteps, they looked up.

A woman with a nametag that read *Maggie* stood gaping, her

face pale. "Forgive my horrid manners. I thought I was seeing things. You look like Emma."

"Emma?" Rainy perked up.

"She used to live around here. Sad story. Her daughter was, well, you look like a carbon copy of her." Maggie shook her head.

"Please, can you tell me—" Rainy came off the barstool leaning across the counter.

"Two specials." Libby bounced out of the back carrying two plates.

Maggie hurried out the front door, a phone to her ear.

April 21, 1997

Dear Claire,

Happy Birthday to my favorite teenager! Are you celebrating with friends? Did you have a big party? In front of me sits the most decadent chocolate cake I've ever seen. I hope you like chocolate. Your dad just stuck a half gallon of Blue Bell ice cream in the freezer. If you've never had Blue Bell, you're missing out. I think they only sell it here in Texas.

Your bedroom at The Castle is getting an update next week. I've taken out the little girl décor and am having it redone. I wish I knew what your favorite colors were. Where is your favorite place to be? Have you visited many places? Did you visit Mount Rushmore last summer? Our private investigator said that there had been a report that you were seen there. It wasn't just a dad and daughter, but a family of four. Do you have a sibling? Before that report, I hadn't even thought of that.

Your dad and I never had any other children.

Every day he checks in with his private investigator to see if they've learned anything new. He's had ten investigators give up already, but he keeps trying. I pray that one day you will meet your dad. He loves you, Claire, as much as I do.

Love,

Mom & Dad

April 21, 1998

Dear Claire,

Happy Birthday! All the birthday cakes seemed too young for a 14-year-old, so I bought you a fruit-topped cheesecake this year.

Without your dad, I would've curled up in your room and cried until my heart stopped. Somehow his strength has been enough for both of us.

Everywhere I go, I look at the faces of the young teen girls hoping that one will look back at me with my eyes or your dad's smile.

I miss you, Claire. We should be shopping on the weekends and getting manicures and pedicures together. Do you have someone in your life that does that with you? I hope so. I hate that it isn't me, but I hope the report we heard last year was about you, that you're growing up with a loving mother, someone to help you with your hair and giggle with you about boys.

I miss you so much.

Love Always,

Mom & Dad

April 21, 1999

Dear Claire,

Happy 15th Birthday! A red velvet cake lavishly heaped with cream cheese swirls sits at the center of the kitchen table.

Your dad is pacing next to me as I write. So far I've managed to hold back my tears, but he knows they're coming.

Did you visit the Grand Canyon last summer? We had a sighting called in that someone saw you at the South Rim. Your picture is on milk cartons all over the United States. I pray every day that someone in your school will see the picture and tell us where you are.

(This is your dad. Happy Birthday, beautiful! Your mom is beautiful, so I know you are as well. Love you.)

Love,

Mom & Dad

Chapter Thirteen

January 11, 2016 – 12:45pm

"That woman's reaction was weird. It was almost spooky. I wanted to run after her, but tackling her would've been in poor taste." I was mad at myself for not at least trying to catch her.

"It was odd, but probably not worth a tackle."

We were half-way back to the cabin when Alex's cell phone rang. "It's DJ. I don't have my Blue Tooth on. Will you answer it?"

"Hello. This is Alex's phone. You're on speaker."

"Kate?" DJ sounded hesitant.

"Yes?"

The silence was so loud. It was like fireworks of quiet exploding. Alex slowed down and steered the truck into the grass.

I stared at him. My heart raced. My name acted as a key. Now that I had it, doors flew open and memories peeked out from their hiding places. The faces of my sister, dad, and mom flashed in my head. I pictured my apartment with boxes stacked in the living room.

DJ's voice startled me from my thoughts. "You still there?"

"She's here. Give her a second." Alex reached for my hand.

"You called me Kate. That's my name. How did you know?"

"I'd rather explain in person. We need to go into San Antonio. Can you pick me up at the station? We'll talk on the way in." DJ's words tumbled out in rapid succession.

"Sure." Alex checked traffic on the two lane road and pulled a U-turn at a wide spot. "Be there in fifteen minutes."

I ended the call. "I have a name again." Tears poured down my face as I repeated my name over and over. Then, my last name popped into my head. "Westfall. My name is Katherine Westfall. Kate for short."

"Nice to meet you, Kate Westfall." Alex reached over and offered his hand.

I laughed and shook it.

He didn't let go. "I guess I can't call you Rainy anymore."

Fourteen minutes later we pulled into the parking lot of the sheriff's office. DJ was waiting outside. He folded himself into the backseat as soon as Alex stopped.

"Where to?" Alex looked back over his shoulder.

"Head toward the mall. The one outside the loop." DJ turned his attention to me. "So, I spoke with detectives in San Antonio. There is a possibility that the car you saw on the news does belong to your sister. Since it seems your name is Kate, it's a strong possibility." He leaned forward, his head between the seats.

"Is she okay?" I popped my knuckles.

"She's alive. I don't want to tell you too much. The detectives are going to ask you lots of questions. I explained that you're dealing with amnesia, but just answer what you can."

Without taking his eyes off the road, Alex reached over and tapped my hand. "You okay?"

I squeezed his hand but stared out the window. "I'm a little afraid of what I might remember."

In the mall parking lot, I inched forward in the seat, looking at every store and restaurant.

Alex pulled into a parking space. But instead of getting out, he turned and laid his hand on my knee. "You remember being here." He said it as a statement, not as a question.

"A little. Walking through the mall may trigger more memories." I clutched his hand. "I know they need me to remember what happened, but..."

He stroked the back of my hand. "I'll stay close."

As we strode toward the sidewalk, I could feel Alex watching me. The two detectives were easy to distinguish from the shoppers. There were not many others at the mall in ties. Detective Miller was middle-aged and stocky. The ring on his finger probably wasn't sliding off without the help of dishwashing liquid. He narrowed his eyes, sizing me up. Detective Torres was younger, somewhere near my age, I'd guess. He had a daily workout routine, based on how he filled out his dress shirt. He was a couple inches shorter than Alex. He greeted me with a smile, and I shook his hand first.

"Detective Ben Torres. This is my partner Jack Miller."

"Hello, we're hoping you can shed some light on what happened here the other night." Miller's smile lacked warmth.

Torres nodded toward DJ before turning soft brown eyes on me. "Thanks for meeting us today. What do you remember about the other night?"

"I only learned my own name an hour ago. Memories are coming back in bits and pieces. Can we walk around a bit and see what triggers?" I surveyed the walkways and stores around us. Landscaped paths meandered through the outdoor mall. Next door to the ice cream shop, strollers surrounded a playscape overrun by preschoolers. Further down, water danced in a fountain and added to the relaxed atmosphere of the mall.

"Lead the way. Anything you can remember might help." Torres kept pace next to me.

Miller lagged behind, but I felt him watching me. DJ walked next to him, asking about the case. Alex stayed next to me, just as he said, brushing his knuckles against my hand each time my shoulders tightened.

In front of a department store, I stopped and pointed. "We stopped in here. There was a clearance rack, and we found these really cute sundresses. Mine was blue and had buttons all the way down the front." I covered my face with my hands and shook my head. "I'm sorry. You don't care about that part, but we were here."

"You don't have to be nervous. Every little thing you can remember is great." Torres glanced at his partner. "You said we?" He had out a notebook and pen ready to write down whatever I told him. His buzz cut made him look tough, but his eyes exuded kindness.

"My sister and I. We were shopping." After I answered, I continued down the sidewalk.

Alex almost ran into me when I stopped abruptly in front of an Asian restaurant.

"This is where we had dinner." I pictured the Moo Shu Pork wrapped up, lying on my plate.

"What did you do after dinner?" Torres scribbled notes as he asked the question.

"We stopped at a few more stores. Anytime we saw a sale sign, we popped in for a look." I pointed at stores where we'd shopped as I continued through the mall. "And then we walked over to the bookstore and got ourselves fancy coffee. After that, we wandered through a few more stores. We stayed until most were closed."

"Do you remember where you were parked?" Miller rattled the keys in his pocket.

"This way, I think." I followed the sidewalk away from the bookstore.

Alex walked next to me as I hurried toward the parking lot.

The walkway split, but I couldn't go any farther. Around the corner, I would've been able to see where we parked, but I stopped. My chest heaved. My feet felt cemented to the sidewalk.

Alex leaned in close. "Rainy, are you okay?"

I shook my head. My eyes pleaded with him to protect me from the returning memories. "I can't go to the parking lot."

He stepped behind me and wrapped both arms around me. "Would y'all mind if we stayed here and let Kate tell us what she remembers about leaving?"

Miller shot me a look someone would give a petulant child. "Young lady, we really need to—"

DJ stepped in front of him and whispered something I couldn't hear.

Torres pointed to a cluster of wicker seating. "Absolutely. Let's have a seat."

I sank into the cushion on the wicker couch and glanced back to make sure Alex was still next to me. "Both of us were carrying several bags. We'd parked way back in the lot. Near some large rocks." I hugged my arms around me and closed my eyes. The memory of running through the lot, plastic shopping bags crinkling in my hand was so real I shivered.

Alex rested his warm hand on the nape of my neck.

"What car were you driving?" Torres glanced from Alex back to me.

"We were in Meg's car. A grey Focus."

Torres and Miller exchanged a look. I guess no one had mentioned Meg's name.

I pressed back into Alex bracing for the memory that hung just out of sight. "She popped the trunk as we walked up to the car. I remember Meg laughing because there were so many bags." I swallowed the fear rising in my throat and chewed my lip.

Torres and DJ leaned forward in their seats. Alex felt me shaking and slipped his arm around me.

"As I dropped my bags in the trunk, someone grabbed me. Meg's face…" I choked back my tears. "She was terrified. I remember the look on her face as she tried to scream. After that there's nothing."

I clasped Torres's hand. "I need to know if Meg is okay."

"She's alive, but she suffered a head trauma and is in a coma." He slid his hand out from under mine. "Can you give us the details of what happened after you woke up in the van? It may help us figure out who hurt your sister."

I recounted the night's events, telling them about the white van and the kidnappers, even though I was pretty sure DJ had forwarded his report to them. I explained how one of them kept referring to a lady—but they never used her name—and how they talked about wanting me to think I was Claire. I mentioned grabbing the photos, escaping, picking my way through the brush, and finding myself at the cabin door as it started to rain.

"Where are those photos?" Torres looked up from his notebook.

"I have them," DJ said. "One of the photos is more recent and has a house number on it."

"I'd like to get copies of those."

"Absolutely," DJ said.

Miller flipped through the pages of his little notebook. "There was no sign of your purse or cell phone in the car."

Alex looked from me to Miller. "She didn't have them with her when she got to the cabin. Is it possible it's still in that white van or the house where she was held? Would her battery have lasted this long?"

"We'll check it out." Miller reached out and shook his hand. "And let you know if we find something." Genuine sympathy showed in his eyes.

Detective Torres placed a business card in my hand. "If you remember anything else, call me. No matter the time."

Alex handed Torres a business card. "Here's my number if you want to ask Kate any other questions."

He slipped the card into his pocket after reading the name. "How do you fit into all this?"

I wanted to hear the answer to that question. *What did I want him to say?*

"She showed up at my door." Alex pressed his hand into the small of my back.

His manner was protective. I wondered what the detectives thought, not both of them, mostly Detective Torres. I glanced up at Alex and felt my heart rate increase. My attraction to him grew despite the constant reminder in my head that he wanted to be alone.

Torres tore a sheet out of his notebook. "Here's the hospital information. Thank you for your time. He shook DJ's hand. "I'm glad you called us."

DJ and Alex looked at me.

"You okay?" DJ sounded concerned.

"Yeah. I will be. And, DJ, thank you. In less than 36 hours, you figured out my name." I hugged him.

"I'm glad I could help. I had to hurry after Alex started calling you Rainy." He draped an arm around my shoulders. "Now I want to catch those kidnappers. Anything you remember, let me know. Y'all head on over to the hospital. Becca is driving in to meet me. I texted her about your sister."

"Tell her I'll call her later."

After a quick tip of his hat, he walked away.

"Let's get you over there to check on your sister." His warm hand pressed into the small of my back.

Room number in hand, we skirted past the hospital information desk headed straight for the elevators. On the second floor, I inquired at the nurse's station about seeing my sister. They pointed me toward the room. I wasn't sure what the visiting regulations were for ICU, so I grabbed Alex's hand hoping that the nurses wouldn't ask if he was family. When we entered room 214, Meg's husband, Tom, looked up. Weariness showed in the lines of his brow. My heart broke for him.

"Kate, where have you been?" He threw his arms around me, then kissed me on the cheek. "It's been horrible." Tears pooled in his eyes as he looked at Meg. "They aren't sure when she'll wake up."

A nurse rushed in and commented on increased activity on the monitors. After jotting notes on the chart, she hurried back out of the room. My sister looked so peaceful with her blonde hair fanned out across the pillow, despite the tubes, wires, and noisy machines.

"Hey, Sis, I'm here. I'm okay. Please wake up. Tom and I are both worried about you." *Guilt.* I knew that I shouldn't feel guilty. It wasn't my fault she was hurt. But if I didn't look so much like Emma, none of this would have happened.

Tom pulled me in for another hug. "I've been so worried about you, Kate. When I got to the hospital and you weren't with her, I was scared something terrible had happened."

Alex took a step back and bumped into the wall.

Tom continued, "I told the police over an over that you wouldn't just leave her in that condition. I knew something wasn't right. I needed to know you were okay."

Alex stepped toward the door. "I'll wait in the hall."

"No, Alex, don't leave." I held out my hand to him. "This is my brother-in-law, Tom."

Alex's shoulders relaxed, and he flashed a weak smile as he

walked back across the room. He shook hands with Tom then laid his hands on my shoulders. "It's awful what's happened."

"Have you talked to the detectives today?" I watched Meg's chest rise and fall in rhythm to the sound of a machine.

"This morning, but they left in a rush without saying much." Tom looked at Alex. "Can you please tell me what happened?"

Alex nodded slowly. "Kate was kidnapped, but incredibly she managed to escape."

"They hurt Meg when they grabbed me." I pressed the heels of my palms to my eyes, hoping to prevent a flood of tears.

"Wait. Stop. Kidnapped you?" Tom clutched the rail on the bed.

I nodded. "I don't know why." I left off the word yet. I didn't want others to know about our online searches.

Tom dropped into a chair rubbing his face.

"I stumbled to Alex's cabin. He's been..." I looked back over my shoulder. "I'm not sure what would've happened to me."

Tom stood and stared at Alex. "I didn't realize Kate was seeing anyone here in town. Why did you go to his place but not call me? Didn't you care what happened to your sister?"

His words stung. *How could he think that about me?*

Behind me, Alex inhaled sharply, then exhaled slowly. "You have it all wrong. Kate was traumatized, enough that she couldn't remember. She's gone days without knowing her own name." He stepped between me and Tom. His words, like daggers, garnered the intended response. "She rushed to her sister's bedside as soon as the detectives told Kate what hospital Meg was in."

Tom paled. "I didn't know."

"And she didn't either." Alex crossed his arms.

"I'm so sorry, Kate." He moved as if to hug me, but backed up when Alex didn't step out of the way. Tom focused on Alex. "Meg would hug you if she could, I'm sure. She'd be inconsolable if anything happened to her sister. Thank you for taking care of Kate."

I rubbed Alex's back hoping he'd relax a bit. "Tom, you look exhausted."

"It's been rough." Tom stepped around to the other side of the bed.

"Why don't you go home? I'll stay here with her tonight." I

slipped my hand under Meg's hoping for the slightest squeeze. "Meg, what about a girl's night? What movie should we watch? Think we can find any good chocolate around here?" Tears dotted the sheet as I leaned over her.

"I appreciate the offer, Kate, but I can't leave her." Tom stared at Meg. "I've got to be here when she wakes up." He pulled a tissue out of the box by the bed and wiped his eyes, then slipped his keys out of his pocket. "You don't have to stay with a stranger. Let me give you the key to the house." He fiddled with a key trying to get it off the ring.

Alex grabbed my hand, and I turned to look at him.

He shook his head. "As your bodyguard, I think you're safer with me."

"What wouldn't be safe about our house?" Tom sounded irritated at the implication.

"As my bodyguard?" I wanted him to answer as Alex, not out of an obligation to protect me.

He leaned in close and whispered, "I can pack a bag and stay with you at their place."

"That would be weird." I almost laughed out loud when he winked at me.

"Then come back to the cabin." He held my gaze and tightened his hold on my hand. "Please."

Our conversation was interrupted when the nurse asked us to step outside.

I hugged Tom. "Keep the key. I'm okay for now."

Alex shook hands with Tom. "I'll bring her back up tomorrow."

He followed us out the door and grabbed Alex's arm before we stepped away. "Kate's important to us. Don't…"

"I won't … let anything happen to her." Alex looked him in the eye. "Detective Torres has my information."

An hour and a half later, we were back in the cabin eating tacos we'd picked up at a taco place in Kerrville.

"These are delicious." I wiped my chin.

"Tacos to Go make the best."

"I can't argue." I tossed the foil wrapper at the trashcan, and it bounced in after hitting the rim. "I know you didn't want me to go to Meg's, but now that I've got an identity again, I could get a hotel room."

"You sure that's a good idea? Those men haven't been caught yet. And you have no ID."

"I'm not in your way?" I slid my chair back from the table, and Bureau jumped in my lap.

"Not a bit." He tapped the table. "So tell me about Kate Westfall."

"Let's get some coffee and go talk in the living room. But first, I'd like to call Becca."

He handed me his phone. "I'll make coffee while you chat."

The bedroom door squeaked as it swung closed. Becca answered after the second ring. "You have a name!"

"Yes, thanks to DJ. I have a name again."

"Is everything okay?" It was as if Becca had known me for years. In two short days, I felt closer to her than many of my friends back home. I wanted to talk to her, especially to continue the conversation from the first time we chatted. "Mostly. I don't know."

"Talk to me, Kate. I'm glad I don't have to call you Rainy anymore."

"Alex talked about losing his wife last night. He didn't say what happened."

"Oh." Becca let her response hang in uncomfortable silence for several seconds. "I'm a little stunned. He rarely talks about it."

"Did you know her?"

"I met Alex shortly after she died." Becca choked up at the mention of death. "Wait. You didn't say a word about it when we talked this morning. Was this when you woke up in the middle of the night?"

"I needed to think about it."

"Did something happen?"

"He said he moved out here to be alone. I'm worried that I'm in his way. Maybe it isn't good for me to be here." I didn't want to tell her about the mug or about running my fingers through his hair.

"He did move out there to be alone ... three years ago. He'll say something if it's a problem."

"Are you sure?"

"Yeah. What else is bothering you?"

"I wonder if he's only protecting me because of what happened to his wife." The words sounded worse out loud than they did in my head, and I wasn't sure I wanted to hear Becca's response.

"You can stay in our guest room."

"Is that your nice way of saying 'Probably so'?"

"I don't want to say anything that Alex hasn't chosen to reveal. But ... this is something you already know. He has walls."

"You don't say?" A humorless chuckle escaped before I could stop myself.

"I don't want to see either of you get hurt. We love Alex."

"I have no intention of hurting him."

"I know that, and I wish things were different."

"I better go."

"Kate, wait."

"I'm a big girl. I'll be okay."

"If it helps, he smiles more."

"I'm not sure it does, but thanks."

I padded out to the living room. Alex sat on the hearth sipping his coffee.

"Thanks. It's an odd feeling to be without my phone, now that I know who I am. My friend, LeAnn, is probably worried sick."

"And she is?"

"My closest friend back in Denver."

"Call her."

"I won't be long." The anticipation of talking to her, the familiarity, pulled at me, but I needed to choose what to say carefully. She knew me well, and saying the wrong thing would invite a long conversation.

"Take whatever time you need." He handed me a mug. "But don't let this get cold."

Back to the bedroom I went, dialing LeAnn's number.

"Hello?"

"LeAnn, it's Kate."

"Kate! I was starting to wonder if you were okay. You didn't respond to my text. I even called earlier today, but it went straight to voicemail."

"I lost my phone, but I'm okay."

"What's going on?"

"Some stuff happened, but things are better now."

"What stuff?"

"I really don't want to go into right now. Please."

"Are you okay?"

"Yes. I'm fine. I just didn't want you to worry about me. I'll call again in a few days."

"You have me a little worried."

"I borrowed someone's phone. I'll tell you all about it later."

"Kate Westfall, you're scaring me. What's going on?"

"Please, LeAnn. I promise to tell you later. You can call this number if you need to get ahold of me. I'll call you when I find my phone."

"All right. Please call me again *soon*."

I walked into the living room and plopped myself down on the rug in front of the fireplace, my cup of coffee cradled in my hands.

Alex sat down next to me. "I should probably get another recliner. Having only one makes it seem like I don't want company, right?"

"Maybe a little."

"So, do I get to hear all about Kate, now?"

"Sure. I guess." I set my mug on the hearth and hugged my knees to my chest. "I grew up in Denver with my mom, dad, and sister."

"I hear it's beautiful there."

"It is." The woozy feeling I got when the teacher made me introduce myself to the class washed over me. "I feel like I'm standing at the front on the first day of school. I'm not sure what to say."

Alex chuckled. "Are your parents still in Denver?"

"No. Mom died in an auto accident. Someone ran a light, and she never made it home. That was several years ago. Dad died last year. Heart attack."

"I'm sorry."

"It was hard. Losing Mom like that stung. One minute everything was fine. She ran to the store, but never came home. I say it would've been easier with some warning, but that's a lie." Again I ran my mouth not even thinking about what Alex had been through. "I'm so sorry. You—"

"Kate, no need to apologize. We've both lost people we love. I asked you about your family. Tell me about your dad."

"Meg was already here in Texas. She and Tom hadn't been married but maybe four months. I sat with Dad until the end. He called Meg to say goodbye." I avoided eye contact with Alex. "She hopped the first plane she could catch, but he knew she wouldn't make it in time. She was on a flight when he died. But in those last few hours, I thought of all the things he did right, the things I'd miss. He wasn't perfect, but he was my dad." I covered my face but held back my tears. I was tired of crying.

Alex draped an arm around me. "You and Meg must be close."

"Honestly, not really. But she's all I have left."

"You don't get along?"

"Meg and I never saw the world the same way. She was the star of anything she did. Everyone loved her. It was easier to just take her suggestions and do what she wanted rather than argue."

"But now?"

"Things are okay. It was her idea for me to move here, but there's not much reason for me to stay in Denver, I guess. But that day at the mall was wonderful. We were enjoying each other's company more than we had in years." I gazed up at him. "What if she doesn't wake up?"

"She'll wake up." He pulled me closer. "Happy memories. Tell me something fun."

I rested my head against him. "When I was six, I walked out to the living room on my birthday, and there was present wiggling on the floor."

"It was moving?"

"Yep. My mom and dad encouraged me to open it. Meg giggled until I squealed."

"What was it?"

"A puppy. She had on a sparkly pink collar with a heart tag that read *Emma*. She was such a good dog."

"Emma?" He raised an eyebrow.

"I'm sure it's a coincidence." Believing anything else required more courage than I had at the moment.

Alex pushed himself off the floor and held out his hand to help me up. "Let's go in the office." Laugh lines crinkled near his eyes.

He pulled up Facebook and turned the screen so I couldn't see what he was typing. His eyes sparkled with mischief when he turned the screen toward me. "Hello, Kate Westfall."

I raced through memories hoping there wasn't anything horribly embarrassing on my profile page. "Uh oh. I'm almost afraid to look." Apart from photos, cat memes, and a handful of shared articles about genealogy and Benedict Cumberbatch, there were very few posts.

Alex laughed and searched his own name. "Just to show that all's fair, here's mine."

As soon as his page loaded, I eagerly leaned in front of him and scrolled through the handful of posts listed on the page. "You're an avid Facebook user, I see. You haven't posted anything in over a year." I scanned the few photos he'd posted. "Your wife was beautiful."

Clouds gathered in his eyes.

"Aww, you don't have any pictures of Bureau on here." I nudged him in the ribs.

"I'll get right on that." He clicked on a family picture. "This is my family. The picture was taken the day my youngest sister graduated from high school."

"Tell me about them."

"Not tonight." He closed the browser screen and leaned back in the chair, clasping his hands behind his head. "What do you do?"

I dropped into the extra chair and crisscrossed my legs. "As a hobby or a job?"

"Job."

"I got paid to design web pages, but my hobby, my passion, is genealogy."

"I can see that."

"My personal research hit a dead end quickly so I built family trees for my friends."

"You have a tree without branches?"

"You're going to make me cry. You wrote that down, didn't you?"

He rolled his chair in front of me. "I can stop listening to you if need be, you know, to prevent tears."

I rested my hands on his knees and leaned in close. He smiled, but swallowed hard. Nearly touching his cheek, I whispered in his ear. "I can't think of anything funny to say."

Apparently I was wrong because he tossed his head back, and a robust laugh echoed in the office.

I sat back in my chair and grinned.

"Back to genealogy, what's your favorite part?" He made no move to shift away, if anything, he rolled even closer.

"The look on people's faces when you can show them an old photo of their grandmother or tell them where their great great grandfather was born is priceless."

Alex studied my face, a grin twitching at the corners of his mouth.

My heart pounded faster. "What? What did I say?"

"You light up when you talk about it."

My cheeks warmed. "People like feeling connected. I thought about trying to make a living as a genealogist after graduation, but it seemed too risky. Building websites paid well, and it was pretty easy to find a job. So I did that."

"Do you like it?"

"Meh."

"You weren't able to find anything about your family?"

"My mom was adopted, and she knew nothing about her birth parents. My dad flat out refused to give me any information. I was never able to find much in my own searches. It was like he never existed."

"I bet you'd be great as a genealogist."

"Not having a family tree of your own isn't great in the advertising department." I'd never told anyone that I wanted to be a genealogist. Around Alex, my thoughts tumbled out without me inspecting them multiple times.

"Maybe one day you'll find something."

"Not much hope of that. Mom understood my frustration. She felt horrible that she had nothing to offer in the way of information. Because of privacy laws with adoptions, I may never know who her parents were. Dad, on the other hand, didn't see the point in finding family roots. The only thing I know from his past is a kolache recipe. I think I posted pictures of them. Go back to my profile."

He pulled up my profile and clicked over to the photos. I scrolled through them and clicked on my family photo.

"Here they are. Gavin and Judy Westfall. And here's one of all four of us."

"Meg looks a lot like your mom."

"Yep. Blonde hair, blue eyes. They looked more like sisters than Meg and I did. Even my dad had riveting blue eyes." I cut the last word short as I yawned.

"You should get some sleep."

"Yeah, okay." I stood up, and as I stepped away, he turned back to the computer.

I hesitated in the doorway. Alex stood facing the screen scrolling through my pictures. He inhaled sharply when I wrapped my arms around him, my face nestled in his back. He pressed his elbows against himself catching my arms in between and laid his hands on mine.

"Goodnight, Alex." There weren't enough words to tell him how protected he made me feel, or how thankful I was for the safety of this cabin.

Alone in bed, more and more memories flooded back—little ones, sensations, feelings. They filled in the empty spaces like sand poured over stones. I remembered the bunny I used to drag around with me everywhere, the thrill of seeing a Hawaii license plate when we were on our summer vacations marking states off the list, and even the fear that soured my stomach when I tried to tell Meg no about almost anything. As if reading through an old diary, I spent time meandering through my memories. Fear swayed or dictated so many of my decisions.

I switched off the lamp by the bed. The darkness folded in around me. My thoughts tumbled back to the horrid closet. I clicked on the lamp, and the light chased away my uneasiness.

Footsteps drew near. "You okay?" He leaned on the doorframe.

"Yeah, I'm okay." I turned off the light. The darkness returned but, this time, like a well-loved blanket.

"Call me if you need me. I'm not far away." His words encircled me, comforting and safe.

At least tonight, there was no reason to be afraid.

April 21, 2000

Our Beautiful Claire,

Happy Sweet 16! I wish you could see your birthday cake. It is a rectangle with a stripe of dark frosting decorated to look like a road running down the middle. Sitting on the road is a plastic red sports car. That was going to be your birthday gift, a new car.

Your dad went to look at a few cars. He wanted to have recommendations if you walked through our door. I couldn't bear it so he went alone.

I try to bury myself in charity work, but the more time I spend on that, the less time I have to spend at The Castle. Your dad and I drove out this morning to be here for your birthday. He is taking this birthday very hard. Some days I forget I'm not the only one that lost you. He lost you before he knew you were his. I feel guilty about that.

Never wait to say something, Claire. Speak up even when it's hard.

I'm trying not to hate the beast, but I'm not very good at it. How do I forgive when hating him for what he's done comes more naturally than breathing?

Your daddy and I miss you.

Love,

Mom & Dad

CHAPTER FOURTEEN

January 12, 2016 – 1:12pm

I hoped that today Meg would be awake. Guilt festered because she was laid up in a hospital bed, and I was mostly unharmed.

Alex pulled into the covered driveway and dropped me near the hospital entrance. "I'll meet you in Meg's room." He saved me the effort of walking from the parking garage.

I felt better, but parts of me were still sore. People filled every seat in the main lobby, and others scurried around like ants in a disturbed mound. Winding between hospital visitors, who wore grim expressions, I ambled toward the elevators. I was three steps away when the elevator doors closed. The empty elevator didn't care. Away it went. By the time another one arrived seven other people waited near me. The stairs would have been faster and less crowded.

On the second floor, I headed directly to Meg's room, but stopped in the doorway. Someone else lay in the bed. Tom was nowhere to be found. Panic, the kind that grips your throat from the inside, moved in without notice. I walked the hall peeking into each open door. I must've been pale because a nurse stopped me. She looked rather concerned. "Are you okay, ma'am?"

"My sister was room 214."

"Let me check on that for you." The nurse picked up a clipboard and scanned the list. "I can't release any information. Talk to someone at the booth in the main lobby."

"What do you mean you can't release…?"

"I really can't say anymore." She hurried off as an alarm beeped in a nearby room.

I told myself Tom would've called if Meg had taken a turn for the worse, trying to find a way to stay calm.

I rushed back to the elevators. Why did they move more slowly when I was in a hurry? Really. Einstein had an entire theory about it. On the ground floor, I ran to the booth. "I need information about Meg Taylor."

The attendant seemed taken aback by my panicked demand. "What was the name again? I'll check the computer." She typed, then frowned. "I'm sorry."

"You don't have any information? But she was here yesterday."

"I can't give out any information." She shook her head.

I walked away without another word. I needed Alex. *Did I miss him? Where is he?* I paced watching the main doors. I spotted Alex as soon as he darted inside. He looked like I felt, frantic. Halfway across the lobby, he halted. His head whipped back and forth scanning the room like an unlatched screen door in a hurricane, the color gone from his face. His jaw clenched, his eyes red, he spied me and broke into long-legged strides.

He neared, and I gave him the update. "Meg wasn't in her room. They said they can't—"

Alex enveloped me in his arms like a young child finding a lost stuff animal. "I just got off the phone with Torres." He stepped back, his hand on my neck, stroking my jawline with his thumb. With his other hand, he rubbed the cleft in his chin. Something was definitely wrong. "Meg's house was broken into this morning. Tom walked in on the perpetrators and was shot."

I was sick to my stomach, and my knees threatened to buckle.

Alex pulled me back into his arms. "He's alive. Tom and Meg are in a double room on the sixth floor. I'm not suggesting that you don't go see your sister, but please keep an eye out for any faces you might recognize."

I scanned the faces of men and women scurrying around the main floor. Worried visitors now seemed sinister. I shuddered. "I have to go see them, but I'm scared." I wasn't sure Alex was going to release me from our embrace.

He could've said "me too" and I would've understood, but Alex thought if he bore the fear, that I might not be as frightened. It didn't work that way. I pushed gently on him, stepping back. A look crossed his face, and, for the first time, I understood that when he held me it was as much for his comfort as for my protection. Unsure of what to do with that knowledge, I slipped my fingers into his hand. The elevator opened, and we stepped into the boarding throng.

The room on the sixth floor was easy to spot. A uniformed officer sat outside the room. When we stepped up to the door, I introduced myself.

"I'm Kate Westfall, Meg's sister. Is it okay if we go in?"

"You may. Detective Torres has your name on the list." The officer looked at Alex. "And you are?"

"Alex Ramirez."

The door opened, and Detective Torres poked his head out. "He's okay. You can let him in."

Questions started as soon as we entered. "Can you think of anyone that would want to hurt your sister and brother-in-law?" Torres's brown eyes bored into me, watching my every move. *Is he worried about me? Or does he think I'm hiding something?*

"No. I was only in town visiting. I hardly know anyone here." I was frustrated that I hadn't learned more from the kidnappers.

"Do you think they went to the house looking for Kate?" Alex didn't look at me as he asked the question, but his hand tightened around mine.

"That's an idea we are pursuing. It seems plausible." Torres exchanged a look with Alex, his lips set in a grim line.

I glanced toward the beds. Tubes and wires covered Meg and Tom. "Am I safe coming here?"

Miller rested a hand on my shoulder. "Just don't come alone." The worry in his eyes frightened me.

Alex wrapped an arm around me. "She won't."

I looked up at him and pointed toward the beds. He nodded.

While Alex talked with the detectives, I stood between the beds. Even in a coma, Meg looked like she could grace the cover of a magazine. Tom was shirtless, his upper left torso bandaged, his arm in a sling. They were both here because of me.

The door closed with a soft click. The detectives must've slipped out of the room. Maybe thought bubbles did appear above my head because how else did Alex know to whisper in my ear, "None of this is your fault." He punctuated his statement with the same embrace like at the mall. He wrapped his arms around me from behind.

I leaned my head back against him. "It doesn't feel that way. There are so many ifs. If I hadn't come to visit, they might not be here … If I didn't look like Emma … If. If. If."

He led me to the bench, and we sat, side by side. I rested my head on his shoulder, and he held me. For almost an hour, neither of us spoke.

On the way home, I wiped away persistent teardrops, and Alex kept checking the rearview mirror. We were in a nightmare without the option of waking.

"When we get back, I want to search for Claire again. I have to find out more about her. All this terrible stuff is happening because some woman wanted me to think I was Claire. I'm not, so where is she?"

"I don't know, Kate." He looked back over his shoulder before changing lanes. "I want to fix it all, but I don't know how. I'm not even sure how to help you find Claire."

"Alex, I'm not asking you to fix it. You've done so much already. I feel safe because you're with me. Together, we'll figure all this out. We have to."

He trailed his fingers down my arm. "We will."

His touch set off fireworks inside me. Clear-headed, I noticed the same qualities I'd admired under the effect of pain medication. But now, as I looked at him, I saw more than a bodyguard or protector. My attraction grew like magical beans after a rain. I admired his strength, his protective impulse. I'd glimpsed his tenderness. I wanted so much more than just a safe place.

At the cabin, Alex sat in the extra chair while I searched for more information about Claire. In a browser window, I navigated to the website for the Kendall County appraisal district. I entered the address of the yellow house in the property search, and in minutes, I had the name of the current owner. At the bottom of the page, the property deed history listed names I recognized. "The yellow house was sold in 1989 by Emma Bentley to the current owners."

"Amazing. I knew that property search was out there, but never used it." Alex shifted his chair next to me.

I searched again for information about the house at the corner of Fourth and Main. "The corner house is owned by Travis Bentley." I pointed at the screen, and Alex leaned in close to look. "His current residence is listed as a San Antonio address."

"I wonder how they found you. There is no database of looka-likes."

"A doppelganger database?"

Alex pressed his shoulder into mine. "Exactly."

"There is more to Claire's story. I know there is. There has to be."

April 21, 2001

Dear Claire,

You're 17. The years have grown wings. I don't wish for time to stop, even though I am missing everything. Enjoy life, every minute.

Before you were born, life felt like it was moving me along. That's not to say I didn't make choices. I did. Some good and some bad. There are some bad choices I would make again a hundred times, and there are others, not as bad, I would never repeat.

In my one session with a therapist, not long after Scott took you, I was encouraged to write down the story of what happened. I wrote it. I've attached the first few pages to this letter. I added a note at the end.

I almost forgot to tell you about the cake. I chose a multi-layered chocolate cake with strawberry filling. On top of the milk chocolate frosting are five chocolate covered strawberries. Delicious! (I know because I snuck a slice.)

You feel so far away this year. I miss you.

Happy Birthday,

Mom & Dad

Summer of '83, Part 1

I'd made meatloaf for dinner. But by the time I sat down at the table, I had no appetite. Any other day, I would've devoured the meatloaf and probably had seconds. But that night my eyes hurt from crying, and worry whispered in my ear. Scott hadn't come home from work. I'd called the dealership only to learn that he left a little early. He'd been so distant and closed off after his father's death. But this took it to a whole new level. Fearful thoughts crept into my brain. I prayed that he hadn't hurt himself. After only a couple bites, I trashed my dinner.

At midnight, I gave up my wait. In the dark, I flipped back the covers and crawled into bed. Lying on my back, I watched the barely visible ceiling fan go around in circles. At 3 am, Scott still wasn't home. No phone call. No note. He just didn't come home.

The Scott I loved had disappeared—but not in the physical sense—when his dad died suddenly two months before. After the funeral, he'd been different, but he'd been home. I worried that all the rumors surrounding my father-in-law's death had taken a toll on Scott.

I'd heard the whispers questioning if it was really an accident. How could the man accidentally hit the only tree on a straight stretch of road in broad daylight? Nothing ever came of the rumors. His death was ruled an accident. Scott was so much like his dad. Had the rumors been too much? Or worse, were they true?

I wasn't sure what concerned me more—that Scott had changed into someone I didn't recognize or that he'd disappeared without a word.

In the morning, Scott was in the kitchen making himself breakfast. I ran to hug him. He shrugged it off and mumbled an excuse about having a lot on his mind.

His brush-off stung. I watched as he moved through the kitchen but avoided my gaze. After he ate, he walked out the door without a goodbye or peck on the cheek.

The screen door slammed behind him.

Added Note: As you read the rest of this story, please know that I once loved Scott, and I never set out to hurt him. I will not accept the blame for his wrong behaviors. Nothing I've done deserves the punishment of living life separated from you. It is a penance too severe.

April 21, 2002

Dear Claire,

Happy 18th Birthday! I'm not sure if my handwriting will even be legible because of the tears blurring my vision. It is unfathomable that I have an adult daughter now.

Would you be surprised to know I spent this last week baking? I baked 18 dozen cupcakes. You've been on my mind for weeks. Not a day goes by ever that I don't think of you, but these last weeks you've been on my mind almost constantly.

Even though these letters are still tucked in envelopes waiting to be opened, I like to imagine that somewhere you are reading my story as I include the pages. But I shouldn't call it my story. It's your story as much as mine.

I almost forgot to add … You will be graduating soon! I wish I could be there to watch you cross the stage. Your dad hired a new investigator last week. If this new guy finds a lead, maybe we'll surprise you at graduation.

Love Forever,

Mom & Dad

Summer of '83, Part 2

After Scott left, I went for a run. Mile after mile, my feet pounded against the black top. Sweat gathered at my hairline then careened into my eyes. I didn't bother to wipe it away. It masked my tears.

I waved when a little red Mazda honked as it passed.

Typically, I visited with my mother-in-law each day. But not that day. I couldn't. The embarrassment of being rejected tugged at me like a whiney child, and the worry about Scott's safety sucked the air from my lungs. I wasn't sure how to even bring it up to her.

All motivation to maintain my everyday routine was gone. Alone, I listened to Billboard's top country hits. Each song sent my emotions in a different direction. The sting of his brush off morphed into the fear that he was cheating. I wanted him home, then I wanted to hurt him. Having shed more tears than I even thought possible, I turned off the radio.

When the small clock on the mantle chimed five o'clock, either from hope or delusion, I went into the kitchen and warmed everything I'd made the night before.

By six o'clock, the food was piping hot and ready to serve, but there was no sign of Scott. My appetite non-existent, I turned off all the burners, changed again, and set off on another run. There were no tears this time. Angered bubbled as I slammed my feet on the ground.

When I got back from the run, I crawled in bed, exhausted, but my pillow harbored thoughts that snuck into my head. The hours crept by slowly. Sleep visited in spurts, interrupted by nightmares and worries.

In the morning, with no sign of Scott, I decided to visit my mother-in-law. Scott's behavior was odd. I needed to speak up about his absence. I walked down the block to her house, and Travis, Scott's older brother, answered the door.

I found Betty crocheting and watching her stories. She clicked off the television as I entered the room.

Travis leaned on the arm of the couch. "Everything okay? I saw you running yesterday. You only run when something's bothering you."

"I run almost every day." Puzzled, I looked up at him for an explanation.

"You jog every day, but you rarely run. What's wrong?" He had me pegged.

I hated that my tears preceded my answer.

He furrowed his brow and waited.

"I'm worried about Scott. He's been so different after y'all's dad died. He hasn't come home for two nights. Yesterday morning he was in the kitchen making his own lunch, but he wouldn't let me hug him. I don't know what to do. He hardly spoke to me at all." Sobs stampeded out of me.

Betty whispered assurances that all would be okay, but her eyes told a different tale. Tears gathered, and worry creased in the corners of her eyes. Travis trudged back to his bedroom. Tears made him uncomfortable. If it wasn't fixable, he had a hard time.

After spilling my secret, I silently panicked that maybe I shouldn't have said anything.

Betty seemingly read my thoughts. "You were right to speak up. Travis will check on Scott."

"Thank you."

Betty and I talked about other happenings around town. I appreciated the ease I felt around her. After we'd been talking and laughing awhile, Travis sauntered into the room dressed in a suit and tie.

"Mom, I'm headed to San Antonio for a meeting. I'll be home late." He kissed her on the cheek and patted me on the shoulder. "You ladies have a nice afternoon."

We heard the screen door slam shut and shortly after, the hum of Travis's Mazda speeding off.

At home, I made sure I had everything I needed to make Scott's favorite dinner, lasagna. Cooking soothed me. Mixing and measuring, I forgot my worries, if only temporarily.

Hours later, Scott still hadn't come home. When the phone rang at 7pm, I answered hoping he'd finally decided to call me, to at least let me know he was alive.

"Hey, Emma. It's Travis. I couldn't get a hold of Scott today. He wasn't at work. I just called to see if he'd made it home and if you were okay."

I struggled to hold back tears. "I haven't seen him since yesterday morning. Maybe he went fishing or something. I thought he was at work." I tried to maintain my composure. "I even made his favorite for dinner. Now I have a full pan of lasagna, but no Scott."

If Scott wasn't at work, where was he? Did he really spend the day fishing? I stopped myself from answering the questions. I wasn't sure I wanted to know the truth.

"I'm just leaving the office. Mom and I eat late when I have meetings. I'll swing by and pick you up. Bring the lasagna. You can stay the night in the guest room if you want."

"Thanks, Travis. I'll see you in a bit." I was grateful for the invitation. Loneliness and worry were unpleasant companions.

When Travis pulled up, he ran up the front steps and carried the lasagna out to the car. I slung my purse over my shoulder and followed him out. At Betty's, we enjoyed an evening of laughter. I almost forgot my husband hadn't come home.

It neared midnight when Travis walked me back to the house. "You sure you don't want to stay the night?" He leaned against the stair rail.

"I better not. I want to be here if Scott comes home."

"I understand. Call if you need anything." He double tapped the rail before pushing off and striding away.

"Thanks, Travis." I closed the door and turned at the sound of footsteps coming up the hall.

"Where were you?" Scott's question was an unveiled accusation.

Anger boiled up, but I took a deep breath grasping at my self-control. "I was having dinner with Betty and Travis. I made you a lasagna, but you didn't come home. I took it to your mom's, and we ate a late dinner."

"Did you bring any home for me?" His tone softened.

I handed him the baking dish and stomped out of the room. Throwing a tantrum wasn't going to help the situation. But I was mad, and my feelings were hurt.

After changing into pajamas, I slid under the covers. I stiffened when he slid into bed next to me and silently prayed he wouldn't touch me. I pulled the covers to my chin. "Did you put the lasagna in the refrigerator?"

"Yes. Listen, Emma, I'm sorry. I don't have a good explanation for the way I've been acting."

"Can we talk about it tomorrow?" I rolled over, giving him my back.

"Sure." He slid up behind me and draped his arm over me. I tensed at his touch, and he withdrew. He slipped out of bed. Minutes later I heard the rumble of his truck pulling away from the house. I wept into my pillow. Eventually, my conflicted thoughts gave way to sleep.

As I slowly became aware of the sun streaming in the window, I heard Scott snoring next to me. I slipped out of bed and pulled on my robe.

I ambled into the kitchen to make him breakfast. Despite my mini-tantrum last night, I wanted things to be good again.

When Scott joined me in the kitchen, he poured himself a mug of coffee, then dropped into a chair. "I took the day off yesterday. Spent the day fishing. Not sure why I didn't tell you. There is this cloud over me ever since Dad died. I thought by sneaking away, I could leave it behind."

I wanted to understand. "I'm here, Scott. Please don't shut me out."

"Thanks, Em." He smiled, the old spark flickering in his blue eyes.

"Your mom invited us for dinner tonight."

"Sounds great. What time is dinner?" He drained the last of his coffee.

"5pm."

"I'll be sure and be home by then. I'm going to help a friend wrench on his car." Scott gave me a quick peck on the cheek before tromping out of the kitchen.

I stood by the sink staring out the window while the dust from his tires settled back to earth. I'd seen a glimmer of the old Scott. In my heart, I thought maybe he'd turned a corner.

Dressed in a yellow sundress, I walked out of the house at 5pm. Alone. Staying on the pavement so that my white sandals wouldn't get covered in dust, I walked down the block. Betty greeted me at the door.

136

"Hello. You look beautiful, my dear. Where's Scott?" Betty pushed open the screen.

"I thought maybe he was here already. He hasn't been home since breakfast. He was helping a friend with his car."

"He's probably just running a tad late." Betty motioned toward the dining room. "Have a seat. I'll let Travis know you're here."

Travis waved as he walked passed the dining room. Betty walked in and took her seat at the head of the table. A minute later, he carried in a platter of brisket and pork ribs and set it in the center of the table. After more back and forth trips to the kitchen, mashed potatoes, green beans, and a garden salad circled the barbeque platter.

"Travis fired up the smoker this morning," Betty said as she passed the potatoes.

Meat and sides were piled on each plate. She guided the conversation in her relaxed way telling us about the latest news she'd heard at her bridge night. When she'd exhausted the local gossip, she nodded toward Travis. "You spoke with your brother today, didn't you?"

Surprised, I turned toward him. A sadness hung in his deep blue eyes. "I did."

Betty pushed for more information. "How is he? Did he say anything about where he's been?"

Travis sprang up out of his chair. "I forgot the barbeque sauce. I'll be right back. Oh, and Scott sounded fine." He added the last bit as he was half-way out the door.

When he returned to the table, he was quiet, polite as always, but he hardly looked my way and only gave short answers when Betty asked him questions. His behavior gave me pause. Normally gregarious and outgoing, the quiet, sullen Travis made me wonder if there was something he was keeping from me, from Betty, or from both of us.

He jumped up again when someone knocked at the door. "I'll get it."

Betty smiled. "It's probably Scott. I told you he'd come."

We heard Travis argue with someone in hushed tones. Moments later, Scott sauntered into the dining room and sat down next to me. He filled his empty plate and apologized for being late. Travis never returned to the table.

Thanks to Betty, the conversation during the rest of dinner flowed naturally. She had an almost magical gift for making you feel at peace, no matter what circumstance hounded you. After dinner, Scott gushed about the food but begged off dessert saying we needed to return to the house.

At home, it was clear why he was in such a hurry. He wanted the comforts of a wife. I cuddled next to him on the couch until his hands started to wander. My heart divided, I whispered in his ear that I was going to take a shower and would meet him in bed. It was my way of delaying, without saying no.

In the shower, I struggled to remember the Scott that won my heart. I hoped those memories would stir passion in me. The Scott that came and went without a word left me cold. I stepped out of the shower, toweled off, and then wrapped the towel around me. I painted a sultry smile on my face and tiptoed into the bedroom. Scott was snoring.

I fished a nightshirt out the dresser and pulled it over my head. Scott lay half-dressed on the bed so I draped the covers over him. Emotionally exhausted, I fell asleep when my head hit the pillow.

In the morning, I squinted at the bright morning light and rolled over. A single piece of blue paper lay on Scott's pillow. The words blurred as tears puddled in my eyes.

Em- I'll be gone for a while, not sure how long. I need to find the other side of this cloud.   - Scott

Chapter Fifteen

January 13, 2016 – 11:42am

Alex jumped when his phone rang. He picked it up and swiped his finger across the screen, answering DJ's call.

"Hey, I've searched using the sketches that Kate helped us with. I think I found something." DJ talked 90 miles a minute. "There is a guy named Corey who matches the sketch. He owns a small house maybe 3 miles from you as the crow flies. We'll go check out that place."

"Any progress on the other guy?"

"Maybe. Corey was once arrested with a Jim, who favors the other sketch. I'm texting you a picture. Have Kate take a look. If she recognizes the man, please let me know ASAP."

"Will do." Alex saved his script before walking away from the computer. A text notification popped up on the screen. He pulled up his messages and called out to Kate. "DJ sent a photo. Have a look." He strode out of the office and found her in the kitchen.

The cabin smelled wonderful. He'd been so immersed in his work he hadn't noticed the delicious scent wafting from the kitchen.

Kate pulled a tray of cookies out of the oven. "Let's see it." When he showed her the photo, she dropped the tray onto the stovetop and wrapped her arms around herself. "That's him."

Alex felt like a heel for being so thoughtless and sticking the picture in her face. He hadn't even warned her that it was a possible suspect. "I shouldn't have been so casual about it. I'm sorry."

She sat down and covered her face with her hands. Seeing the picture of the kidnapper surely brought back memories of the night in the closet. Alex stood next to her and quietly texted DJ one word: *kidnapper.*

Alex poured two glasses of milk and put a few cookies on a plate. Returning to the spot next to her, he set the snack on the table and gently rubbed on her back. Without a word, she leaned on him. Minutes ticked by with her shoulder against his hip, her head on his waist.

His fingers buried in her curls, he rubbed her neck. He hated to see her upset but relished the fact that she rested on him for comfort. Feelings and longings stirred inside him. *You've only known her a few days. Slow down.*

She straightened and wiped her face. "So they know who he is now." She sighed deeply. "Have they arrested him?"

"His name is Jim. They haven't arrested him yet, but at least they know who they're looking for now." He was glad for the photo as well. Now he wasn't trying to protect her from an unknown enemy. The kidnapper had a face. "What do you say we drive into San Antonio and go up to the hospital? We'll see Tom and Meg and then have dinner here in Kerrville. LaFours has good shrimp." Alex would be surprised if they found those men at that house. Surely, by now, they were long gone, running from consequences.

"Sounds good. Let me get cleaned up." She turned off the oven before padding off to the bedroom.

Alex slipped into the office, closed the door, and called DJ; but the phone rolled to voicemail. "Hey, DJ. She recognized the man, and it really shook her up. Please let us know when you make an arrest. I know she'll breathe a little easier. I will, too." He hung up the phone and trotted into the kitchen. "Here, Bureau. Ready for food?"

Kitty kibble clattered in the small metal bowl, and Bureau skidded into the kitchen as if he'd been starved. While the cat crunched food, water sloshed over the sides of the bowl as Alex carried it from the sink. Bureau recognized the splash of his special treat and focused his attention on the water bowl. The ice Alex added buoyed to the surface each time the black paw plunged it under the water. But, when Kate opened the bedroom door, Bureau left his treasure and ran to her.

Alex delighted in the way her brown eyes sparkled when she looked at him. It was a recent change in her already pretty face. Her safety wasn't all he cared about. "He likes you."

During the ride into town, Alex asked follow-up questions to their conversation from last night. "So were you planning to move soon?" Besides the awkward conversation the first night, she hadn't said if she was single, and knowing that detail became increasingly more important to him. He worked his way to the question.

"Yeah. I was hunting apartments."

"You said Meg was all the family you had left?"

"Yeah."

"So it's ... just you, then?" He tried to sound casual, but it tumbled out more like a freshman asking the prom queen to dance.

She turned her head toward the window. If she wasn't single, some guy was going to be extremely put off by the way Alex had treated her these last few days.

What started out as a giggle blossomed into a full-bodied laugh. "It's only me."

"You were pretty loopy the last time we talked about it." His cheeks warmed, which meant his ears were probably red. *Way to be smooth.*

Kindly, she skated past his juvenile question and changed the subject. "Last night I had a weird dream. I dreamt about that small, yellow house in Schatzenburg. I was sitting on the floor in a room that had blue floral wallpaper, but only on one wall."

"A memory?"

"No. I think Claire is taking up residence in my subconscious. I want to find her. Maybe she can answer some of the oddities. All that happened to me was somehow because of her. I guess I feel connected to her now. I know that sounds strange. That's weird, right?"

"Maybe a little." Alex winked to let her know he was teasing. "When we get back to the cabin later you can work more of your magic online. I think you have a knack for finding people."

August 18, 2002

My Beautiful Claire,

I forced myself to stop dancing long enough to write this letter. We received a picture of you today. I've spent the last two hours staring at your beautiful face. Your dad has been on the phone with multiple private investigators trying to pick up your trail. What an unexpected surprise to receive your photo. It came with a note attached. The note read *Claire at Graduation*. It was signed *J*. (I've wracked my brain trying to think of who may have sent it, but I have no clue.)

(To J: I thank you because I can finally picture my daughter. And I hate you because you know where she is and you know where I am, yet you keep us apart. How can anyone with a heart do such a thing?)

Are you enrolled in a university? What major will you pursue? I am SO PROUD OF YOU. My heart feels like it will explode right out of my chest. I've missed so many milestones, but it seems like Christmas just to have a glimpse of you.

(This is your dad. The letter was postmarked in Cheyenne, Wyoming. Your mom and I have a flight booked already. We leave tomorrow morning. Be on the lookout for us. I'll be the guy standing with a lady who looks just like you. You're beautiful just like your mom!)

He is so excited. I don't think I've ever seen him so happy. I hope this is the clue we need to find you. Maybe in a few days, you'll be reading this very letter.

Eternally hopeful,

Mom & Dad

April 21, 2003

Dear Claire,

After seeing your photo, I can imagine your smiling face as people wish you happy birthday. I wasn't sure what kind of cake to buy for a 19-year-old, so I went with chocolate. Can you tell that I like chocolate? It is a three layer chocolate cake with white chocolate shavings on the top.

Is there a man in your life? It is better to finish school if you can. Men can be such a distraction. But I know that loves comes in its own time. That thought brings me back to the story. When Scott shrugged off my hug, it stung bitterly. I put walls up that day, protecting myself from further pain, but in doing that, I walled him off.

The next part of the story is attached.

Love Always,

Mom & Dad

Summer of '83, Part 3

Hurt, anger, and worry swirled inside me as I crumpled Scott's note. I threw on my running clothes and headed away from the house. The breeze dried the tears that wet my cheeks. My ponytail swung back and forth as I pumped my arms with each stride. My frustrations were pounded into the pavement with each thump of my heels.

Instead of heading straight home, I walked to Betty's as I cooled down. I knocked, but no one came to the door. Only the screen was closed, so someone was home. The door squeaked as I pulled it open. "Hello? Anybody home?"

In the kitchen, I poured myself a glass of sweet tea. There was always a pitcher of sweet tea in Betty's refrigerator. Surprised by footsteps behind me, I whirled around to see Travis in a towel running toward the utility room just off the kitchen. He saw me about the same moment.

"Oh! Hey, Emma. I didn't know you were here, obviously. I was just getting clothes out of the dryer. Mom is out playing bridge, I think."

I covered my eyes. "Sorry to barge in."

"No problem. I just didn't expect anyone to be here. I'll be back out in a minute or two." With clothes tucked under one arm, he gripped the towel with the other and trotted down the hall.

When he was out of sight, I poured myself another glass of tea and dropped into a chair at the table. Three minutes later, Travis emerged wearing corduroy shorts and a button-down shirt with the sleeves rolled up. He almost always looked like he'd just stepped off the cover of a magazine, even in just his towel.

He poured himself a glass of tea and sat down opposite me. "Sorry about that."

I dismissed it with a wave of my hand.

"You just get back from a run?"

"Scott left." I drained the rest of my tea.

The table shook and tea splashed out of his glass when Travis brought his fist down hard. "Son of a ... How could he? What did he say?"

"He left me a note, on his pillow. He said he'd be gone for a while, but didn't know how long."

"I'll try and talk to him. I'm so sorry."

"It's not your fault, Travis. You didn't do anything wrong. Just let me know what you hear. I want to know he's safe."

Travis slid his fingers under mine and ran his thumb over my knuckles. "I'll keep you updated." His tenderness was comforting and dangerous.

"I better go. I need a shower, and I haven't eaten much of anything."

"You run home and shower, and I'll make us a stack of pancakes. How does that sound?"

"Delicious. Thanks, Travis." I jogged back to the house and told myself that it was good to have a friend at a time like this, especially someone that understood Scott and loved him as much as I did.

After a quick shower, I ran to the dresser and yanked on the drawer handle. I chided myself for giving a second thought to what I should wear. I threw something on, then pulled my hair into a banana clip as I walked back to Travis's house. I stepped into the kitchen as he lifted bacon off the griddle.

We spent the next two hours eating, laughing, and talking.

When Betty got home from her bridge club, I told her about Scott's note. It was difficult. I emphasized my hope that Scott wouldn't be away too long. She insisted I stay the afternoon, and I didn't argue. Alone, my thoughts invented every horrible outcome imaginable. In company, I could almost forget Scott didn't want me.

I stopped in the doorway as I was leaving. "Thank you. Both of you. I'm not sure how I would've made it through this day without you." I pushed open the screen but turned when I didn't hear it snap shut behind me.

"You shouldn't walk by yourself in the dark. I'll walk you home." Travis slipped on his loafers.

Gravel crunched under our feet as we walked along the side of the road. I waited for him to speak, unsure of what I wanted to say. He stayed quiet.

Travis stopped at the bottom stair. "Night, Emma."

In my nightshirt, I stared at the queen-sized bed. Two pillows and too big. I gathered my pillow and quilt and lugged them out to the couch. With the television on, I snuggled up. The lull of the voices chased away the loneliness and allowed sleep to envelop me.

Sunday morning dawned lazily, and rain pattered against the windows. I got ready for church and was just about to leave when I heard a car horn. Betty's Lincoln Town Car stopped in front of the house.

146

I slid into the backseat. "This is a nice surprise. Thanks for picking me up."

"No sense in you going all alone." Betty looked back over her shoulder from the passenger's seat.

Travis smiled at me in the rearview mirror. "Sleep well?"

"Surprisingly, yes."

Faces at church were full of questions when I walked in with my mother-in-law and brother-in-law but no Scott. I evaded all questions about Scott's whereabouts from the town busybodies. I wasn't ready to air my marriage troubles.

Polite smiles and overly friendly greetings swamped Travis. I hid a smile as ladies fawned over him. Poor Travis, if the ladies of the congregation awarded titles, he would definitely win "Most Eligible Bachelor" and possibly "Best Dressed" as well. I expected he had a little black book full of names and phone numbers, but he never brought any lady friends around his mom's place.

After church, I spent the afternoon with Betty and Travis. Laughter made the day without Scott seem shorter. Early that evening, I jogged with Travis alongside me. His company slowed my paced and lightened my mood.

CHAPTER SIXTEEN

January 13, 2016 – 1:44pm

When Alex and I approached room 614, the same officer we met the other day greeted us. He shook Alex's hand and opened the door for us. Meg sat up in bed. An afternoon talk show played on the television, and Tom snored quietly in his bed. She put her finger to her lips and then stretched out her arms.

I don't think I'd ever been so happy to see my sister. I ran to the bed and hugged her. "Are you really okay, Meg?"

"I am now. I'm so happy to see you, Kate." She nodded toward her sleeping husband. "My poor Tom." Her eyes brimmed with tears. "I'm just glad he's going to be okay. How are you? The last time I saw you, men were dragging you into a van."

It was my turn to tear up. "I'm okay." I motioned for Alex to join us.

"I remember it vividly. I was terrified." Meg let her tears fall freely. "I wasn't sure I would ever see you again."

She flashed Alex a tight smile before looking at me, a question in her eyes.

"Meg, this is Alex. Alex, Meg."

Alex offered his hand, but Meg ignored it. Alex and I listened as she recounted her memories of the awful events in hushed tones.

"We hurried to the car after the mall closed."

"I remember that." I smiled as Alex slipped his hand in mine. "It was a long way to the car."

"I opened the trunk and put our bags in. Are they still in the trunk?"

I shrugged. I hadn't thought to ask that question.

"I remember a van parked next to us. And a man jumped out." Meg stared at the wall, reliving that night.

"I guess I didn't see that." I took a deep breath, and Alex squeezed my hand.

"The man grabbed you. Put something over your face."

"That I remember." I shivered, and he stepped behind me and rested his hands on my shoulders.

"I tried to get to you, but another man caught me and threw me to the ground." Meg's heart rate monitor started beeping. She looked at me again. "I don't remember anything after that."

"Don't think about it anymore." I leaned over the bed and patted her arm. "You need to relax."

"Have you told this to the police?" Alex kept his hand on my back.

"Detective Torres and Detective Miller came by earlier. The nurse called them when I woke up."

"Oh, good." I wondered if her information had helped the case.

"Detective Miller was so kind. I'm not sure about the other one. He's too intense. He asked a lot of questions about you, though."

My sister and I clearly had differing opinions of people. Miller wasn't awful, but I preferred dealing with Detective Torres.

Alex slid a chair close to the bed, and I sat down. He whispered that he would be right outside the door, then turned to face Meg. "It was nice to meet you, Meg."

"Likewise, Alex." Her words, though polite, sounded flat.

He wanted to let us talk privately, but any farther than outside the door stretched the distance where he felt he could watch and protect.

As soon as he disappeared out the door, Meg raised her eyebrows. "What's the story, Kate? You two are pretty chummy."

I'd have steered the conversation back to recent events, but that would only cause more beeps, so I took a deep breath and tried not to think of it as a grilling. "I'm not sure there is a story. When I escaped, I ended up at Alex's cabin. He's protecting me." I hoped the short version would satisfy her.

"From what?"

"The kidnappers are still out there somewhere." I dialed back my sharp tone. The last thing I wanted was to set off her monitor again.

"Your luggage is at the house. But ... Is it serious between you and Alex?"

"Meg, I only just met him. And don't worry about the luggage. I'm okay for now. I'll get it when you go home from the hospital."

"What are you wearing?"

I looked down at my outfit. "What do you mean?"

"Where did you get clothes?"

"He had a friend buy me some."

"Tell me about him."

I'd heard Meg's tone before, so I chose my words carefully. "He's kind. A little quiet. A widower, his wife died three years ago."

"Don't waste your time. Those brooding types are a drag. And gosh, a dead wife? That's a lot of baggage."

I leaned down to tie my shoe. I didn't want Meg to see the lasers shooting out of my eyes or the flames escaping my nostrils. *How is it possible that we shared the same parents?* After several awkward minutes of knotting and unknotting my laces, she noticed my silence and back-pedaled.

"Sorry." She rarely apologized.

I forced a smile. We'd always had different opinions on men, but I hadn't expected such a reaction from her.

Meg tried to move the conversation along and asked what happened to me after she fell. I told her about waking up in the back of the van, my stay in the closet, and my well-executed escape. Including almost every detail of my run through the brush, the retelling felt almost as long as the escape itself. Alex walked back in as I told Meg what the doctor said about my amnesia. "He was right. My memory returned, most of it, anyway. But listen, I've talked your ear off. We need to go so that you can rest."

Meg didn't argue so I knew she was tired.

I hugged her. "I'm so glad you're okay."

Reaching for Alex's hand, I made sure Meg saw the smile I flashed him. Petty? Yes. Instead of resting his hand in the small of my back, he put his arm around me letting his fingers rest in the curve of my neck.

Outside her door, out of earshot of the officer, Alex chuckled. "She doesn't like me, does she?"

"I'm so sorry. How embarrassing. I can't believe she treated you that way."

On the way to the restaurant, I stewed about my sister's behavior. She and I never saw eye to eye, but I usually acquiesced to her ideas. I'd trusted her opinion. *I trusted her opinion because I was afraid to have my own.* She was beautiful and had impeccable taste in clothes. It seemed logical to trust her in other areas, but it was easy to see where that had gotten me, 31 and single.

April 21, 2004

Dearest Claire,

Happy 20th Birthday. How are you celebrating today? I bought a lemon meringue pie for you today. I'm guessing you're out enjoying time with friends for this birthday.

I still have the same housekeeper at the San Antonio house. She is very reliable. We have a Christmas party every year that is so much work to put together. I couldn't do it without her.

Travis started a tradition a few years after you disappeared. A month before Christmas he and I shop and shop. When you were little, it started out as shopping for you, but keeping wrapped gifts for years and years wasn't going to benefit you, and it sure wouldn't help me. Just before Christmas, we'd donate all that we bought. Now we shop and shop for kids, even though you're much older. The gifts are donated in your name every year.

Don't be mad at Travis for his choices. It is hard for us to regret what brought you into our lives. The world is a better place with you in it, even if I never see you again.

Love,

Mom & Dad

Summer of '83, Part 4

At the end of every day, I went home to an empty house. I became accustomed to sleeping alone. After a week, I moved back to the queen-sized bed. Most mornings I jogged and showered before walking to Betty's and often stayed until well after dinner. I didn't restock my refrigerator for almost a month. I watched the little savings

Scott and I accumulated shrink. He somehow expected me to pay the bills with no income.

Late one evening, Travis held open the screen as I unlocked the front door. "Night, Emma. Call if you need anything."

"Goodnight." I slipped inside and closed the door.

I peeked out the window and watched as he lingered on the steps. They creaked as he slowly plodded off the porch. At the bottom step, he turned back. Skipping every other one, he ran back up to the porch. He raised his hand to knock but drew it back. Hands burrowed in his pockets, he marched off the porch. Part of me wanted him to knock. I stayed at the window until he was out of sight.

Following my normal routine, I prepped the coffee maker for the morning, moved a load of laundry to the dryer, and stepped into the shower.

My head full of shampoo, suds sliding down my face, I felt a hand touch my hip. My scream echoed off the tiled walls.

My terrified greeting offended Scott. He grabbed his clothes and stamped out of the bathroom. I rinsed the soap off and almost tumbled out of the shower. By the time I rushed into the bedroom, he was in his jeans, his shirt draped over his shoulder.

"I'm sorry, Scott. You startled me. You haven't been home. I wasn't expecting anyone to touch me in the shower." I fought with my robe, trying to pull it onto my wet body.

"Whatever. I wasn't who you expected more likely."

"No, sweetheart, please. Don't leave. Let's start over. I'll get back in the shower. Please don't leave again."

Turning around, he charged toward me. I searched his face for passion or regret but saw that his blue eyes were cold and angry. It scared me.

He got so close I could feel him exhale. He spat as he enunciated the words. "Never again. I won't touch you ever again. You don't want me. I can see it all over your face."

He stormed out of the room, swinging his arms, knocking knickknacks off the dresser. I heard dishes smashing against the floor in the kitchen. Scott ranted as he destroyed whatever fragile piece he grabbed. I cowered in the corner of the bedroom for nearly ten minutes. The whole time, I could hear things breaking throughout the house. Each crash initiated a new outburst from Scott and more sobs from me. I didn't recognize this Scott. A sudden silence filled the house. The pulsing of my heartbeat swooshed in my ears until the back door slammed. He was gone.

I grabbed the phone on the bedside table and called Betty. Travis answered.

"Scott ... just ... left." Shuddering sobs interrupted my words. "He was so angry." Two minutes later I heard the back door open.

"Emma, where are you?" Panic resonated in Travis's voice.

"I'm in the bedroom. Be careful for the glass." Perched on the edge of the bed, I wiped at my tears.

He hurried to the bedroom. Stepping around shards, he squatted beside me, his jaw clenched. "Did he hurt you?" He glanced sharply at the glass scattered on the bedroom floor.

"No. He didn't touch me."

Travis scooped me into his arms. "I don't want you to stay here. You'll be safer at mom's house."

I didn't argue. I wrapped my arms around his neck and leaned my head on his shoulder. I was glad for the cover of darkness. If someone saw the two of us, I could only imagine the salacious gossip that would ensue. As he carried me back to his house, I cried into his shoulder. He shushed me as he walked into the house and whispered, "I don't want mom to know about this. Scott's actions would break her heart."

He carried me into the guest room and put me down just inside the door. Every muscle in his body was taut. He ran both hands through his hair lacing his fingers behind his head. His pulse throbbed in his tightened neck muscles.

I adjusted my robe, making sure the edges overlapped. "I won't say anything about it to her."

"You can sleep in here. I'll be back in a while with your clothes." He didn't wait for me to answer before leaving the room.

Once he'd closed the door, I crawled into bed. Scott's words, *never again*, echoed in my head. I wept using the pillow to muffle my sobs. Closed eyes brought visions of shattered glass and shards all over the house. I would have to deal with that in the morning.

The longer Travis was gone, the more I wondered where he was. I started to worry that he'd gone after Scott. When I'd conjured up the worst possible scenario and imagined them coming to blows, I heard the doorknob turn. Travis slipped in and shut the door. Without turning on a light, he set a bag on the floor and perched on the foot of the bed.

"I cleaned up the mess. You don't have it waiting for you. Your clothes are in the bag." He stood up and paced back and forth along the side of the bed. "I'm so sorry about this. I'm not sure what's going on with my brother."

I couldn't see him in the dark, so I leaned over and switched on the bedside lamp. I didn't even think of how red and swollen my face was from crying.

When he saw me, he dropped to his knees next to the bed. "Oh, Emma. Don't cry. Please don't cry." His anger melted away. Tears pooled in his eyes as he pleaded with me.

His tender words evoked unstoppable tears. He tucked a strand of hair behind my ear and wiped tears from my cheek. (I remember how warm his breath felt when he leaned in close and whispered I was safe.) When his lips brushed my cheek, I turned. His lips sought mine. I welcomed it. When he kissed me, I laid my hand on his cheek. He snapped back and stood up. (I made a choice in that moment that was wrong, but, well, I don't regret it.) Before he could apologize, I pulled back the covers in invitation.

Chapter Seventeen

January 13, 2016 – 5:12pm

Alex held open the door to the restaurant and waved at the waitress as he steered Kate to a table far from the door and away from the windows. He pulled out a chair, and she took a seat. Rather than sitting across from her at the square table, he sat to her right. The close proximity allowed them to converse quietly and gave him a clear view of the door.

The waitress laid menus on the table. "What can I get you two to drink?" She nodded when they told her their drink order and hurried toward the kitchen. On the way, she stopped at two other tables, refilled tea, and dropped off a check.

"So what's good here?" Kate laid the menu open on the table in front of her.

"I usually get the shrimp." Alex tapped his finger on her menu, pointing out his favorite platter.

"That's what I'll have then."

The waitress returned with two glasses of sweet tea, pulled out her notepad, and jotted down their order. She picked up the menus and smiled. "It'll be right out."

They sat in comfortable silence. Kate drew circles in the condensation on her glass. A grin teased at her lips.

"What?" He glanced over his shoulder then raised his eyebrows, unsure what amused her.

"We've talked about me, and I don't want to talk about the kidnapping. So all there is to talk about is you or Bureau. And you already told me about your cat."

"Fair enough. Want to start with my Facebook profile?" He laid his phone on the table.

"Nope. Not enough info. I prefer the third degree."

The waitress overheard their banter and grinned as she set plates—seasoned shrimp on beds of dirty rice with a side of roasted vegetables—in front of each of them. "Can I get y'all anything else?"

"No, thank you. It all looks good." Alex turned back to Kate. "Go easy on me with the questions. Will you?" Despite the visit to the hospital and the kidnapping mess, this felt like a date, and he was happy about that.

"Of course. Let start with something easy. Where did you grow up? Tell me about your family."

"I grew up in San Antonio. I'm the oldest of five. Three of my siblings—my two brothers and a sister—live out of state. My youngest sister lives in Austin. We keep in touch during the holidays, but we aren't especially close. My mom wouldn't approve of the way things are."

"And your parents?"

"They both died in a car accident the day after my youngest sister graduated from high school. She still started college at the end of the summer. It was one of the bravest things she's ever done. She and I are probably the closest. We see each other a few times a year."

"I'm so sorry. I can't imagine the pain of losing both at once."

"I miss them. Remember how I told you that I wanted to find my roots? So much died with them. It was too hard searching with so little information. It's been almost seven years since the accident."

She moved the questioning along. "Did you play high school sports?"

"Ha! Do I look like I played high school sports? I was not one of the cool kids."

She relaxed into her chair and gave him the once-over. "You must've changed significantly since then."

"I do *not* want to talk about high school."

"Where did you go to college?"

Between bites, he shared more and more details of his life. His one line answers evolved into stories. Long after their plates were empty, they sat at the table enjoying coffee and conversation.

Alex glanced up at the door as Kate asked him about how he'd met DJ. Mid-question, he leaned in and kissed her. He put his hand to her cheek, covering the entire side of her face. Keeping his hand there, he slid his lips close to her ear. "Jim and another guy just walked into the restaurant." He could feel her body tense. "We need to keep your face hidden until we can think of a way out of here."

She brushed her lips against his stubble and hid her face in the curve of his neck.

He pushed her hair to one side letting it block her face from view. Massaging his thumb and forefinger up and down her neck, he continued whispering to her. "Jim is sitting with his back to us. The other guy is facing this way."

Alex slid his phone off the table and texted DJ while still entangled with her: *Kidnapper at restaurant.*

DJ was quick to respond: *Where?*

Alex responded with the name of the restaurant. Kate burrowed into him, one hand clutching his shirt. Her tears trickled down his collarbone. He couldn't tell her not to cry. "I'll figure something out, Kate. Keep your face buried against me." Massaging her neck again, he whispered a suggested plan in her ear. She nodded into his shoulder and, barely lifting her head, located the cocktail sauce and passed it to him. He shook it onto her hand. "Whenever you're ready." He hoped the charade would work.

"Ah-Choo!"

"Oh no, dear, are you okay? Not another nosebleed." He stood up. Hovering over her and waving his hands as he spoke. He made a bit of a show. *Loud, obnoxious people get ignored, right?*

He tossed cash onto the table, enough to cover the bill and a tip, and wrapped his arm around Kate, who had her head raised and her hands over her face. He guided her to the door. Once outside, they ran to the truck. Alex yanked open the passenger side door and helped her inside. He dashed around and climbed into the driver's seat. He threw the truck into reverse and backed out of the space. They passed a white van in the parking lot before turning onto the street. She only nodded as they drove past it. He drove several blocks, then pulled off the road into a crowded lot, and parked between two other trucks.

Kate's face was still covered in cocktail sauce. He handed her tissues. They both jumped when the phone squawked.

"Y'all okay?" DJ's voice had an edge Alex rarely heard.

"We just left the restaurant. There were two of them. I don't think they saw her." Alex forked his fingers through his hair repeatedly.

Kate pushed back the cuticles on her fingernails.

"The team was geared up and halfway to their place. We just turned around. It'll take us twenty minutes to get to the restaurant."

"Keep us posted." Alex hung up and pinched the bridge of his nose. "You want me to find a closer place to park so you can watch the arrest?"

"I don't want to see them." Her voice wavered.

"I understand. Whatever you want." He wanted to reach for her hand.

She tucked her arms around her. "Please, let's go home."

She called it home.

They rode along in silence. He glanced at her as she stared out the window. *Guilt.* She'd relaxed so completely into his embrace before he whispered about Jim. His first impulse was to hide her face, but he hadn't thought beyond the immediate threat. *What is she thinking?* His guilt now wasn't from feeling unfaithful. Now he felt guilty because she thought he kissed her without any other motive. The irony was that he'd wanted to, but the kidnappers crashed their evening. He had to be more careful. Until DJ gave them more news, they'd have to keep close to the cabin. He couldn't let his feelings interfere with protecting her.

As soon as they arrived at the cabin, Kate headed straight for the shower. The cocktail sauce was matted in her hair and had left a sticky residue on her face. Alex paced in the living room, listening to her cry in the shower, while he waited to hear from DJ. *Please let this nightmare be over tonight.* Kate hadn't spoken a word on the way home. *You have to explain.*

His phone barely made a sound before he answered. "Did you get 'em?"

DJ sighed. "No. They'd left by the time we got there."

"What?"

"They were waiting on food to go. We missed them. Be careful."

When she stepped out of the bathroom, Alex handed her a cup of coffee. "They were gone when DJ and the team arrived."

"Oh." She gripped her coffee cup as if it were a source of strength. "I wanted it to be over."

He rubbed her back. "Me, too."

What happened at the restaurant was quietly ignored, and searching for information about Claire helped pass the hours. Kate searched marriage and birth records again.

"Alex, look at this." She reached for his arm, but pulled back before she touched him.

He leaned in close to look at the screen.

"She married Travis." Kate's voice was barely a whisper.

"I thought she married Scott."

"She did. But then she married Travis. I should check the divorce index." She pulled up Claire's birth certificate again. "I missed something the first time. The certificate was revised in 1989. The father's name was originally left blank but was updated to add Travis Bentley as the father."

Alex wanted to hold her, tell her he'd keep her safe, and beg her to forgive him for his rash charade.

She googled *Claire Bentley.* Pages of results popped up just like before. She skipped to page three and researched the links. None of them seemed to be the Claire from Schatzenburg. Then Kate pointed at the screen. "I wonder if this is her. It's not the barrel rider, at least."

The Claire appeared to be the right age, but as they scanned the page, they saw that Bentley was her married name.

"She's not the Claire we're looking for." She crossed her arms in front of her.

"You didn't to that thing with your hand."

She looked at him like he'd turned purple. "What are you talking about?"

"Star Wars. You know, the line about the droids."

She shrugged. "Haven't seen it."

"Any of them?"

Kate shook her head, then focused on the computer. She searched for *Emma Bentley*. The first result was an obituary.

She gasped. "She died. Emma Bentley died last April. Claire is listed in the obituary as her only surviving child."

A few clicks of the mouse and the printer spewed out a copy. Copies of the marriage records slid out after.

"No wonder the lady at the restaurant looked like she'd seen a ghost." Kate yawned. "One more search, then I should go to bed."

She pulled up the divorce index and searched for Emma and Scott. There was a listing for a divorce granted in Texas in 1988. "I wonder what happened."

"Travis fathered Emma's child. That's what happened."

"I guess you're right." Kate shut down the computer. "I'm going to head to bed. This is getting interesting, but I'm tired."

There was no hug tonight. She hadn't even touched him. *Why were you so rash?* He rechecked every lock on the windows and made sure the cabin door was bolted.

She disappeared into the bedroom, joined by Bureau. Alex laid back in the recliner with a quilt draped over him. His mind would not shut off. Every sound had him wondering who was crouched outside the door. He replayed the scene in the restaurant over and over in his mind. After a half hour, he padded back into the office and started working. Buried in code, he lost track of time.

Dishes clinked in the kitchen. Alex immediately regretted staying up the rest of the night. He rubbed his eyes and stretched. Kibble clattered in the bowl. When he stood up, whatever didn't pop screamed in pain from sitting for so many hours.

Kate offered him a cup of coffee as he ambled into the kitchen. "Hey." Her brown curls hung loose, dancing as she moved.

"'Morning."

"Alex Ramirez, you look terrible. Did you sleep?"

"Not really."

With one hand on her hip, she pointed at the bedroom with the other.

"But…" He was taken aback by her silent demand.

"I won't open the door, for anyone."

Too tired to argue, he trudged to the bedroom and slid under the covers. The pillow and sheets smelled like Kate. He inhaled deeply and drifted off to sleep.

Three hours later Alex's ringing phone pulled him out of a deep sleep. "Hey, DJ, what's up?"

"Are you where we can talk?"

"Yeah." Alex sat at the edge of the bed, rubbing his eyes.

"I wanted to say…that…"

"Spit it out, DJ." Alex yawned.

"She's been through a lot." DJ sounded a little uncomfortable. "If you don't…"

Alex waited while DJ hemmed and hawed on the other end of the line.

"Just be aware of what signals your sending her way."

"Is that all?" Alex wandered out of the bedroom with the phone to his ear. Kate met him in the living room. Quietly she listened, searching his face, trying to decipher what DJ was saying on the phone.

"We're geared up and ready to head to Corey's house." DJ was back in business mode. "I'm headed this way, and I can bring the item you requested."

"Oh, good."

"Should I bring it?"

"Please." Alex smiled as he thought about her reaction. As soon as he hung up, he filled her in on the search.

She sat down in the recliner, crisscrossed her legs, and stared at the non-existent fire. "Do you think they'll catch them?"

"Kate, seeing them in that restaurant unnerved me. I can't fully comprehend how you must've felt." He took a seat on the hearth opposite the recliner. "About last night. I'm sorry. Kissing you was the first thing that popped into my head. I wanted to keep them from seeing your face. But … I'm sorry."

She stared at him for several seconds before responding. He would've paid money to know her thoughts. There was an awkwardness between them, but then something melted in her brown eyes. "I'm thankful they didn't see me."

April 21, 2005

Dearest Claire,

A toast, to you, our grown up little girl on her golden birthday! I have a plate full of truffles for this birthday. It seemed a good accompaniment to a glass of wine. Happy Birthday!

Your dad and I still get you a gift on every birthday. Most of them we donate after a few months, but the one we bought today we'll keep until you come home. Your dad picked it out. That man has very good taste.

Love and Cheers,

Mom & Dad

Summer of '83, Part 5

I woke up with the sunlight on my face, feeling loved. But when I looked beside me, I saw the empty space. There was no note, no written apology, but I knew. Seeking comfort, I'd offered the apple.

I laid my hand on the empty pillow and closed my eyes, remembering. Guilt swept over me. I sprang out of bed, trying to distance myself from the memory. I pulled out clothes and dressed quickly. I could hear Betty humming in the kitchen. All the way down the hall, I silently rehearsed what to say.

"Emma, you're awake. Travis said that you came back after I went to bed. He headed out early this morning."

"Scott ... um ..."

"You don't have to explain, dear. Travis told me that you and Scott had a disagreement. I think that was his nice way of saying you argued. Can I get you some breakfast?"

"No, thank you. I should get home." I hurried out, clinging to a memory that I needed to forget.

After Scott's tirade in late July, I didn't hear from him at all in August. Visits with Betty were a daily ritual, but I retreated to my own house before Travis returned from the office. Limited contact seemed the best prevention against any further trysts. I longed to be in his arms again, to feel the comfort, but I was a married woman.

By late August, I suspected I was pregnant. One afternoon when Betty was playing bridge, I drove into San Antonio so that no one would recognize me in the pharmacy. I wove my way through the aisles until I located the pregnancy tests. At the register, I placed it in front of a disinterested clerk and wiped my sweaty palms on my jeans before fumbling in my wallet for cash, then I grabbed my purchase and hurried out of the store.

At home, I made sure all the doors were locked before closing myself in the bathroom. Step by step, I followed the directions listed on the back of the box. Then I waited.

The test confirmed what I already knew in my heart. I was pregnant.

I agonized over how to tell Travis. I assumed he'd be disappointed. I imagined his dark blue eyes boring into me as I tried to explain about the baby. He'd never been cruel or even cross with me, but I worried that a family wasn't what he wanted. A disappointed Betty flashed before me. I imagined the whispers moving through the pews. And again there was Travis. I couldn't bear to face him when he learned the news.

Scott was absent from my nightmare because he was absent from my life. There wasn't any way to pretend Scott was the father.

I pulled stationery out of the drawer and wrote a note.

Travis - I'm pregnant. I wanted to tell you face to face, but I just couldn't. I don't know what to do. – Emma

I tucked the card into an envelope and scrawled his name on the front. *Travis.*

The day after I wrote the note, I delayed my daily visit until the time Travis was usually home. But Betty and I talked for a long while without any sign of him. Finally, I asked. He was at a dinner meeting with out-of-town clients and wouldn't be back until very late. Reluctantly, I left the note with Betty and asked that she give it to Travis. Betty slipped the envelope into her apron pocket and promised to deliver it.

After returning home from Betty's, I ate a small dinner then dressed for bed. I was tucked in when I heard keys jingle in the lock. Scott was home. No one else had keys. Cautious, I waited to see his mood. Minutes later, he sat next to me on the bed. Tears brimmed in his eyes.

"Em, I'm sorry. There's no excuse for the way I've behaved. I want to come home. Will you have me?"

Glimpses of the Scott I married stirred emotions more recently felt for someone else. Without the option to wait on Travis's response to my note, I sided with my fear. "Yes, Scott. Of course."

He kicked off his shoes and slipped under the covers. I laid my head on his chest. He ran his fingers through my hair, and the silence of untold secrets hung between us.

From that night, it was as if Scott had never left. He came home after work, was in our bed every night, and woke beside me every morning. After a month, I decided that it was time to tell him that there was a baby on the way.

I'd gotten no response from Travis.

One night as Scott and I were snuggled in bed, I whispered in his ear that I was expecting a baby. Scott assumed that the baby was his, and I didn't correct that assumption.

Added Notes: My biggest mistake was writing that note. Never put in writing what you should say face to face. And assumptions are horrid things, dangerous landmines waiting to wreak havoc. Watch out for them. Looking back, nothing about my decision to welcome Scott back made sense.

Chapter Eighteen

January 14, 2016 – 12:24pm

The timer beeped. I grabbed a hot pot holder and pulled a tray of golden brown cinnamon muffins from the oven. While Alex slept earlier, I prepped two delicious options for a late breakfast. I came to terms with that fact that stress and danger brought out my urge to bake. I'd resisted the urge at first, but making cookies yesterday calmed me so much, I craved the peace that baking brought.

After Alex's apology, he took a shower. I pondered what he said and what he didn't. My hands stayed busy adding fillings to the kolaches and spooning batter into tins while my brain picked apart his words. No matter how I replayed what he said, his kiss was an act. I couldn't pretend it was more.

The aroma in the kitchen pulled me back to my childhood. Mom used to bake cinnamon muffins. When she did, I got to mix the streusel topping. And when I was just tall enough to see over the counter, my dad taught me to make the kolaches. It was the one family thing he treasured, an old family recipe.

When Alex padded into the kitchen in his stocking feet, wearing jeans and a flannel shirt hanging open over a tee shirt, I'd just finished drizzling icing on the muffins.

"Smells delicious in here."

The single-serve coffee maker grumbled as it heated water, then spewed out a piping hot cup of coffee. It needed to be descaled. Plates and silverware were already on the table.

"You've been busy." Alex swapped out the filled mug for an empty one and brewed another cup.

"Baking calms me." I shrugged my shoulders.

"It is an odd but tasty problem to have." Alex winked as he sat down.

The steam coming off the kolaches carried their delicious aroma. Alex snagged one off the platter and juggled it in his hands. I set the muffins on the table.

He'd tasted one bite when someone knocked at the door. "It must be DJ."

I added another place setting and made another cup of coffee as Alex went to answer it.

"Come in. Kate made the best kolaches I've ever had."

"A little late for breakfast, isn't it?" DJ set a box wrapped in plain brown paper on the floor, then lifted his Stetson off his head and smoothed his hair.

"Are you saying you don't want any?" Alex lifted his eyebrows and grinned.

"That is not at all what I'm saying. Just making an observation." DJ tapped the box with the toe of his boot. "Becca sent this over. She said you asked her to get it."

"Thanks." Alex pulled out his wallet and handed DJ several bills. "I was up all night. I slept a few hours this morning. Woke up when you called. Head on into the kitchen. I'll grab another chair."

It was entertaining watching to the two of them banter.

Once we were all seated, DJ told us about the planned search. "There's a team headed to Corey Reynold's house. We're going to send in a team on foot to verify that the van's there, then we'll all move in. It'd be best if you two laid low in the cabin for a while."

DJ raved about the kolaches. He slathered butter on a muffin, and crumbs dusted his shirt as he took a bite. "Please give Becca these recipes."

After our late breakfast, Alex cleaned up the dishes, and DJ called to get an update on the search. I scanned the bookshelves looking for something to read. I picked up *The Blue Rebozo* and settled in the recliner.

I'd just finished Chapter One when Alex tore the paper off the box DJ brought. "What do ya think?"

I crawled out of the recliner and walked over to him. When I saw the new two serving coffee maker, my heart pounded a little faster. "When did you...?"

"I asked Becca to get one. Last night." His green eyes twinkled. "It makes *two* cups at the same time." He held up two fingers and grinned.

I couldn't help but giggle at his wonderfully boyish grin.

He played with an errant curl hanging loose from my ponytail. "I didn't have time to get a second recliner, but this is a start."

Earlier, I'd come to terms with the fact that he truly wanted to be alone and protecting me was his only goal, but now a sleek, black coffee maker offered the slightest possibility I was wrong. "I like it. A lot."

"I'm going to set it up." He carried the box into the kitchen.

I followed him.

DJ met us in the kitchen. He planted himself in a chair and kicked his feet out. "Hopefully, after today, you won't have anything to worry about." There was a playfulness in his blue eyes when he wasn't in business mode.

"I appreciate everything you and Becca have done."

He shook his head. "They must've holed up at that house until last night. Except they showed up at Tom's place. I can't believe no one spotted that van." When he referred to the kidnappers, the playfulness disappeared altogether.

"They probably got tired of pot pies, frozen dinners, and tomato soup."

DJ's ringing phone drowned out my comment, and he answered. After a quick nod, he hung up. "They spotted the van. I'm off to meet up with the team. You two stay put until you hear from me." He ran out the front door.

Alex darted to the door and locked it. Silence hung in the air. I glanced at Alex, his brow scrunched into tight wrinkles, his hands clenched.

"This might all be over soon." It was more of a hope than a statement.

"I'm going to grab some wood. I want to have a stash in here so I won't have to wander out near the shed later." He carried the large canvas bag outside and returned two minutes later with it full of oak logs.

I bolted the door behind him as he hurried in.

"Thanks." He dropped the bag near the fireplace. "It's hard to believe that less than a week ago you were banging on my door in the middle of the night. Even if they catch these guys today, don't feel like you need to be in a hurry to leave. You're welcome to stay as long as you'd like." He tossed a few logs onto the grate.

"Thanks, Alex. I'm thankful I ended up here." I hoped his answer would be "Me, too."

"I guess this was the first place you stumbled on?" He tucked paper under the logs and lit it.

"No. One place was empty, and I skirted around another place. It was all lit up and surrounded by beer cans. I could hear guys talking loudly. They all sounded drunk, then started fighting so I kept going."

"So what made you stop at my place? No beer cans?" He sat down on the rug next to me.

"Bureau. He was silhouetted in the window." I stroked the kitty who had sauntered up on cue, focusing on the softness of his fur. I battled the impulse to bury my face in the curve of Alex's neck and snuggle against him. It wasn't a matter of feeling safe. His quiet brooding stirred my curiosity, and his touch channeled electricity through my nerve endings. But I thought better of tackling him. "I know I've said it before but thank you. Thank you for opening your door, for driving me around, and for following your instincts to keep me safe." *I think I just thanked him for kissing me.*

"I'm glad you showed up at my door." He traced the pattern in the rug, moving his index finger slowly toward mine. When he covered my hand with his, the sweat on his palm surprised me. "Rainy, last night, I…"

My gaze riveted to his face, I nodded involuntarily. I wasn't sure how he planned to finish that sentence, but since he'd called me Rainy, anticipation exploded inside my chest.

He put his hand to my face like he had at the restaurant. "… wanted to…"

If he said anything after that I didn't hear it. My heart thumped excitedly on my eardrums. I closed my eyes. Excitement frolicked on my skin as I felt him lean closer. I smelled the crisp mountain scent I breathed in each time I nestled to his chest. His breath danced on my lips.

Buzz. Buzz. Buzz.

Please don't answer the phone.

Aware of the danger that lay outside, he answered with a sigh. I nestled up against him hoping that after he hung up, we'd pick up from where we were interrupted. Alex draped an arm around me.

DJ didn't even wait for Alex to say hello. Alex gripped me tighter after the first few words. As soon as he hung up, I raised my eyebrows afraid to ask.

"They didn't find Jim. They think he ran off into the woods. They found Corey shot in the head. He was airlifted to the hospital." As he uttered the last sentence, he jumped up off the floor and checked the window locks again. It didn't help my fear to see him so nervous. When he returned from the bedroom, I could see the worry engraved in his brow.

He sat back down on the floor next to me, but the soft kisses and longing gazes evaporated with the news that Jim was out there looking for a place to hide. Huddled on the rug, we waited for him to find us. At least that's how I felt.

I rested my head on his shoulder. "I'm scared."

He wrapped an arm around me. "He'll have to shoot me first," he said, the recent tenderness replaced with protective words and body language.

I ran my finger down the cleft in his chin. "That doesn't make me feel better."

Alex's emotional walls, which were crumbling moments ago, were firmly mortared now.

He kissed the top of my head. "DJ is sending a car."

Next to me sat my bodyguard, but I wanted the tender man, with sweaty palms, whose eyes danced. He wanted to let his walls down and let me in, but I wondered if he could.

CHAPTER NINETEEN

January 14, 2016 – 11:44 pm

Alex inhaled the lavender and chamomile scents of Kate's shampoo. Her curls lay draped over his arm and across her face. *Tell her you don't want to be alone anymore.* When she'd dozed, after hours of waiting on news of the search, she'd rested her head on his shoulder. He'd leaned back and gently let her slump across his lap.

Goosebumps erupted on her arms, and he stretched back, yanking his grandmother's quilt off the recliner. With the fire almost out, a chill settled in the cabin. He tucked the quilt around Kate and brushed curls out of her face. Holding her, he could pretend that their world was safe.

But it wasn't. Unable to sleep, he kept watch, rubbing the cleft in his chin. He wanted to protect her. He needed to protect her. It wouldn't bring Ellie back. But his choices now had nothing to do with Ellie, not anymore.

Leaves rustled outside, and he shifted scanning the front windows. Kate stirred, but he laid his hand on her hip and gently patted until she soothed back to sleep. A spotlight swept back and forth through the trees. Thankful that DJ sent them, he trusted that the two officers parked outside had everything under control.

As Alex focused on the warmth of Kate's body and the slow rhythm of her breathing, a calm washed over him. His eyes red and burning, he tilted his head back against the recliner and gave up his battle against sleep.

She'd been using his right arm as a pillow for hours. He didn't want to disturb her, but his knees were stiff and both his arm and his backside were asleep. The slightest movement danced prickles up his arm. His knees popped loudly when he bent them.

Kate stiffened and lifted her head, looking around.

He stroked her hair. "Sorry I woke you."

A contented smile danced on her lips. She leaned on his chest and rubbed her eyes. "What time is it?"

Alex checked his phone. "2:36am."

"Any word from DJ?"

"They called off the search for the night. Officers are outside."

"Did you sleep at all?" She sat up and stretched, her skin peeking out from under her shirt.

"A little." He wanted her to snuggle back into him.

"I'm hungry."

"There are a few kolaches and muffins left. Is that okay with you? We won't make much noise that way."

"Yeah, that sounds good." She started to get up.

"I'll get it." He patted her knee and pushed himself off the floor. Every joint creaked and popped as he hobbled to the kitchen.

When he returned to the living room and saw that she'd changed into yoga pants and his sweatshirt, he smiled. He adored the way she looked in that over-sized sweatshirt, his sweatshirt.

She yawned as she took the plate from him.

"Are you even awake?" He sat down with his back to the recliner and held out his arm inviting her to nestle against him.

"Only sort of." She obliged him with a smile.

"Kate, until Jim—"

She shook her head. "Let's pretend that there's no Jim outside. Please. Talk to me about something else."

"All right." He ran his fingers through her curls. "What do you want to talk about?"

"You were about to tell me how you'd met DJ when we were, um, interrupted." She brought up the restaurant kiss without mentioning Jim.

"I was, and we were." Alex gulped down a swallow of Coke. "DJ and I lived in the same dorm when we were in college. He lived in the room across the hall. I wouldn't say we were especially close, but we hung out from time to time."

"I'd like to see pictures of the two of you from back then."

"Not possible. I'm sure they've all been burned. Anyway, after graduation, DJ and I lost touch. Three years ago—when I was driving home after viewing this property—I was driving a tad over the speed limit. I wasn't in a good place, one look at me, and anyone could see that."

"Was that right after your wife…?"

"Yeah. Well, a patrol car came up behind me, lights flashing. Out steps DJ. He recognized me as soon as he walked up to my window but also recognized I needed a friend."

"He let you off with a warning?" Kate popped the last bite of her kolache into her mouth.

"Nope. I got a ticket that day and a good friend. He gave me his number and made me promise to call. He had my name and number, so I knew there was no avoiding it."

"You needed a friend."

He closed his eyes. "You asked about what happened to my wife."

"You don't have to tell me, Alex."

He wrapped both arms around her drawing strength to relive the memory. "It was a Friday night. Ellie had always wanted to see Peter Pan. Ever seen it?"

Kate shook her head.

"Well it was in San Antonio so I surprised her with tickets. But I was late getting out of the office because I'd gotten wrapped up in a project debugging some code …" A deep breath pressed down his emotions as guilt pounded in his chest. "As I was leaving the office, I called her. She suggested we meet downtown instead of me driving across town to pick her up." He tensed.

Kate slid her hand down his arm and tangled her fingers with his. "Did she make it to the theatre?"

He nodded. "We met outside the box office. After the show, we strolled to a nearby restaurant and enjoyed a quiet dinner."

"Sounds romantic."

"We were two weeks away from our first anniversary."

She choked back a cry which came out sounding like a squeak.

"After dinner, we got into separate cars and headed home, but I stopped to buy us a bottle of wine. Ellie loved a good Merlot." Alex wiped his eyes.

She tightened her grip on his hand and held her breath.

"When I got back to the house, her car was in the driveway, but the front door hung open."

"Just like when we pulled up to the cabin."

Alex ran his fingers through his hair. "I found Ellie on our bedroom floor—" He choked on the words and swiped at the tears he tried to hold back.

Kate stifled a sob. She ran to the bathroom and returned carrying a box of tissues.

"I was too late. She'd interrupted a burglary. The thief even took the rings right off her fingers." He twisted tissues in his hands.

"Alex, I'm so sorry." She touched his arm.

"If I hadn't worked late, she wouldn't have arrived home alone. Or if I hadn't stopped for wine, I would've been the first one inside." He tore the tissues into shreds.

Kate scooted closer and laid her hand on his knee.

He clasped her hand in both of his. "I'm sorry for ..."

"Feeling?" She rested her head on his shoulder. "Please don't apologize for that."

"I'll do whatever I have to do to keep you safe, Kate. But I failed Ellie."

She shifted so that she faced him. "Alex, please look at me."

He met her gaze, blinking back tears.

"It wasn't your fault. You shouldn't feel guilty."

"I want to believe that." He buried his face in her sweatshirt. Tears that he'd held far too long poured out.

She circled her arms around him and pressed her cheek to his head. "It wasn't your fault."

Ten minutes later, Alex sat up and used his tee shirt hem to wipe his face. "Go crawl into bed and sleep for a while. I'll keep watch."

"Are you okay?"

He breathed in deep, then exhaled slowly. "Yeah, I'm okay."

Halfway across the room, she stopped and ran back to him, throwing her arms around his neck. He hugged her close, wishing Jim never existed.

Kate kissed him on the cheek. "Goodnight."

He pulled her tight before letting go. "'Night, Kate."

Emotionally exhausted, Alex settled in the recliner determined to keep watch, but after a half hour, he dozed. He dreamt of Ellie. Standing just out of his reach, she ran her fingers through her short blonde hair, then blew him a kiss. He reached for her, but she shook her head and waved before she strolled away.

The dream was new. Usually, he dreamt he watched her walk into the house. He always called out, tried to warn her not to go in, but she never heard. That dream always ended the same way, as it had in reality. But this dream was different. She didn't go into the house. She only waved and drifted away.

Alex bolted out the chair and shook off his haze. He'd have to stand if he wanted to stay awake.

Moments later, Kate opened the bedroom door. He grinned at the sight of her ponytail askew but sobered when he saw her red, puffy eyes.

CHAPTER TWENTY

January 15, 2016 – 4:45am

My emotions on a roller coaster, my brain on a tilt-o-whirl, I shuffled out of the bedroom, too wrapped up in my thoughts to sleep. The police hunted Jim, yet I felt like the prey. On the high side, Alex had opened up. Protective and tender, he embodied so much of what I wanted. I hoped that whatever we'd sparked wouldn't die out when the danger disappeared.

"You didn't sleep long." Alex motioned toward the kitchen.

"I can't sleep."

"Care to talk about it?" He brewed two cups of coffee with the new pot.

"Too many thoughts. Too much worry." I dropped into a chair. "Did you get any sleep? The police are outside to keep watch."

"I slept a little, but I dreamt about Ellie." He set my coffee in front of me.

I tried not to cry. *He will never be over Ellie enough to love again.* She still inhabited his dreams. I didn't have a chance against that. My heart shattered. I focused on keeping the pieces from spilling onto the table.

After two cups of coffee, I searched for *Travis Bentley.* Alex went to take a shower.

A few quick searches turned up several informative links. He was a businessman in San Antonio, Texas. He played high school football in his younger years.

I heard Alex near the office door and glanced back over my shoulder. "Since we haven't heard anything, I guess Jim is still hiding somewhere."

"He may have found a vacant place to lay low."

I whipped around. He grinned knowing we'd had the same thought.

He called DJ, but it went straight to voicemail. "DJ, call me back."

Minutes later, his phone rang.

Alex didn't wait to tell DJ our idea. "When Kate escaped, she passed a place full of rowdy drunks but didn't stop. We don't know that Jim traveled the same direction, but if the drunks are gone he could be hiding there. Some of those cabins are only used only one weekend a month."

I watched Alex's face for cues to DJ's reaction. As soon as he ended the call, he filled me in.

"They've checked every house and cabin in a five-mile radius." Alex rested his hands on my shoulders. "Also, they got an address for Jim Smitty and went to his house at the crack of dawn. He wasn't there, but they're sweeping his house looking for leads."

"Are they still searching out here?" I tried not to sound panicked, but I wanted to know that they hadn't given up the search.

"Yes. DJ said to expect guys out front most of the day. There are another couple guys at Corey's searching the area from there." He sat down in the extra chair. "Do you mind if I work for a little while? I need about two hours to wrap up this project and send it off to the client. If that's a problem—"

"That's fine. I'll go watch television or read. I promise not to bake." I headed for the bedroom intending to watch television, but when I laid down in the bed, sleep tackled me. Instead of a peaceful, angelic slumber, it was a drooling and snoring kind of nap.

Pop!

What is that noise? I'd barely opened my eyes when Alex came barreling through the door.

"Get down onto the floor!"

I scrambled off the bed, and he pulled me next to him. Our backs against the bed, we stayed clear of the windows. Every muscle in his neck pulled taut, and I could feel his heart pounding in his hand. Or maybe I imagined that. He tensed. I trembled.

Pop!

Pop. Pop. Pop. Pop. Pop. Pop. Pop.

The half second of silence seemed like an eternity, then commotion and hollering started.

We both jumped when Alex's phone rang.

A look of relief spread across his face. *DJ's team must've arrested Jim.* I hugged Alex while he listened. He draped an arm around my shoulders, but the relieved smile faded from his face. He jumped off the floor and called over his shoulder as he ran to the door. "DJ was shot."

I stayed right on his heels but paused at the front door. Outside, chaos reigned. Deputies darted back and forth. A couple of them stood around the shed. DJ leaned on the bumper of his Tahoe, his sleeve soaked in blood. Alex led him toward the cabin. I ran and grabbed towels from the bathroom.

DJ grinned as he flopped back into a chair. "We got him." The grin masked his wincing.

"Where's Jim? Is he...?"

Alex looked from DJ to me. "He's dead."

"Hey, would you go pick up Becca so that she doesn't hear that I was shot from some rookie officer who'll only tell her that I'm on my way to the hospital." DJ pressed the towel to his arm.

Alex nodded, but rested his gaze on me, concern etched in his brow.

I swallowed back my pleas for him to stay with me. Deputies were all over the place. "I'll stay here with DJ. You go get Becca." I slipped my hand in his. "I'll call her as soon as the ambulance arrives and keep her on the phone. I won't mention anything that happened."

Alex studied me another few seconds, then squeezed my hand before he rushed out the door.

"Let me hold that for you." I pressed the towel to DJ's arm. "What happened? I didn't even know you were here."

"We'd just pulled up when one of the guys heard something in Alex's shed. As we approached, that son of a gun took a shot at us. It zipped past, and we took cover."

I managed to keep pressure on his wound despite my shock.

"I motioned for the guys to circle around, and when I did, I heard another shot. Then my arm felt like it was on fire."

"DJ, I'm so sorry."

"He opened the door of that shed, gun raised, and it was over in a matter of seconds."

Alex hadn't been gone more than ten minutes when the ambulance arrived. The paramedics circled around DJ, and I called Becca.

"Hey, DJ." Becca sounded as chipper as always.

"It's Kate. DJ let me use his phone. Do you have a minute?"

"What's up?"

I ducked into the office but left the door open. I wanted to keep an eye on what happened with DJ, but I didn't want her to hear the paramedics. And I didn't want DJ to hear my conversation. Although, I knew eventually he would hear all about it. "Alex and I had a conversation last night. I understand about the walls now."

"Is he with you?"

"No."

"The fact that he even said anything is monumental."

"But…" I sighed. "He can't move on from Ellie. I'm not sure he ever will."

"Did DJ take over what Alex asked me to buy?"

"Yeah. I think maybe he wants to, but he can't. He told me he dreamt about her."

"What are you going to do?"

We wouldn't be talking about any of this after she got news of DJ, and I couldn't think of any other subject that would keep her engaged without suspicion. "When this is all over I'm headed back to Denver. I'll put off the move for a while."

"Oh, Kate. I don't want you to leave."

"I have to."

"What if he asked you to stay?"

"He won't."

"This seems so sudden. What did he say? Hold on. There is someone at the door. Alex is here. Why is he here?"

"I'll talk to you later, Becca." I hung up, and DJ called me. "Time to go, Kate."

At the hospital, Alex and Becca were pacing when the ambulance arrived. Becca rushed to DJ's side and took hold of the hand on his good arm, kissing it over and over as they wheeled him back to a room. Alex and I wandered into the waiting room.

"Is he really okay?" Alex leaned forward, hands clasped together, and rested his elbows on his knees.

"The paramedics didn't seem worried. In fact, they were laughing and joking with DJ about *flesh wounds*."

Alex chuckled. The reference clearly meant something to him, but I didn't understand it.

"Did he say what happened? I know they got Jim, but what's the full story?" He leaned back and slouched down in the chair.

"DJ had just pulled up when one of the deputies heard something in your shed. He motioned to the others. As they approached the shed, Jim shot at them. A few seconds later, he fired again and hit DJ in the arm. All the officers returned fire."

"I'm glad DJ had a car out there."

"Me, too."

Alex crossed his arms. Laugh lines creased near his eyes. "My life was boring before you arrived."

"Sorry." DJ's phone, cradled in my hand, lit up and started ringing. "What should I do? With everything going on it might be important."

Alex reached for my hand. "Let's take it to him."

The doctor walked out of DJ's room, and Becca fussed over her patient.

I whispered in Alex's ear. "Becca is watching DJ like a hawk."

He leaned down to respond but stopped when DJ's cell phone rang again.

I handed DJ the phone. "It rang two minutes ago, too."

"Hello." He flashed Becca an apologetic grin, then focused his attention on the phone call. "Great. Okay. Thanks for letting me know. I'll head that way in a few minutes."

Alex looked down at me and winked.

"And where exactly do you think you're going?" Becca asked, hands on her hips. Her auburn hair stuck out where she'd run her fingers through it.

"That was the hospital in San Antonio. Corey Reynolds is awake and asking to talk to police. I need to talk to him."

"DJ, please. You've been shot. Can't someone else go? And look at you. You can't go like that."

"I'll grab a fresh shirt from the office and follow all the doctor's orders. Alex can drive me there. You'll be there to watch over me, too. But I need to do this." He draped his arm around Becca's shoulders and kissed the top of her head. "For Kate."

Becca glanced my way. "Okay."

DJ looked at Alex. "You don't mind driving me, do you?"

"Of course not. Whatever you need" Alex winked at me again. "For Kate."

"Torres is meeting us at the hospital. And don't forget to run by the station. I need to look presentable." DJ turned around and smiled at Becca. "You okay, sweetheart?"

"No, my husband was shot." She patted his uninjured shoulder.

"If you turn left here, it's faster than going all the way to Main." DJ's adrenaline rush hadn't completely subsided.

Alex complied without comment. After a quick stop at the Sheriff's office for a clean shirt, we were on the road. As we entered the highway, Becca leaned forward, the seatbelt fully extended. She reached around the seat and caressed DJ's uninjured arm again. He sighed.

"Becca, I'm sorry I didn't say anything on the phone, but I couldn't. I hope Alex delivered the news gently."

"Thank you for the distraction. I would've been a mess if a uniformed officer had shown up at the door."

"I'm so relieved."

Quiet settled in the cab for a few miles, but after a third sideways glance from Becca, I prepared myself for questions.

"Are you sure you want to leave?" She nodded toward the driver's seat.

I noticed Alex look at me in the rearview mirror. *Did he hear what she asked?*

DJ walked into Corey's hospital room and greeted Detective Torres, who stood just inside the door. Becca, Alex, and I waited in the hall. DJ left the door open.

"A nurse called and said you wanted to make a statement." He addressed Corey.

"Yes. I tried to tell the nurse, but she wouldn't listen. Then, I tried to confess to him, but he insisted I wait for you." Corey pointed at Detective Torres, whose notebook hung open ready to take notes.

"I've never had someone so eager to confess before." Torres smirked.

DJ sat down in the chair next to the bed. "So what is it you wanted to tell us?"

Corey inhaled deeply and coughed. "Jim called me a few days ago and asked for my help."

"What did he want?"

"My help."

"With what?"

"I didn't know anyone would get hurt. He asked me to help him grab this lady. He wanted to use my house to keep her until Lorraine told us what to do next."

"Who's Lorraine?"

"Don't know. Ask Jim."

"Why the rush to tell us this?" DJ crossed one leg over the other.

"Jim shot me! I wasn't going to let him pin all that other stuff on me. He's the one that hurt that other lady."

"Why'd Jim want to kidnap the woman?" Torres glanced at me.

"A lady named Lorraine hired him to do it."

"But you don't know who she is?" DJ leaned forward.

"She's the one that hired us to kidnap the girl. I just told you that. Jim always talked to her."

"And what did Jim do to the other lady you mentioned?"

"He threw her to the ground."

"Where?"

"At the mall. I saw her hit her head." Corey moaned as he shifted. "She didn't, did she?"

"What else can you tell us?" DJ uncrossed his legs and leaned forward, maintaining a stern expression.

"Oh, no. She died." Corey rubbed his face. "I didn't have anything to do with that. I only tried to kidnap the other one."

"Why were you supposed to grab her?"

"She was going to be Claire." Corey stared at DJ. "I've told you everything. Will I still have to go to prison?"

"You committed a very serious crime, and someone *almost* died because of it." Torres closed the flap on his notebook.

"She's alive?" Corey looked upward. His lips moved, but no sound came out. "Thank God."

"I appreciate your honesty."

"You'll tell the judge I helped you?"

"Yes." DJ sauntered to the door of the hospital room and leaned out.

Corey craned his neck trying to hear what DJ whispered to me. I peeked into the room, far enough so that Corey could see me. I expected to be frightened or overcome with emotion, but instead, I pitied Corey, the tiniest bit.

He waved at me. "I'm so sorry, miss. I didn't mean for your friend to get hurt."

"Okay."

"I'm glad you escaped."

"Me, too." I nodded as if DJ needed more confirmation.

Torres stifled a laugh and shook his head.

"Thank you, Mr. Reynolds." DJ walked out of the room, trying to hold back his chuckles until he'd at least cleared the doorway. He conferred with Torres in the hallway before we said our goodbyes.

Before heading home, Alex and I stopped in Meg and Tom's room to tell them the news. Tom breathed a deep sigh of relief.

Alex patted Tom's uninjured shoulder. "I'm really glad this is all over for you both."

Meg motioned me over to the bed. "You just missed Jerry. He was so worried when he heard what happened to you."

"He must've been horrified by what's happened to you all."

"Did you understand me, Kate? Tom's brother asked about you. He said he'd tried to call, but you didn't answer."

"My phone is still MIA."

"I thought maybe you were ignoring him because of..." She stuck her chin out toward Alex in an unglamorous move. "...that guy."

I hated that my sister might be right again and that Alex might have too much baggage, but I'd never admit that to her. "Meg, he's only helping me until this whole thing is over."

"Well, it's over now. Why don't you go back to our place? Tom will give you the keys."

"No, thank you." I glanced at Alex, and he swooped in.

"Ready to go, Kate? DJ and Becca are waiting." His hand felt like the summer sun, warm on my neck. "Meg, Tom, heal quickly. If you need anything, call us. Tom has my number."

A quiet settled in the cab of the truck as we drove out of San Antonio. I debated whether or not I should mention that Alex and I had been searching for information about Claire, a fact I'd avoided any mention of. The possibility DJ might be able to help in the hunt swayed my decision.

I leaned forward. "DJ, please don't be upset with me, but I had Alex scan those pictures before we handed them over to you." I held my breath unsure how DJ would take the news.

"Please tell me you aren't conducting your own investigation." He eyed Alex.

"You want to hear what she uncovered so far?" Alex's eyes danced as he looked at me in the rearview mirror.

"As long as it was legally obtained and no one was injured." DJ feigned irritation but winked at me, and Becca chuckled.

"You made it sound like the 1986 picture wouldn't fit into your investigation at first, that it wouldn't help catch the kidnappers."

"We used the more recent one and discovered a few interesting things."

"Like what? You didn't say anything." Alex tightened his grip on the wheel.

"It was an investigation. There were several things I didn't tell you." DJ turned to look at me. "That picture by the car was taken in front of your sister's house. Someone was…stalking you. For lack of a better word."

"And you didn't think to tell me this?" Alex's shoulders tightened.

"Calm down. I told you what I thought you'd need to know to keep Kate safe." DJ reached back to hold Becca's hand.

"What are you doing to find the woman that hired the kidnappers? Can you tell me that?"

It bothered me to hear them at odds, to know Alex was angry. I leaned close to the driver's side window and whispered, "Please, Alex. Don't be mad. You've kept me safe."

Alex shook his head and sighed. I sat back, trying not to cry, wishing I'd kept my mouth shut.

Becca raised her eyebrows and pointed at Alex. "Are you sure about, you know?"

I ignored her question.

DJ noticed Alex's change in demeanor and answered his earlier question in a measured tone. "Jim took that information to his grave so we're short on leads. We're looking at known associates of his." DJ shifted to face me. "Kate, tell me what y'all learned."

"I searched for a Claire born to an Emma in 1984. I found one born in Kendall County that seemed like a strong candidate."

"Was there an address?"

"In Schatzenburg. Ever heard of it?" Alex, calmer now, glanced over at DJ.

"Have I heard of it? I just about grew up there." DJ looked from me to Alex.

"You did?" My voice squeaked with excitement.

"I grew up in the metropolis of Kerrville, but my grandma lived in Schatzenburg. I spent endless hours at her house. Gram still lives there."

"Think she would know anything about Emma and Claire?" I hoped she could fill in the life between the documents and explain some of the oddities we'd uncovered.

"I'll ask her." DJ picked up his phone, and we all waited quietly.

"Gram, it's DJ… I'm fine. Who told you I'd been shot?" DJ looked at Becca, who shrugged. "No, Gram, I'm not in the hospital."

He tilted his head back as he listened. "I'm really fine. It just grazed me … yes." He cleared his throat. "A friend of mine is looking for information about a Claire Bentley, who was the daughter of Emma." DJ pulled the phone back from his ear. "… No, she doesn't know where Claire is. She's trying to learn more about her because…" DJ inhaled deeply. "…because she was kidnapped, whoever did it wanted her to think she was Claire… Who's Travis?" He rubbed his face. "Would you mind if they came to talk to you?" DJ looked at Alex. "Now?"

"Point me in the right direction." Alex drummed on the steering wheel.

"Gram, we are headed over… Okay, I'll tell them." DJ tucked the phone in his pocket. "Gram says she'll brew coffee and set pastries out for us."

"Thank you, DJ. She sounded excited when you mentioned Claire." I tried to reign in my expectations.

"She was but explained that she couldn't tell me over the phone. She says she has quite the story to tell."

The large, neatly kept, white Victorian sat on a large lot two down from the house at the corner of Fourth and Main. Flower pots dotted the porch.

DJ leaned forward in his seat, smiling. "Just pull in the driveway."

As soon as Alex threw it in park, DJ swung open his door. He at least remembered to open Becca's door before hurrying to the porch.

Gram, a tall lady with silver hair drawn back into a loose bun, stood on the porch. "Come in, all of you. DJ, let me see you." She hugged her grandson. "Becca, he's going to be impossible to keep in line while he heals."

"Tell me about it." Becca tucked her arm around DJ.

"These are my friends Kate and Alex." DJ pointed toward Alex and me.

"You two are just adorable. Come on into the kitchen." Gram patted me on the back as I stepped inside.

"Mrs. Crawford, thank you so much for having us." I bubbled with anticipation.

"Please call me Gram. That's what most people call me. Mrs. Crawford is much too formal."

In the kitchen, a tray full of cinnamon rolls, bear claws, and apple fritters sat in the middle of the table. Gram poured us each a cup of coffee, then passed the sugar and creamer around the table.

"Thank you for seeing us on such short notice." Alex seemed just as taken with Gram.

"DJ said that you wanted information about the Bentleys." Gram skipped the small talk to get to the heart of things. I liked that.

"About Emma and Claire, yes."

"I can't tell you about Emma and Claire without first talking about the Bentley family." Gram pointed to the kitchen window. "They lived two houses down from here. That way." Even sitting at the table, we could see the house at the corner of Fourth and Main. "Betty was my dearest friend. Wonderful family, Betty and James and those two boys." She pulled a tissue out of her apron and stared at the table for several seconds. When she looked up, there was a sadness in her eyes. "I won't give you the Christmas card version." She focused on me. "I think you need to know the real truth." She sipped her coffee, then folded her hands.

"The two boys, Travis and Scott, looked alike, but were so very different. Everything Travis did was lauded, and Scott lived in his older brother's shadow."

I glanced at Alex, remembering the article about the brothers. Most of it discussed Travis, the winning quarterback, but it closed with one line about Scott scoring the winning touchdown.

"They loved each other, but Scott always watched for a way to get an up on Travis. I remember the look in Scott's eye when he saw his opportunity." Gram shook her head. "It was summer. Emma was in town visiting and the boys were around most of that summer."

"Did Emma live here or did she know someone that lived here?" Alex leaned on the table.

"She visited Beth, but that's another story entirely." She waved her hand. "Anyway, anyone could see that Emma adored Travis. His affection wasn't quite as obvious, but he didn't act on it. He had a plan for that summer and wooing a girl wasn't part of it. So Scott stepped in."

"Scott liked her, too?"

"That, I can't say, but he chased her. I'm not sure what Travis was thinking, but he didn't do anything to stop it. After Scott's third proposal, Emma said yes."

"She married Scott?" I knew the answer, but I hoped the records had been wrong, hoped that the hero stepped in before it was too late. It was the kind of ending that made you want to throw a book against the wall.

"She did," Gram said softly.

Alex leaned back in his chair and crossed his arms. "What about Travis?"

"He acted like a big brother to Emma, never gave a hint that he regretted anything." Gram sipped her coffee. "Scott and Emma were happy, I think, for a while."

A sad silence settled in the room. The way Gram told the story, Emma married the wrong brother.

"But when Scott and Emma had been married about two years, everything changed. James died in a car accident." Gram dabbed her eyes. "I knew the day would come when I'd tell this story, but… it makes me wish all over again life worked out differently."

"I don't remember any of this, Gram." DJ picked up an apple fritter.

"You were probably only two or three when that happened. Betty and I met when I was still young. We'd known each other for years. Seeing her so devastated was heartbreaking." Gram noticed that Alex had less than half a cup left. "Can I get you more coffee, love?"

Alex shook his head. "No, thank you. Not right now."

"We really worried about her. Travis, moved back home. He'd

been living in San Antonio but came back to his mom's after his dad died. That was good for her. He was very good to his mother. Betty couldn't have asked for a better son."

I wrestled with what Gram was telling us. I knew what names were listed on the birth certificate, but what I wanted to know was why, why the lady with the face like mine cheated on her husband. To balance that awful word, I sought justification for her actions and for Travis's.

"I think maybe I do remember Travis. Tall, blue eyes, dark hair?" DJ added a cinnamon roll to his plate.

"Yes. Travis was wonderful. Everyone loved him. Anyway, we were all so focused on Betty that no one really realized how hard Scott had taken his dad's death. Betty told me that he would disappear for days without a word to Emma."

"But I thought Emma was married to Travis. They lived in that house, right?" DJ pointed toward the corner house.

"You're getting ahead of my story." She patted his hand. "Emma spent a lot of time with Betty and Travis when Scott was having such a hard time. There was one night when something happened, but I'm not sure what. I never even mentioned it to Betty, but I'll tell you. The Lord knows I am not trying to gossip."

"Gram, we all know that you're not that kind of person." Becca squeezed her hand.

"Thank you, dear. My DJ sure picked a good one, didn't he?" Gram chewed a bite of her cinnamon roll, and we all waited to hear what happened.

After she wiped the icing off her lips, she began again. "I heard shouting late one night, so I peeked out the window. It sounded like it was coming from the direction of the yellow house, but I couldn't see that far. Just before I gave up looking, Travis ran by my window from the other way, from his house. He was in jeans, but he had no shirt on. I remember because it was so unusual, but not as unusual as what I saw next."

I slid my plate to the center and leaned forward.

"Minutes later, Travis strode passed the window with Emma in his arms. She was in a bathrobe. He carried her to Betty's. I've never told anyone what I saw, not even Mr. Crawford, God rest his soul."

"He carried her all the way from that house to the corner?" Alex seemed to be calculating the distance in his head.

"Do you remember when that happened?" DJ shifted his sling.

"I think so. From what I saw, they came from that direction and ended up at Betty's. The yellow house is up on the next block." Gram turned to DJ. "Summer of 1983. Let me think. It must've been about late July."

I did quick math in my head. Counting nine months from the end of July led right at the end of April. Claire's birth record listed her birth month as April, but I couldn't remember the day.

Gram cleared her throat. "Eventually, after a few weeks, Scott came back around. I don't know all the details of what happened to bring him back, but he came back and things with Emma seemed good again. Very soon after Scott returned, it was announced that Emma was expecting." Gram choked up. "Children and grandchildren are some of God's greatest gifts. As you can imagine, Betty was thrilled to hear that she'd be a grandma."

Becca slipped out of the kitchen wiping her eyes.

"DJ, is she okay? I didn't mean to upset her."

"I'm sure she's fine. Let me run and check on her." He hurried to the door. "Could you wait to tell the rest?"

Gram nodded. "How did you meet?" She glanced from Alex to me.

"Go ahead, Kate." Alex slid his hand down my back.

"I ended up in trouble, and Alex helped me."

"I see. DJ mentioned a kidnapping."

"Yes." I glanced down at the table and fidgeted with my coffee spoon. I realized how nervous I looked and dropped my hands into my lap.

"Did all this happen recently?" There was a presence and a vitality about her that made her seem years younger than I guessed she was.

"It happened a week ago." Alex tangled his fingers with mine under the table.

"Some things are just meant to be." Gram walked to the stove and lifted the percolator. "Half a cup?"

"Yes, please." Alex slid his cup toward her.

Dumbfounded, I checked that my jaw hadn't hit the floor. *Meant to be?* She didn't know that he had thick walls around him. Becca had warned me about them, but now, even she acted as if they'd come down. I wanted to believe both of them, but then I remembered Alex's comment about the dream. After a big sip of tepid coffee, I scrunched up my nose.

"Warm up, dear?" Gram eyed me; a mischievous spark twinkled in her eye.

"Yes, thank you." My cheeks grew as warm as the coffee.

She read my thoughts, I think, more than that maybe. She saw something I couldn't see and watched expectantly for my reaction to its discovery.

I wanted to steer the conversation away from me. "Have you lived in Schatzenburg all your life?"

"Most of it." Gram's cheeks colored a soft pink. "I moved here in my late teens. That was a *long* time ago."

"You must love it, to stay here that long."

"I know too many secrets about this place to leave now." She winked as DJ and Becca strolled back into the room hand in hand. Becca's eyes were still red, but a smile graced her face.

"Now where was I?" Gram tapped a finger on the table.

"Grandchildren." Becca cut her bear claw into bite size pieces.

"Ah, yes. So then Claire was born. It must've been about 1984. She was a beautiful child, absolutely beautiful. If Betty and I hadn't been so close, I would've thought everything was wonderful for Scott and Emma. But mothers know things. She confided in me, and I won't break that confidence. But I will say that she worried for that little family. So I did, too."

I still wanted answers. There were gaps in her story, and I didn't understand.

"Betty worked hard to keep things happy. Oh, she loved that little Claire." Gram choked back a sob and waved her hand in apology.

DJ looked frantic to see his Gram so upset. "Can I get you anything?"

"No, I'll be okay." She patted his hand. "Betty got sick. Cancer. By the time they caught it, it had spread too many places in her body. Travis took care of her right up until the end."

"Does Travis still live on the corner?" Alex cradled the mug in his hands.

"I'm not to that part yet. Be patient with me." Gram wiped her eyes. "I wish I knew more to tell you about what happened next, but I only know what I heard from Emma and the rumors of all sorts that buzzed through the pews."

"You make it sound almost scandalous, Gram." DJ downed the last of his coffee.

"It was. The whispers made me wonder about the night I'd seen Travis carry Emma to his house, but I kept my lips sealed. That was not for me to spread around. But whatever happened, Scott left, and he wounded Emma in the worst way possible."

"What did he do?" Alex and I asked in unison.

"He left with Claire." Gram stared at me.

I wasn't sure I heard her correctly.

"Where'd they go?" Alex gripped my hand tighter.

"Disappeared." Gram stood up and walked to the sink.

DJ, Becca, Alex, and I looked at each other. The reality of what happened, like water droplets on a blanket, slowly penetrated our shock.

Becca teared up. "What type of heartless person takes a child from their mother?"

"I sat with Emma many times in those horrible first few weeks, not that the later days got any easier for her. She'd cook and cook. It calmed her."

"But she never said why?" As soon as my question slipped out, I regretted asking it.

Gram gave me such a kind look, I nearly cried. "Emma never explained. I wish I knew what else to say."

I hadn't missed the little details, waving like flags, trying to get my attention. She gazed at me with the same look from before, only more somber, waiting for me to see what she saw. I wasn't willing to look where all the flags pointed.

"So Claire was kidnapped? How old was I when this happened?" DJ rubbed his forehead.

"You were probably six or seven. You were staying with me most of that summer. I had to be careful so that you didn't find out. I didn't want to scare you." Gram sat back down at the table.

"Did they ever hear from Scott?" Alex looked from me to Gram.

"I was getting to that. Emma searched and searched for her baby, but they never found her."

"Never? Where are Emma and Travis now?" Alex leaned forward in his seat. He already knew part of the answer but probably didn't want to believe it, just like me.

"They married a while after Scott left, then moved to San Antonio. Emma used to come out several times a year. But she died last year, days before Claire's birthday."

Gram, Becca and I were all in tears, even Alex and DJ looked misty-eyed.

"That was a hard funeral. Emma died so young, and Travis was despondent. To answer your question," Gram turned to Alex. "he still owns that house, but lives in San Antonio." She swallowed down her coffee. "Look at me. I'm being such a ninny. I hope this story helps you find what you need. It would be wonderful if someone could help Travis find Claire. That man wants nothing more than to see his little girl, though it seems funny to call her a girl now. She's over thirty."

"Thank you for telling us the story." I wiped my face.

"It was the talk of the town for a long while. Even thirty years later, people still bring it up from time to time. You know how people like to whisper about things."

"We discovered that. Alex and I ate lunch at the drugstore a few days ago. One of the ladies acted like she'd seen a ghost."

"So that was you? Yes, people talked about that." Gram reached out and patted my hand. "Looking at you makes me miss Emma. You do bear a strong resemblance to her."

What if...? I couldn't force myself to finish the thought. I'd only just remembered who I was, now my brain murmured questions. I glanced at Alex wishing for thought bubbles. *Does he think I'm Claire?* I smiled awkwardly at Gram not knowing how to respond. *I can't be Claire. I just can't.* My heart started racing, and the room tilted as if it would spin at any moment. I wanted to leave. I looked up at Alex and tugged at his hand.

An understanding settled in his green eyes, and he squeezed my hand in response. He turned to Gram. "Thank you so much for meeting with us. I hate to run, but I have a cat that'll be upset if he doesn't get his food."

The drive to Becca's house seemed long. Instead of talking about Claire's story, we rode in silence. When we pulled up to the curb in front of their house, Alex jumped out and walked to the porch with DJ.

Becca hugged me. "Please reconsider your decision. Please." She glanced over her shoulder. DJ and Alex were out of earshot.

"I'm not sure what he said to you, but maybe Gram is right. Maybe it is meant to be." She hugged me again. "And I want you to stay because you're my friend."

"You weren't there when Gram..."

DJ called out, and Becca climbed down out of the truck. I moved to the front seat as Alex slid into the driver's seat.

He drove several miles without saying a word. I stared out the window. Grass that could barely be called green grew in patches on the medians. Bushy evergreens intermingled with scrub oaks along the side of the road. From the safety of the truck, I could appreciate the rugged beauty of the landscape.

"I apologized to DJ." The strain in his voice caught my attention. "Please forgive me. I don't want you to think I'm a hot head who can't control his temper."

"I don't think that at all." While the strain of the conversation made me uncomfortable, his intensity lit my insides. I found the combination of protectiveness and tenderness provocative. My thoughts drifted back to when he wrapped his arms around me at the mall. "Not at all."

He sighed. "I'm not always so intense."

A few miles down the road, I'd tamed my inner turmoil about who Gram thought I was. "I almost can't wrap my head around Gram's story. But what she told us explains so much. After Scott left, Emma and Travis married."

"That story about Travis carrying Emma, wow. I wonder what

all the hollering was about at the yellow house that night. That was in late July?"

"Yep. Nine months before April."

"Oh. *Ooooh.*" Alex glanced at me with eyebrows raised. "How long did they wait to marry after Scott left?"

"Not sure because I don't know when he left, but she probably had to wait a year for a divorce to be declared because of abandonment. Sometime after that she married Travis and updated the birth certificate. I wonder…"

Alex turned down the one lane road near his cabin. "Yes?"

"Think he married her because he felt guilty or because he loved her?"

"He loved her." Alex slowed down to avoid hitting a deer. "What do we do now?"

"Part of me wants to keep looking for Claire knowing that she was taken from her parents. And I feel like I should talk to Travis. I'm not sure how to start that conversation."

"Yeah."

"That's a conversation that needs to happen face to face. What if that woman, Lorraine, finds someone else that looks like Claire? I would hate for him to be tricked after all he's been through. When we get back to the cabin, I'll look up a phone number for him."

Knowing the story fed my desire to find Claire. How could I face Travis, warn him that someone wanted to trick him, and not have any information about his Claire?

April 21, 2006

Dear Claire,

Happy Birthday! We've missed so many of your birthdays. This year there is a Tres Leches cake on the table. My sadness is stirring a hunger that may require the entire cake.

Storms are threatening as I write. It seems so fitting to the way I feel. I can barely write today.

Love,

Mom & Dad

Summer of '83, Part 6

The morning after I broke the news, Scott called Travis and Betty before I climbed out of bed and asked them to come to breakfast. You can imagine my horror. I worried more about the look on Travis's face than the possibility that Scott might learn the truth. I set out plates, napkins, and silverware. Scott stirred the gravy, then pulled the biscuits out of the oven.

Betty and Travis were barely inside the door when Scott announced that we were expecting a baby. I knew Betty would be excited. Her face lit up, tears glistened in her eyes. Travis patted Scott on the back and offered me sincere congratulations. He seemed genuinely happy for us, which surprised me. It stung. Afraid of his disappointment, I wasn't at all prepared for him to act as if the baby wasn't even his.

For the next several months, I held my breath hoping that whatever magic spell had brought Scott back to me would not be broken. I buried my hurts and relished in the perfect-looking life that I'd somehow achieved despite the bumpy road to get there.

Added Note: Reading through this story again, I experienced waves of guilt and sadness. Oh, how clear hindsight can be.

April 21, 2007

Dear Claire,

Happy Birthday! I was very unoriginal this year. I bought another decadent chocolate cake. Oh, how I wonder what you're doing with your life. Are you married? Do you have any children?

My dream was to get married and be a mom. As you read the attached pages, I hope you feel how excited I was about having a baby.

Happy Birthday,

Mom & Dad

Summer of '83, Part 7

The nurse laid you in my arms, and my heart melted. From that moment, you were my world. Big, grey-blue eyes gazed at me in wonder. You were perfect.

Scott was so excited. He commented on how much you looked like him. Travis and Scott looked alike, but there were noticeable differences. You favored Travis. I kept my lips sealed.

When Betty came in, I let her hold you. Oh, what joy lit up her face. Travis snapped picture after picture.

Betty and Scott were cooing over you when Travis stepped up next to the bed. He rested a hand on my shoulder. "She's beautiful, Emma. Congratulations." His clear, blue eyes sparkled with delight, without a hint of accusation or regret.

The day you were born, Scott became a new man. He was so excited to have a baby girl. You became his entire world, and I took a backseat. (For you, it was a price I paid willingly.)

As you grew up, your eyes changed to brown and you started to favor me. (At least I hoped!)

CHAPTER TWENTY-ONE

January 15, 2016 – 5:06pm

The cabin seemed to open its arms in welcome each time I stepped inside. The fire died out long ago, but the faint scent of oak lingered. Bureau slept on the rug, curled up in his favorite spot. The quilt draped over the recliner added to the postcard-perfect picture of home. *Home.*

Outside, the wind whipped, and large raindrops pounded the ground. "Late afternoon storm. We got home just in time." Alex rested his hands on my shoulders.

"Yeah."

After a shower, I pulled out the bread, cheddar slices, and butter. There were a few slices of leftover bacon so I tucked a couple slices in each sandwich. I'd just pulled the first sandwich out of the pan when Alex wandered into the kitchen.

"Sandwich? I'm making bacon grilled cheese." I pointed at the pan with my spatula.

"I'm getting a bit spoiled having someone cook for me. I haven't had such a variety of hot food in years."

Alex set mugs on the coffee maker. "Want a cup?"

"Please."

He brewed the coffee. "I wonder why they snatched you. You do look like Emma, and you're about the same age as Claire, I'd guess. But nothing in Gram's story explained what reason they'd have to kidnap you."

"I didn't see any rewards offered for information about Claire when I searched, but maybe it's something like that."

"Do you think someone was trying to defraud Travis?"

"It's possible."

"When was Claire born?" Alex barely finished his question before he darted out of the room. He returned carrying the birth certificate. "April 21, 1984. If you have a similar birthday, maybe that's why they chose you."

I hadn't noticed the day. I'd only remembered the April part. *How did I miss that?* "That *is* my birthday. I know what you're thinking, but I can't be Claire. I had two parents and grew up in Denver. My dad's name was Gavin, not Scott."

Alex reacted to my tone and put his hands up in defense. "I wasn't saying that, Kate. People have doppelgangers. How would the kidnappers know birthdates?"

"In Texas, birth indexes are public information. It's the same in Colorado."

"So did they pick you because of your birthday? I can't imagine it was random."

"I don't know."

"I know baking helps you think. If you need to bake a multi-tiered cake, I can probably borrow pans from Becca." Alex grinned that boyish grin I'd only seen a few times before.

"You know me well, it seems. I was thinking cookies of some sort." I flashed him my cheesiest smile and opened the pantry. While I scoured the shelves for cookie fixings, Alex collapsed in the recliner with his book.

Knock. Knock.

Alex jumped out of the recliner. "Who would show up here on a Friday evening?" He opened the door only after I dashed off to the bedroom.

With my ear to the door, I listened.

"Captain Crawford asked me to drop this by. It was recovered from the white van yesterday. He asked that Ms. Westfall let him know if there is anything unusual or helpful to the case." It must've been someone from the Sheriff's office.

"Thanks. We will." Alex locked the door before bringing me the purse.

I looked into the bag, checking the various pockets. Then I dumped everything onto the bed and started going through each piece.

Alex sprawled out on the bed next to me. He watched as I dug through the contents.

"Nothing unusual. Just what I'd expect to find in a purse. My cell phone—which needs to be charged—and the charger cord are both in here. My return flight ticket is here, too."

"When were you flying home?"

"Monday."

"So soon?"

"I should call Travis Bentley. If he has time, we can meet before I leave."

Alex handed me his phone, then grabbed my phone and charger and plugged it in.

I dialed the number I'd scrounged from the internet. My hands shook as it rang and rang. Alex sat down next to me just as the machine picked up.

"Hello. This is the Bentley residence. Please leave a message."

Beep.

"Hi. My name is Kate Westfall, and I wanted to talk to you about Claire. Please call me when you get a chance."

Alex held up a piece of paper with his number written on it.

"I can be reached at 210-555-1993. I look forward to talking with you." As soon as I hung up, I thought of all the things I should have said. "I didn't tell him that I didn't know where she is. He'll be excited when he gets the message."

"Don't fret it. He'll call back, and you can say whatever you need to say." Alex tucked a few strands of hair behind my ear.

Kiss me. Ask me to stay.

"You're right." My phone buzzed on the dresser as it came to life. "I should see who's been trying to contact me."

My handful of friends from back home probably thought I dropped off the map. Hopefully, LeAnn spread the word I lost my phone.

I sent out a group text. "I have my phone again. Exciting vacation. I'll see y'all when I get home. Monday."

"I'm sure they miss you. And were probably worried sick."

"It helped that I called LeAnn earlier this week. Mind if I call her again?"

"Is that code for please leave?"

"Yes." I shrugged. "I'd rather talk about you behind your back." I grinned, hoping my humor covered the truth.

"Very funny. I'll leave." He sauntered out of the room without closing the door.

"LeAnn, I got my phone back. Hold on." I swung the bedroom door closed. "All the stuff that was going on with me is over so I think I can talk about it without melting into tears."

"You sound so serious, Kate. What's going on?"

"You have to promise me that you won't say a word. To anyone. I really don't want to answer a million questions over and over."

"I promise."

I recounted to LeAnn all that had happened. I did well holding it together until I told her about our meeting with detectives at the mall. I was somewhere in the middle of telling her about how protective Alex had been when I burst into sobs.

"Kate, are you okay?" He knocked at the door.

"Hold on, LeAnn." I opened the door and grabbed his hand.

He followed me to the bed and laid down.

"I'm back."

LeAnn's voice dripped with concern. "You okay? You sounded so upset."

"Yeah. I'm okay ...now."

Alex rubbed my back, reason enough to have him next to me.

I'd have to be vague and creative with my words. "Anyway, that's the story."

"Is he single?"

"Uh huh." I didn't even touch on the whole Travis part of the story.

"You aren't coming home, are you?"

"I leave Monday."

"Does Mr. Bodyguard have someone else?"

"It's hard to say."

"Is he sitting right next to you?"

"Uh huh."

"Well give him a hug from me for keeping you safe. Kate, I know you. You're smitten. I can hear it in your voice. I can't wait to hear all about him when he's not beside you."

"I'll call you when I get back in town." I ended the call.

Alex rolled to his back and tucked his hands behind his head. His grin lit up his face like a bronze statue in the sunlight. "You *were* talking about me."

"How much did you hear?"

"Only you, but watching you blush is cute." He jumped up off the bed. "Ready to search for Claire?"

"Lead the way."

I googled again adding *1986* and *Scott* to the search words, *Claire Bentley.* Tears sprung up when I clicked on the missing children links. "She was on milk cartons."

"I guess we can blame the barrel rider that we didn't see it earlier."

"I added search terms which bubbled these results closer to the top." I wiped my eyes.

"You okay?" He squatted by the office chair.

"Yeah. It's just so…" I clicked to the next page of results and then on the article listed at the top. "This says that Scott left with Claire after discovering he wasn't the father. Gram didn't tell us that."

"Gram wouldn't say that even if she knew."

"You think it was the night that Travis…"

"Yes. Men don't carry women in their bathrobes an entire block unless they're protecting them, in love, or both."

"So which do you think it was? I'd guess protecting since there was hollering."

"Both."

"This article was informative, but it doesn't help me find Claire."

"Scott likely changed their names, so that they wouldn't be found. We just have to think like Scott." Alex stood up and laid his hands on the back of my chair.

"If we found Scott, he would lead us to Claire."

"Then how do we find Scott?" He grazed his fingers along my shoulders.

"I don't know." I was disheartened. Finding records in spite of typos or misspellings was possible, though hard. Finding records when someone purposely deceived others and hid information was impossible. "I don't know how to find her, Alex. I'm going to have to meet with Travis without offering him any hope. It makes my stomach hurt thinking about it."

"Stop thinking about it. Think about something else." He scooted the extra chair next to me.

"Like what?"

"Help me with my family tree."

With a new mission, thoughts of Claire were put aside, and I searched for Alex Ramirez, born in San Antonio in 1981. No results matched my search criteria. "I guessed that you were born in 1981. Was I wrong?"

"Close. 1980." The teasing sparkle in his eyes made me wonder what I was missing.

I searched with the new date to no avail. "I still can't find you."

"Try searching my real name."

"What kind of secrets have you been keeping?" I clutched my hand to my chest and acted shocked.

A robust laugh bubbled out of him. "Alejandro S. Ramirez." The r's rolled off his tongue like a cat's purr.

"What's the S stand for?"

"You tell me." He leaned so close, his breath tickled my cheek.

I searched again using his given name. "Found it!"

"Did you figure out the S?"

"Are you a saint?"

He winked. "My mother probably wished she named me something different when I was two."

On a yellow pad, I drew branches up from his name for his father and mother. I wrote in their names. "Did I get it right?"

"So far so good."

"It's common for Hispanic men to have their mother's maiden name as a middle name, isn't it?"

"It wasn't as common when I was born, but my mom insisted. My brothers have different middle names."

As I searched for records, he stayed close beside me. I wanted to crawl into his lap and bury my head in his shirt. I loved the way he smelled. With him right next to me, concentrating took more energy.

He pointed above his mother's name. "I only know my grandma's married name."

"Here's your mother's birth certificate." I pointed at the screen.

"That's incredible. It has my grandmother's maiden name."

"Yep." I added two lines going up from his mom and wrote in the names *Rosalinda Navarro* and *Enrique Santos.*

I turned my attention to his father. "Let's see what we can find out about your dad."

Branches spread up the page and his online family tree grew. As new people were added to his tree, little leaves appeared. We followed each lead. Caught up in the search, we spent over an hour in front of the computer.

When I yawned, Alex moved his chair. "It's really late. I shouldn't keep you up."

"I usually like being up late, but I'm tired."

"Will you be able to sleep? You can curl up in my lap again if that's better."

"Tempting, but I think I can sleep now that the kidnappers aren't out there lurking." Given my feelings, I didn't trust myself to sleep in his lap.

April 21, 2008

Dear Claire,

Happy 24th Birthday! I bought an assortment of fancy cupcakes. You dad is sitting next to me sipping a cup of coffee and enjoying a carrot cake cupcake. He's not pacing today, which means I'm doing well controlling my tears.

I've joined a website called Facebook. I am gathering as many friends as I can and posting your graduation picture. There is some way that my friends can share that photo with their friends. Even our housekeeper shared the photo. Poor lady, I've talked her ear off about you.

I don't understand how everything works yet, but maybe Facebook will help us find you. It's given me a glimmer of hope.

The story I wrote talked about Scott's reaction when you were born, but I didn't write about anyone else. Travis brought Betty to the hospital as soon as he heard Scott and I were on the way. He paced in the waiting room with Scott, taking picture after picture. He took hundreds of pictures during the first week of your life.

You filled my heart in a way unmatched by any other person alive. From the moment I felt you move inside me, I loved you. To lay eyes on you was like a glimpse of heaven. (Living without you is my own personal hell.)

Scott doted on you. Betty spent more time at our house the first few weeks of your life than she spent at her own house. I didn't mind. I never thought too much love would cause any problems.

I remember (here come the tears) the first time I laid you in Travis's arms. You were four days old. We'd just come home from the hospital, and he'd been so caught up in taking pictures he hadn't held you.

With Betty in the kitchen making dinner, and Scott at the store, it was just the three of us: you, me, and Travis. He laid the camera on the coffee table and sat down nervously. I placed his hand under your head and the other around your body. As I pulled my hands away, leaving you in his arms, tears streaked down his face. I mistook those tears for guilt. They weren't. I know that now.

I picked up the camera and snapped a picture. I hope you some-day get to see it. Have you ever wanted to say something, but words refused to leave your lips? That was how I felt. I wanted to talk to him about you, our shared life, but I let fear stand in my way.

I love you, Claire. Learn from my mistakes. Never let fear stop you.

Forever Love,

Mom & Dad

April 21, 2009

Dear Claire,

Happy Birthday! Your graduation photo is sitting in front of me as I write. I am trying to imagine what you look like as a 25-year-old woman. I chose a strawberry pie for this birthday. Not knowing what you like makes it hard to choose.

You were loved so much. Scott was giddy the first time you smiled at him. Betty cheered you on as you rolled over more than a week before the milestone expectation. We were all convinced you were the smartest child ever born. At six months, you were almost ready to crawl. Travis would come over after work and stretch out on his belly on the floor, drumming his fingers on the rug. You'd rock back and forth, trying to coordinate your arms and legs to move. Three evenings in a row, I watched the same routine. Sadly, I never thought to take a picture.

He was still dressed in his slacks and dress shirt. One evening he even had on a tie while he laid on the floor. It was such a sight. The third night, you found your groove and scooted toward him. You scrambled across the floor, then grabbed a handful of his hair. He scooped you up and blew raspberries on your tummy. Oh to hear that belly laugh of yours once again.

Love you,

Mom & Dad

P.S. I have over 300 friends on Facebook, but no one has seen you.

April 21, 2010

Dear Claire,

Happy 26th Birthday!

Travis holds me while I cry, and when my tears have all run out (or so I think) he hands me paper and a pen. If you ever read these letters, thank your dad. He is the one that encourages me to write every year. It's too hard. I miss you and mourn all the milestones I've missed.

This year I opted for something more grown up than a cake or cupcakes. I bought a chocolate fountain. It's great for dipping pretzels and strawberries.

You were born when I was 26. Thinking of that makes me wonder if you're married. Have you met someone special? I've often daydreamed about watching you walk down the aisle. I imagined Travis would give you away, and Scott could hear about it from his jail cell.

I keep reminiscing about the days when you were with me. The day you took your first steps, all four of us (Scott, Betty, Travis & me) were surrounding you, cheering you on. Scott had his arms spread wide ready to catch you. I think your grandma actually danced a jig she was so excited, and Travis snapped pictures. There is an entire series of photos of your first steps.

For the first two years of your life, everything was near perfect, at least on the outside. Scott and I got along, but I felt alone. I had you, but he wasn't really mine anymore. He'd come home smelling of perfume. (And I never wore any), but I ignored it. Looking back, that was a mistake.

I hope when you find your love, he finds his comfort in your arms.

Love,

Mom & Dad

April 21, 2011

Dear Claire,

I am writing alone right now. Your dad will drive out after work today. He usually takes the whole day off, but a client came into town at the last minute. This house always feels more like a castle when your dad is here. Have you ever met someone that made you feel safe and protected? That's the way I feel with Travis, safe, but he's not here so bear with me as I try to write.

Happy Birthday! How are you celebrating your 27th? With friends in a swanky restaurant? With a boyfriend at a candlelit table? With your husband and kids around the kitchen table? I want so much to see you, to know about your life.

I'm eating a third slice of chocolate cheesecake. That's what I bought for your birthday.

I drove to The Castle this morning. Have I ever written why I call it that? I called it The Castle because it was where I felt safe, and my charming prince lived there. It's silly, I know. We would never dream of selling this house, but it is so much easier on Travis to live in San Antonio. (I admit that it is easier for me, too.) But I love this house. Being here makes me feel more connected to you. I know it seems crazy since the time that you were with me, we lived in the yellow house. But this house is my castle. Someday I hope it's your castle, too.

More than anything, I want you to know how much you were loved. I've attached more pages, the next part of the story, to this letter.

Love,

Mom & Dad

Summer of '83, Part 8

When you were two and a half, Travis came to the house one afternoon. Scott wasn't home from work yet. I'll never forget the sad smile on Travis's face as he stood outside the screen.

You and I were in the kitchen. Pots were scattered about the floor, and you were banging wooden spoons on them. With every bang, more giggles erupted from you. I danced to your beautiful music.

I waved Travis in when I saw him, but his eyes stopped me cold. "What's wrong?"

He looked terrible. His eyes were red and puffy, the color gone from his face. My stomach sank. I knew something was horribly wrong.

"Is Scott here?"

"He's not home yet."

"Y'all need to come over when he gets home. Mom has something she needs to say."

"Travis, you're scaring me. What's wrong?"

"Honestly, I don't know exactly, but Mom is sick. She was in her room talking to Dad about saying goodbye."

My hands flew to my mouth and the wooden spoon in my hand bounced across the linoleum floor.

"Come over when Scott get home. I'll make dinner." Standing in my kitchen, Travis looked like a scared little boy.

I wanted to wrap my arms around him in comfort. But when I touched his arm, tears spilled from his eyes, and he quietly whispered: "I can't."

In that moment, I understood. Travis loved me, and I loved him. Part of me had known it all along.

"She needs me to be strong right now." He let the screen slam behind him and made his way back to the house.

The creak of the screen announced our arrival. Travis filled serving bowls with the taco fixings and pulled the warmed tortillas out of the oven.

Scott's somber nod told Travis I'd conveyed the warning. I nestled you into your highchair and handed you a tortilla. We all took our seats and waited for Betty to join us. Avoiding our gaze, she took her seat and reached for the food. Travis followed her lead and passed the tortillas, meat, and toppings around the table. Tacos were built, but no one spoke more than a "yes, please" or a "thank you."

Betty noticed when all the plates were filled and looked up from her plate. She wiped the corners of her mouth and cleared her throat. Her eyes roamed from face to face landing finally on yours, Claire. Betty's gaze lingered on you as she spoke. She explained that she was dying. Cancer had spread throughout her body. The doctor offered her condolences rather than treatment options.

Scott bolted from his chair and dropped to his knees next to his mom, weeping.

I hugged Betty, then tried to gently pull Scott away. It concerned me to see him so upset. Travis glanced at his mom. Worn and weary eyes pleaded with him to help her out of the dining room. He rubbed his eyes and drew up to his full height. His mom needed him more than ever. His grief would have to wait. Shuffling down the hall, Betty leaned on Travis. Her plate was still full of food.

The next several weeks blew through at hurricane speed. Betty withered away. I spent every day with her. She loved watching you play. I also made sure dinner was in the oven or on the stove each evening before leaving.

Travis took over the vigil when he arrived home from work. I worried about him. He wasn't getting much sleep those few weeks.

In the final week of her life, Betty didn't leave her room. Travis stopped going to the office and traded the comfort of his bed for a chair near her bedside.

Scott was just as torn up, but he handled it so differently. He escaped to a place where the pain was far away. He'd stop over to see his mom each day, but he dealt with his grief by spending time with you. Rocking you to sleep each night was his escape.

Added Note: Seeing Travis upset was a rare occurrence. He almost always maintained control. It was as much a virtue as a vice. He couched strong emotion, and that was sometimes the wrong thing to do. I loved his restraint at times but hated when he withdrew and seemed cold because he couldn't let his emotions show. He's changed some in the years since you were born. You were the one that brought out his strong emotions. Remember the day he held you and cried? Maybe his heart knew even then that you were his little girl.

CHAPTER TWENTY-TWO

January 16, 2016 – 9:15am

Alex stretched and smiled as he heard her in the kitchen. From the sounds of cabinet doors banging, pans clanking, and the oven beeping, he decided Kate was baking. Again. He wasn't sure what bothered her.

He headed straight for the coffee. "Is there a problem?"

"Not really. Meg and Tom are being released from the hospital today. I'm trying to decide what to do."

"You mean about your ticket?" Alex sipped his coffee, letting the caffeine do its work. "I hope you figure it out soon. I've gained five pounds this week." He winked as he took a muffin off the counter.

"I'm going to read while this batch bakes." She grabbed her book of the table and skirted past him.

He leaned on the doorframe and watched her drop into the recliner. *No point in trying to work.* Focusing on projects was more difficult with her around, but it wasn't because she was a distraction, per se. She was more interesting than Java or Perl, or any other scripting language. He quietly slipped up next to her and whispered in her ear. "I think I'll read, too."

She gave a slight shriek. "You surprised me. Want the chair?"

"Nah, I'll sit on the floor." He picked up his book.

She pulled her legs up. "Lean against the chair at least."

He scooted in front of the recliner and leaned back, but he didn't get much reading done. Kate fidgeted more than she read. The recliner moved every four seconds, then her knee bumped the back of his head.

"Sorry." She tapped his shoulder.

He tilted his head back and looked up at her. "Want to talk about it?"

"About what?"

He waited.

"No. Well, maybe." She stared at her book. "I think—"

The timer beeped, and she launched out of the chair.

He followed her into the kitchen.

"You're out of flour." She shrugged apologetically after pulling the pan out of the oven.

"That's not what you were going to tell me."

She sat in a chair and buried her face in her hands.

"What is it?" He slid into the chair across the table from her. "Talk to me."

"I'm not changing my ticket. I'm going back to Denver on Monday. I need to go back to where I grew up. I'm not sure for how long. I may not move here right away. A big part of me wants to stay here, but..."

Alex wasn't prepared for the ache he felt hearing her say she was leaving. He walked to the window and watched a squirrel jump from tree to tree. "I'll be sorry to see you go." *Kate, please don't leave.*

When he turned around, she was next to him, and he wrapped his arms around her. "You want to go home. I understand that." He wiped a teardrop from her cheek with the side of his finger. "I won't ask you to stay."

"Meg and Tom should be home by now. Would you mind if we took them dinner?" Kate twisted her hair up and then let it fall.

"That'd be fine. She'll be thrilled to see me, I'm sure."

"Tom likes you." Kate grinned and hurried off to the bedroom.

Alex's phone vibrated in his hand. As soon as he answered, DJ started talking. He didn't even wait for a hello. That was never a good sign.

"The Lorraine lady called Jim's phone and left a message. She is going to try and find Kate on her own."

"Crap." Alex clenched his fist.

"We don't know what Jim told her. So I don't know if she'll even try and find your place."

"DJ, how dangerous is this woman? Who is she?"

"I don't have any other information, Alex. I'm sorry, but I wanted to give you a head's up. Looks like Kate's not out of the woods yet. Want me to send a car?"

"Not right now, we're leaving in a few minutes. But I'll text when we're headed back if you could have one here overnight."

"Will do. Call if you need anything." DJ sounded upset.

Alex fished a business card out of his wallet and dialed the number. "Detective Torres, it's Alex Ramirez."

"Kate's... friend?"

"Yes. Kate would like to visit her sister. I know one of the photos was taken of her there. Is it safe?"

"Meg and Tom were driven home from the hospital, and there'll be a car out front 'round the clock."

Alex relaxed a little knowing there'd be a police presence. "So it's safe then."

"I wouldn't let her go alone."

"I wouldn't think of it."

"Could you hold for a second?"

"Sure." Alex drummed his fingers on the table. At least they had someplace to go where police were nearby.

"Alex, that was Crawford. He filled me in."

"Yeah. I haven't told her yet."

"Let me know if I can be of help."

Alex laid his phone on the table. He was glad Kate hadn't overheard the call. He didn't want to tell her that someone was still after her. He laid his head down on the kitchen table and listened as Kate sang in the shower. Instead of the protector rising up inside him, his heart broke at the thought of seeing fear in her brown eyes.

He jumped when she bounced into the room. "Kate, could you sit for a second?"

Her face full of questions, she dropped into a chair.

"That lady is out looking for you. We don't know what Jim told her. She may have no idea where to look for you, but…"

"The one that Corey mentioned? She is seriously determined to find a Claire." She slumped down in her chair. "How do they know?"

"She left a message on Jim's phone."

"So she doesn't know he's dead." She folded her arms on the table and rested her head on them. "Meg wants me to come stay with them until I fly to Denver."

"She's your sister." He didn't want her to leave. "But I'd rather you didn't. They have police parked in front, but I'd feel better if you stayed here until…"

"I don't want to stay with her." Kate sat up and tapped the table-top. "Let me finish getting dressed, and we'll head over there."

Alex caught her hand. "I'll do whatever I have to do to keep you safe."

She squeezed his hand. "My bodyguard?"

"If that's what you want to call it."

Alex and Kate stopped on the way to San Antonio and bought two dozen pizza rolls. The aroma made it hard not to sneak one before they arrived at Meg's.

"You're sure it's safe to come here?"

"I called Detective Torres earlier. He isn't taking any chances." Alex pointed at a patrol car parked in front of the house. "We'll have dinner, but not linger too long after that. I wonder how long they were watching you here."

"Not sure. But let's not say anything to Tom or Meg, please."

"We'll see. Meg doesn't need the stress, but Tom deserves to know."

Tom greeted them at the door, his arm in a sling. In the den, Meg was propped up on the couch, resting as ordered. Alex set the box of pizza rolls on the coffee table, and Tom brought in paper plates from the kitchen.

"I haven't had pizza rolls in ages." Tom helped himself to a couple pieces.

"Kate, all the stuff you bought at the mall that night is in the bedroom if you want it." Meg pointed down the hall.

"Thanks. I'll get them when I grab my luggage."

"You aren't staying here?" Meg set her plate on the coffee table and stared at Kate.

"No. I'm going back to the cabin. Are you still planning to go to Colorado in, when is it … April?"

"End of March, yes." Meg wiped off her fingers. "Do you have nightmares?"

"Not really." Kate shook her head.

"I wonder why they grabbed you."

"I only know that it has something to do with a girl who was taken from her mother years ago. Other than that, I don't know. Where will y'all stay in Denver?"

"It's all so weird. It must've been so frightening in the back of that van."

"It was." Kate looked down at her empty plate.

"Were you afraid they were going to hurt you?"

"I was." Kate stood up and walked toward the hall. "I'm going to gather my luggage while I'm thinking about it."

"Need help?" Alex was already by her side.

"Yes."

He heard Meg complain about how strange Kate was acting and rolled his eyes. He completely understood Kate's frustration with her sister.

She closed the guest room door behind him. "I know she's trying to deal with everything. That's why she wants to talk about it."

"She doesn't realize that you don't want to talk about it." He rubbed her arm. "Show me what you'd wear if Becca wasn't shopping for you."

Kate opened the suitcase, and Alex laughed.

"What's so funny?"

"It looks like the stuff she bought you."

folded the sweaters and other tops and stuffed them in her

. She laid the sundress inside before zipping it closed. "An-

Meg continued to ramble about the kidnapping, Alex mo-

"I'm glad Meg is recovering. I can't say that I'm the least bit sorry

what happened to the men that hurt her." He glanced over his

. *She's eavesdropping.*

"Agreed. All of us can sleep more easily now." Tom didn't sound

either.

"They still haven't caught the one that hired them. The police

this morning to warn us. That lady is looking for Kate."

"Oh, no." Tom's face went pale.

"She is not after you or Meg as far as we know."

"But if something happened to Kate, I'm not sure Meg would

." Tom's voice was strained.

"I'll do whatever I have to do to make sure nothing happens to

." Alex snuck a peek at her reaction.

Tom dropped his voice. "It seems like you have strong feelings

Kate."

Alex nodded. "It's been quite a week."

"Kate!" Meg gave an irritated sigh.

Alex leaned around the door and startled Kate. "Your sister is

to you."

She jumped, that beautiful sparkle twinkling in her brown eyes

she gazed at him.

"Kate! Are you even listening to me?" Meg waved her hands.

224

"What?" Kate rolled her eyes, then turned toward Meg.

"The guy at the grocery store. He looked like Dad."

"What are you talking about?"

"Tom saw a guy at the store. He looked like Dad."

"When was Tom at the store?" Kate leaned back into Alex when he stepped up behind her.

"Before you came. He ran to get a few things."

"I never met your dad's family, but this guy could've been his brother." Tom perched on the couch next to Meg.

"We never met Dad's family either, but he never mentioned any siblings." Kate shook her head.

Alex's phone rang, and he stepped into the kitchen to answer it.

"Hello, my name is Travis Bentley. Kate left this number when she called about my daughter Claire."

"Oh, yes. Can I have her call you back in about 5 minutes?"

"I'll be waiting for her call."

Alex rushed up to Kate. "We need to go."

"Everything okay?" Tom stood up.

"Yes. I just noticed the time. We've got a long drive back to the cabin." Alex picked up the suitcase and grimaced dramatically, drawing a chuckle from Tom.

"Don't make me laugh, please." Tom shifted the sling and flinched.

Kate hugged Meg. "I'll call you before I get on the plane."

"You sure you won't stay here at least until you leave?" Meg shot Alex a look, and he took a small step back.

"Alex invited me to stay at the cabin. You need quiet and rest to heal quickly."

"You okay?" Alex tossed the suitcase into the backseat.

"Yeah. I want to be back at the cabin. And you aren't a good liar. What was the phone call really about?"

"Travis called back."

Kate's eyes widened. "What am I going to say?"

"You'll figure it out. Just do it on speaker so that I can hear, please."

Alex pulled away from the curb as she dialed.

"Hello."

"Mr. Bentley, my name is Kate Westfall."

"Yes. I'm sorry I missed your call yesterday. I just got back into town." Travis's voice was electric with excitement. "Messages played as I put away my groceries. I almost fell over when I heard yours."

"I'm sorry to say that I don't have any information about Claire's whereabouts."

"But your message said it was about Claire." His disappointment was unmistakable.

"I'd like to meet with you. It does relate to Claire."

"I guess it's too late to meet now. Tomorrow at 1pm?"

"That works. Text us the details." Kate hung up, and tossed the phone in the cup holder. "Should we tell DJ that we're meeting with Travis?"

"Why? He's supposed to be home recovering. If we tell him, he'll insist on coming with us."

April 21, 2012

Dear Claire,

Your dad is right here next to me. I wish you could see the cake we bought this year. It is completely covered in edible flowers. Happy 28th Birthday! How do you spend your days? Do you work? Are you raising a family? It frustrates me that I don't know these things.

I've backed off on my charity work. I don't have as much energy as I used to. Now I only coordinate our Christmas charity.

Hugs and Kisses,

Mom & Dad

Summer of '83, Part 9

Travis knocked at the door as the first rays of light broke over the horizon. Scott and I both knew she was gone. I watched my husband collapse into Travis's arms. My heart ached to watch them grieve their mother. I wondered if Scott would run off again, and it pained me that I couldn't comfort Travis.

The first few weeks after Betty died were subdued. We hardly saw Travis. He buried himself in his work. Despite the way I felt, I couldn't let Scott and Travis drift apart as brothers. Even though it was hard for me to be around Travis, it was equally as hard to be apart from him. Scott needed Travis, especially with his mother gone. It took several invitations, but finally, Travis came for dinner.

He hugged you that night like he hadn't seen you in a year, and he brought you a floppy rabbit. You dragged it around with you everywhere.

At dinner, Travis told us he planned to move back to San Antonio. He asked if Scott and I wanted to move into The Castle. We jumped at the opportunity.

The following weekend we started cleaning out The Castle. There was so much in that house. It took us several weekends of sorting, but finally, we were close to the end. The last room to sort was Betty's. We all knew it would be hard, but none of us had any idea of how it would change our lives forever.

April 21, 2013

Dear Claire,

Happy 29th Birthday! Your dad bought you the most beautiful flowers, and we got you a sumptuous chocolate cake. (I snuck a slice again.) I hope you're having a wonderful life.

The attached pages were the hardest to write. I couldn't even bring myself to read it again.

Love you,

Mom & Dad

Summer of '83, Part 10

One Saturday, Scott, Travis, and I joined forces to clean out Betty's room. You played on the floor with blocks while we sorted. I folded linens and emptied bathroom cabinets. Travis and Scott sorted through clothes and boxes in the closet. The guys laughed at treasures dug up that morning.

After hours of cleaning, I decided in was about time for lunch. With the closet finally empty, the guys moved on to other tasks. Travis pulled open one of the dresser drawers. Scott pulled out a pile of papers from the nightstand. They continued to sort while you giggled each time your blocks tumbled over. I padded into the kitchen and made sandwiches.

I called out when the sandwiches were ready, and Travis came tromping into the kitchen with you on his hip. Scott followed.

Scott devoured his sandwich, then stood up. "Emma, I'm going to take Claire home for a nap. You can stay here and keep sorting through mom's room." He pulled you out of the high chair. "Give Mommy a kiss." He stood by the door as you ran to me. (Looking at the kitchen door even now, I can still see you, with your arms spread wide waiting to be scooped up.)

I picked you up and hugged you close, and you pressed your puckered lips to my cheek. "See you later. Be good for Daddy."

Scott carried you out of the house.

After finishing our sandwiches, Travis and I set back to work. I started with the pile Scott had pulled out of the nightstand. Betty had used the nightstand drawer to tuck away notes from friends and, the most treasured find, her journal. I set it aside. It was too soon to read it, but it couldn't be thrown away.

Two hours passed, and Travis was still sorting through the dresser. Four drawers hadn't yet been opened. I joined him in the task.

"The nightstand is empty. Sorry it took me so long. Some of the notes to your mom were so sweet. I kept so many. It seemed wrong to toss them. I'll start at this other end of the dresser." I pulled open the drawer and gasped.

"What's wrong?" Travis stepped up beside me.

"She left us letters. There is an envelope addressed to each of us, even Claire." I handed Travis his envelope.

He sat on the bed and ripped it open. I watched as tears gathered in his eyes, but I didn't offer comfort. I couldn't.

I opened mine. The letter detailed some of what Betty loved and appreciated about me: my steadfast love for Scott, even when things were hard, and the way I mothered Claire. I cried. Guilt and grief knotted in my gut.

"I'm going to take Scott his letter and tuck Claire's in the baby book. She's too young right now."

"I'll go with you."

Instead of walking in through the back door, near the driveway, Travis trotted to the front door, as he always did. He pushed on the door expecting it to swing open, but it didn't. I tried the handle.

It was locked.

We skirted around the house and walked to the back door.

"His truck is gone." Travis said it as a statement but a question hung in the air.

We found the back door unlocked. I ran to the nursery. You weren't in the crib. Travis ran through the kitchen and living room looking for any sign of Scott or you.

I looked in my bedroom. An envelope lay on Scott's pillow. (What a horrible flashback to times past.) The flap side was up and opened. When I flipped over the envelope, I screamed. Travis rushed into the bedroom.

Scott must've found the note in Betty's nightstand.

Travis ran up next to me. "What is it?"

"Your mom was supposed to give this to you a long time ago." I handed him the note and waited as he read it. "When I first discovered I was pregnant. The night I left it with her you were working late. That was the night Scott came home. When you didn't say anything, I just assumed that you …"

"You mean … Claire?"

"Yes. I thought you knew." I should've told him face to face and not in a note.

(Only Scott knows if it was open when he found it. I don't know if Betty knew the truth, suspected the truth, or just forgot to give Travis the note.)

"You thought I didn't want her? You thought I wouldn't take care of you?" Pain flashed in Travis's eyes.

I covered my face. "I didn't know what to think. I was scared. I'm scared now. Where is he?"

"He's not coming back, Emma." Travis's words were sharp, his eyes red.

"No. It can't be true. He'll come back. Maybe this is like when his dad died. Don't you think?"

He shook his head. "No, Emma. I don't think he's coming back." His tone was soft and sad.

I fell against him pounding on his chest. "He has to bring her back!"

He pulled me to his chest, holding me while I sobbed. Tears streamed down his cheeks.

Travis dragged his sleeve across his face. "I think we should call the police."

"Will they do anything? Everyone thinks he's ..." I let the words dangle.

"We know he's not." He rested his chin on my head. "She's ours."

I nodded, and Travis picked up the phone to call the sheriff's office. Our hunt for you began that day.

Added Note: Those first few days were so hard. I couldn't be consoled, and Travis was heartbroken. He held me while I wailed, but life had taught us a painful lesson, so we maintained boundaries. Besides, at the beginning, there was only minimal comfort in his embrace. The feeling of comfort and protection I had with Travis was gone. After a time, it returned.

I sometimes wonder how we made it through those first three days. He could've hated me for not telling him, but I suppose grief shared is easier than if we each bore the weight of it alone.

CHAPTER TWENTY-THREE

January 17, 2016 – 10:27am

"I wonder what Travis is like." My knuckles crackled as I pushed back my fingers. "He texted you the address?"

"Yes. You nervous?" Alex changed lanes to avoid the traffic entering the highway.

"Very. I wish I had more to offer him."

"Hopefully, breakfast will help calm you, even though you didn't make it yourself."

"You're so funny."

"Kate, once you talk to him, I bet you'll think of something. Was that Meg that called you after we got back last night?"

"Yep. She's not happy that I'm leaving."

"I certainly—" Alex hit the brakes as a driver, busy texting, cut him off. "Put your phone down."

Thirty minutes later, he pulled into the Cracker Barrel parking lot. The restaurant was crowded, and we had to wait for a table. We strolled around the little gift store at the front. Winding through racks of knickknacks and kitschy tee shirts, he asked me about my apartment in Denver.

"It's on the second floor. The back patio overlooks the mountains. I have coffee out there some mornings." I picked up a wind-up car. "Hardly anybody sells this kind of cool stuff anymore."

We were staring at the wall of candy when they called Alex's name. The hostess led us to a table not far from the fireplace, which helped keep the dining room warm and cozy.

"How long will you be in Denver?"

"I'm not sure." I didn't want to talk about it.

"Will you miss … this?"

This, as in being with you? Yes! "Being kidnapped?" I shook my head. "Not so much, but yes, everyone here has been great. I'll really miss Texas."

Alex rolled his eyes and laid his hand open on the table. "That's not what I mean."

When we were ready to leave, Alex picked up the check and headed toward the registers in the gift shop. I visited the ladies' room. He was signing the receipt when I came up beside him. There was a brown paper bag in his hand.

"What did you get?"

"Candy." He handed me one of those soft peppermint sticks, the kind that melts when you rest them on your tongue. But he didn't pull the candy out of the brown bag. In the truck, he laid the bag of peppermints on the center console and stashed the brown bag behind the driver's seat.

While Alex drove to Travis's house, I texted Becca: *On the way to Travis's place. Alex says it's a nice area.*

Send me the address … Any news? … Still leaving? Becca sent the texts in quick succession.

I texted her the address and then shot off an answer: *He hasn't asked me to stay.*

Becca wasn't ready to give up. *I think you're overthinking his dream comment.*

Me overthinking? Never. I made sure Alex couldn't see my phone. *Will call after. We're here.*

Large homes sat on acre lots, each different from its neighbor.

"You see what I mean about a nice neighborhood." Alex turned into the circular driveway.

I checked the address to be sure we were at the right house. "Travis has done okay for himself."

"He has. It must've have been horrible for them to have all this, but not what they wanted the most."

I knocked at the dark-stained double doors. We waited. I was surprised when a middle-aged woman answered the door. *Is she the housekeeper?*

"Mr. Bentley said you were coming. Come in. He's on his way." She stepped back to let us enter and pointed toward the left. "You can wait in the library." She was curt but not rude. There was something almost familiar about her.

In front of us, a staircase curved up to the second floor. To the right, we saw a living room larger than Alex's entire cabin. We passed a music room as we followed her to the left down a short hall then turned and continued down another hall.

I admired the décor and decided it would be easy to get lost in this house. Alex walked right behind me, his hand on the small of my back.

The housekeeper pushed open a door. "Please have a seat."

Bookcases lined the walls on opposite ends of the stately room. A leather loveseat and two high back chairs faced a massive desk stacked with files and papers. Windows covered the entire back wall of the room offering a view of the manicured back lawn.

I perched on the loveseat and noticed the art collection that hung on the wall near the door. Alex grabbed my hand and inhaled sharply.

The housekeeper held a gun. "I don't want to use this so please listen carefully."

Alex scooted closer to me, and I squeezed his hand hoping he knew what to do. I didn't.

"When Travis arrives you're going to convince him you're Claire, then sign the money over to me. I found you."

"I don't know how to do that. I'm not his daughter."

"Don't give me that nonsense."

"Honestly, I'm only here to offer my help to find her."

"Liar, you're trying to get Emma's money. You stroll in with your smile and brown eyes knowing he will give you anything you want. *I am the one* that found you. *I* deserve the money."

"What money?"

"Please, don't hurt her." Alex stood up.

What is he doing? I jumped up and pressed into his back. "Either of us."

"Stand still. Emma left everything to Claire, but you already know that or you wouldn't be here."

"How did you find me?" I glanced around the room.

"Luck! I saw you at the grocery store and followed you home." She waved the gun as she talked. "But Jim messed up."

"How did you plan to get the money? I'm not Claire."

"Brainwashing or, if that didn't work, threatening. All you have to do is convince him you're Claire and then sign over the money to me."

Every muscle in Alex's body tensed as if he was about to pounce. *What is he going to do?*

She pointed the gun at Alex. "I'm guessing you'll do just about anything to avoid seeing him hurt." Her icy glare scared me. What she said was true. I inched my way closer to the desk.

Alex shifted slightly. "Lorraine, you don't have to do this."

Her eyes widened. "How do you know my name?" She was stunned. "I can't believe my brother betrayed me! When I get my hands on him, I'll wring that grimy little neck of his."

Yelling about what she would do when she got her hands on Jim, she didn't see me lean over the desk. I shot Alex a glance and then swiped at the tall stack of files, sending them crashing to the floor.

Lorraine spun toward the desk.

Alex yelled, "Run, Kate!" as he launched himself toward the lady with the gun.

They hit the floor and wrestled for the weapon. I crouched under the desk and yanked my phone out of my pocket.

I texted Becca: *911 send help.* I jammed the phone back in my pocket.

Around the edge of the desk, I saw Alex on his back with the gun pointed at his face. *I have to do something. I can't let her hurt him.*

"You can come out from under the desk." Her cold, heartless voice made me sick.

Do something. My advantage was that I was behind her, and she didn't dare take her eyes off of Alex. "Don't hurt him. Please."

"That's entirely up to you." Her voice made me want to wretch.

"Get out of here, Kate. Run!" Alex's voice didn't even waver.

"I'm coming out." I stood up and stuck my hands in the air. "I'm walking toward you. Please don't hurt him. I beg you."

When I saw the floor lamp, I knew I had to risk it. I side-stepped slightly to be sure I could reach it.

"Hurry." She spat out the word without turning around.

"Okay." I grabbed the lamp and swung. The bulb shattered when the lamp connected with her head. The gun skittered across the floor.

Lorraine was still standing!

In a full run, I tackled her. She screamed in pain as her head hit the rug.

Alex jumped up and scrambled for the gun. "Get up, Kate. Are you hurt?"

"I think I'm okay." I hurried toward Alex and tucked behind him. "You?"

"Yeah." His chest heaved.

"What do we do?" I rubbed my arms trying to chase away the icy feeling.

Lorraine moaned.

"Hold this." He tucked the gun in my hands.

"But—" My hands shook.

Without taking his eyes off Lorraine, he stilled my hands. "Just squeeze the trigger to shoot."

"Where are you going? Please don't leave."

"Keep your eyes on her." Alex yanked the electrical cord from the base of the lamp.

Lorraine glanced at Alex's back, then up at me, an eerie grin on her face. She started to push up off the floor.

"She's getting up!" I didn't even tried to hide the panic in my voice.

Alex spun around. He pushed her back to the floor and grabbed one of her hands. She struggled, spouting profanities, but he wrangled the other hand behind her and, using the cord, tied her up. Without taking his eyes off of her, he backed toward me and took the gun from my shaky hands. "Call the police."

I nodded, determined to hold back tears. I hadn't even gotten the phone out of my pocket when Torres and Miller came barreling through the door.

"How?" Alex backed away and handed Torres the gun.

"I haven't called you yet." I hated that I sounded stupid.

"DJ called me an hour ago when he figured out that Lorraine, Jim's sister, was employed by Travis. He didn't know you were meeting with Travis." Torres waved in the other officers who arrived on the scene.

"When his wife told him you were here, he called us again. But it looks like your friend saved you." Miller grinned at me but pointed at Alex.

Alex shook his head. "No. Actually, she saved me."

I threw my arms around him, nearly knocking him over.

He pulled me tight and held my head against his chest for several minutes. "You don't listen very well. I told you to run."

April 21, 2014

Dear Claire,

Happy 30th birthday! Your dad is prepping the grill for steaks, and I am chilling a bottle of wine. I wish you were here. For dessert, I bought a Boston cream pie.

Mrs. Crawford stopped by today. She was one of Betty's longest and dearest friends and has always been kind to me. She's the only one around here that still asks about you. Everyone else smiles and waves, but they don't know what to say. She always seems to look inside me and say what I most need to hear.

I almost hesitate to write about this. The doctor gave me some bad news last month. I was diagnosed with cancer. The outlook isn't good, but I'm a fighter. I intend to stay around as long as I can. Your dad is worried. He doesn't wear his emotions on his sleeve, but if you look into his blue eyes, his heart is written there. Never seeing you and leaving him alone are thoughts too awful to contemplate. I have to beat this.

I'm sorry to say that the story doesn't have a happy ending. In fact, it has no ending. I've included the last few pages of what I wrote. At the end I added another part, an update.

I want you to know that I don't hate Scott anymore. I don't write that lightly. He's still a beast, and I can never forget what he did. My forgiveness doesn't free him of any guilt, but hopefully, it will stop bitterness from eating away my insides. Looking back, I see all the things I could have done differently. A thread runs through all of those bad choices. I was afraid. Please remember, Claire, don't let fear stop you.

Until Next Year,

Mom & Dad

Summer of '83, Part 11

Sheriff Jacoby tipped his hat before plodding down the porch steps. I watched him leave until his taillights disappeared from view. Helpless didn't begin to describe how I felt. I hated myself for trusting Scott. The thought that I might never see you again pounded nails in my heart. All hope of finding you rested on a sheriff that had never handled a kidnapping case before. After hours of answering questions, I was exhausted, but sleep eluded me. Without you, how could I sleep?

I wandered into the nursery. The empty laundry basket that had held the outfits I'd folded earlier in the day taunted me. Scott packed most of your stuff before leaving. I sat in the rocking chair and hummed the same tune I did every night.

Travis stood in the doorway and listened. When I reached the end of the song, I turned and looked into his sad blue eyes.

"It's nearly midnight and we haven't eaten since lunch. Come and eat." He stepped to the chair and offered his hand.

The strong hand that gave comfort when Scott disappeared three years ago, was little comfort now, but I took it and followed him into the kitchen.

Travis had thrown together ham and cheese sandwiches. Neither of us felt like eating, but we knew it would be a difficult few days. Eating was a must.

Travis focused on being strong for me. That was a role he knew how to play.

I stood up from the table, my eyes blanketed in a vacant haze. "I am going to lay down. I doubt I'll sleep."

"Can I stay the night? I'll stretch out on the couch."

"Yes. I'll get you a pillow and blanket."

At 9am Travis and I were sipping coffee when the FBI knocked on the door. Travis had called them. I scurried to the bedroom to change out of my robe, and Travis answered the door.

Introductions were repeated when I joined them, and the questions started again. I explained all that had happened and let Travis cut in with the story about the note. Our darkest secret, we were now repeating over and over as officers recorded it in their reports. When they asked if I had any warnings or if Scott had ever shown any signs of erratic behavior, I sobbed. Yes, he had shown erratic behavior, but it was more than two years ago. No, I didn't have any warning. While we shared stories, the agents scribbled notes. Pausing the interview to get fresh cups of coffee, the agents called into the office asking for updates. There were no reports on the truck or its passengers.

After two hours, the agents left promising to let us know of any updates.

I heard Travis on the phone letting the office know he'd be out for the next few days when I stepped into the kitchen. I opened the refrigerator and stared inside.

"If only we'd seen the note earlier … How can this be happening?" Travis slammed his fist into the wall, leaving a gaping hole. "I'm sorry, Emma. If I hadn't …"

"Claire would never have been born." I closed the refrigerator. "I'm numb, Travis. It hurts too much to hurt anymore. Maybe I should go for a run."

"I'll stay by the phone."

Ten minutes later, I was sprinting away from the house, ponytail swinging back and forth.

As I pushed the screen door open, the phone rang. Travis answered. I watched his expression. He hung up after only a minute.

"Scott and Claire haven't been spotted, but he did withdraw a large amount of cash yesterday before leaving town. He cleaned out the account."

I buried my face in my hands. "What am I going to do?"

"We'll figure it out. If they can figure out which direction he went, then they can begin a more intense search."

After a shower, I scoured the cabinets and refrigerator for the ingredients for lasagna. My clanging brought Travis to the kitchen.

"I can go pick up some food. You don't need to cook."

"I do need to cook. It'll help pass the time."

When the timer buzzed, I didn't have to call Travis to the table. He was hardly ever more than a few steps away.

Silently we ate, the chatter and laughter that marked our friendship hidden by pain. At the first blip of a ring, I ran to the phone. Scott's truck had been spotted in Albuquerque. It was parked at a bus station. One ticket agent remembered selling a ticket to a guy with a young child. He thought they headed to Phoenix.

After a week, the updates stopped, and Scott's trail had gone cold. I knew Travis needed to return to work, but he didn't want to leave me alone.

One evening over another elaborate dinner, I broached the topic. "Travis, I know you need to go back to work. And that's okay."

"Emma, I can't provide for you if I don't work, but I feel guilty leaving you."

I interlaced my fingers with his. I kissed his hand and held it close to my mouth. "I'll be okay. Thank you."

Mrs. Crawford stopped by often after that. I wondered if Travis arranged for it.

In the days and weeks that passed, we shared more than a hatred for Scott and the pain of a missing child. Knitted together through the most horrible of circumstances, our friendship deepened. But Travis kept strict boundaries. He held me when I sobbed and cursed Scott under his breath, but didn't offer comfort the way he did that night in the guest room.

That's my story, your story.

Part 12, An Update

A year after Scott left, I was granted a divorce on the grounds of abandonment. Two months after that, Travis asked me out on a date. It was cute. We saw each other almost every day as it was, but on the night of our date, he showed up with flowers. We went to a fancy restaurant.

After a few months of dating, he called and invited me for dinner. When I stepped into The Castle, I could smell the Chinese takeout. We enjoyed dinner, then he handed me a fortune cookie. The little slip of paper read *Will you marry me?*

Travis and I married, and that feeling of comfort returned. For the first time since Scott stole you away, I didn't cry myself to sleep every night. Travis couldn't chase away my grief, a grief he understood all too well, but sometimes his arms were the fortress I needed to recover from the never-ending ache.

Travis was the only one that understood why I teared up when I saw a mom with her little girl. He knew not to ask when I suddenly became quiet. I didn't need words with Travis.

CHAPTER TWENTY-FOUR

January 17, 2016 – 2:10pm

Alex hovered just outside the kitchen watching Kate as he updated DJ. "Kate is answering Torres's questions."

"When Becca told me..." DJ's voice was drowned out by the pounding in Alex's ears when Detective Torres patted Kate's shoulder and handed her a tissue.

Alex swallowed hard and looked away struggling to control the flare of jealousy. It defied reason to feel that way.

"Alex?" DJ's tone brought him back to the conversation.

Alex dropped his voice to a whisper. "I could've gotten her killed."

"You could've told me you were going."

Alex turned around giving his back to the kitchen. "I brought her thinking she would meet her—"

Torres laughed out loud. "You crack me up, Westfall."

Alex spun around. "I gotta go." He hung up before DJ could respond and started toward the table.

Torres met his stare. "Mr. Ramirez, I'm ready for you."

Kate pushed back from the table and accepted the proffered card from Torres. Alex caught her arm as she passed him on the way out of the kitchen. "You okay?"

"I will be." She squeezed his hand.

"The detective seemed amused."

"I told him I should have recognized the resemblance. With stubble, Lorraine would look like Jim's twin."

Alex slid his fingers down to her hand. "Let me give my statement, then I'll get you home."

Alex hardly took his eyes off Kate as he recounted the events and answered questions. She paced outside the kitchen while talking to Becca on the phone.

"So Kate tackled Lorraine?" The detective's question irritated Alex. Kate already answered these questions.

"Yes." Alex glanced at Torres. "Are we almost done?"

"Just about."

Alex looked back toward Kate. The color left her face. Storm clouds filled her eyes. It was as if she crawled inside herself and closed the door. She stared at something he couldn't see. When the phone slipped out of her hand and hit the floor, Alex jumped up, toppling his chair. He crossed the room and nearly crashed into a well-dressed man who looked frantic. Alex stepped aside and pulled Kate to his chest.

The man picked up the phone and handed it to Alex. "Where can I find Detective Torres?"

"In the kitchen."

The man started talking before he even crossed the threshold. "Detective Torres, I'm Travis Bentley. I just pulled up, late for a meeting, and the officers outside said to talk to you." He looked like Kate's father, maybe not as tall, but he had the same blue eyes.

Torres shook hands with Travis. "This is Kate Westfall and her friend, Alex Ramirez. They said they were here to meet with you."

"Yes. I got stuck behind a car accident and was delayed getting home. My housekeeper should've let them in. Where's Lorraine?" Travis stared at Kate.

Alex heard yelling from the phone in his hand and remembered Becca. He didn't listen to what she was saying. He only said, "Let me call you back." He looked down at Kate and panic filled him. She wasn't crying. Stone-faced, she leaned against him, her eyes glazed. He led her to the sofa. "Could I get a glass of water over here?"

When he sat her down, she grabbed a fistful of his shirt, keeping him near.

"What happened?" Travis handed him the requested water.

"I need to take her home." Alex put the glass to her lips. "Please, Kate, take a few sips."

She did as he requested, her expression unchanging.

Torres stepped up holding Kate's purse. "What can I do?"

Alex pulled his keys out of his pocket. "I need to get her in the truck." He tossed them to Torres.

"Give me a few minutes. It's blocked in." He ran out the front door.

Travis paced, fingers interlaced behind his head.

Alex sympathized with the distraught man. "She flies back to Denver tomorrow. Perhaps we can meet in the morning."

Travis stopped pacing. "I'll meet whenever. I need to know about Claire." He wiped his eyes.

"I'll text you."

Ben Torres opened the front door and pointed over his shoulder. "Truck's right by the door. The path is clear."

"Thanks." Alex walked her to the truck, keeping her pinned to his side. He lifted her in, prying her fingers from his shirt. When she made no move to buckle in, he secured her seatbelt before hurrying to the driver's seat.

"We're headed back to the cabin. Are you hungry? Want me to stop and grab food?"

She blinked slowly but didn't even turn her head to face him.

"Kate, I'm really worried. Do I need to get you to a hospital?" He reached for her hand.

She emphatically shook her head and clasped his hand.

At the cabin, still silent, Kate waited in the passenger seat until

Alex helped her out of the truck. Once inside, she stood in front of the stone fireplace, staring into the absent fire. Alex didn't have to ask what was wrong, he knew. He just didn't know what to do or say about it. "What can I do, Kate?" He didn't wipe away his tears. "Please tell me how to help you."

She turned from the ashes and buried her face in his chest. He wrapped his arms around her. After several minutes, he scooped her into his arms and sat down in the recliner. She nestled into his lap without saying a word.

After nearly an hour of sitting silently in the chair, someone knocked at the door. He shifted her to the recliner and got up. "Sit here a minute. I'll be right back."

He opened the door. Becca ran past him looking for Kate. "Is she okay?"

DJ followed carrying a bag of tacos. "We brought food."

"Alex, eat. I'll sit with her." Becca knelt by the recliner. "Kate, would you like some food?"

Kate shook her head slightly and hugged her arms around herself.

"Torres told me what happened." DJ pointed to the kitchen. "You should eat."

Alex stepped back toward the recliner. "Just hand me a taco. I want to stay next to her." He reached down, and Kate grabbed his hand. "I appreciate y'all bringing food, but she..." He shrugged and shook his head.

"We won't stay." DJ caught Becca's arm and shot her a look when she started to object. "But let us know if you need *anything*, anything at all."

Alex nodded. "Thanks."

After they left, he bolted the door. He walked back to Kate, aching at her silence. He squatted in front of the recliner. "Please, talk to me."

For the first time since she'd seen Travis, she met Alex's gaze. Fear and uncertainty pooled in her dark eyes. "What if I don't know who I am?"

The silence was easier than seeing the look in her eyes. Alex held out his hand. "Come here, Rainy. Let me hold you."

She touched his hand, and one solitary tear broke free of the pool. Holding his hand, she followed him into the bedroom. Tucked under the covers, he clutched her close against his chest as she started to cry. He didn't shush her. All the words he'd wanted to say that evening, he held inside. He kissed to top of her head, listening to her sobs, as his tears puddled on the pillow.

It was a long few hours while she cycled between tears and quiet. The whole time, she stayed snuggled to his chest. Finally, she spoke. "I'm sorry."

"For what?"

"Today. The woman with the gun. Falling to pieces. Everything."

He pressed his cheek to the top of her head. "No, Kate. No apologies."

"The way Travis was staring at me... He thinks I'm Claire."

Alex stroked her hair. "He sees the resemblance between you and Emma."

"If that were true, that would mean Judy wasn't my mom." She choked out the last word.

Alex rubbed her back and let her continue without interruption.

"It means my dad... did the unthinkable." She sat up and wiped her face. "I would feel something, know somehow that I wasn't theirs."

"How would you know?" He regretted his question almost immediately.

Anger flashed in her dark eyes. "It can't be true." She jumped off the bed and paced. "I couldn't have ... have lived my whole life with strangers ... and not know." She stopped and stared at him. "Could I?"

Alex had no idea how to respond. He opened his arms, and she crawled back onto the bed next to him. All he wanted was to help her feel better. "Do you still want to meet with Travis?"

"No ... Yes ... I don't know."

He brushed the hair out of her face and looked her in the eye. "Whatever you want, Kate. You don't have to."

"What good would it do?"

"You're good at researching genealogy. How different can it be to find someone not dead? Maybe you can help him."

She ran her finger along the veins in Alex's hand. "I'll meet with him if he can do it before I leave."

Alex turned off the bedroom light and fished his phone out of his pocket. After hours talking about Denver, national parks, Texas Aggies, and any other random topic that popped into their heads but avoiding any mention of Travis or Claire, Kate tucked into bed.

He dropped into the recliner and checked his messages.

Becca had texted an hour ago: *How's Kate?*

He tapped out a reply: *Better. She's sleeping.* Then he replied to Travis's earlier text checking on Kate: *Calmer now. Will meet. Tomorrow at 10am?*

Travis replied quickly: *Yes. I'll make arrangements and send info.*

He hadn't even laid his phone down when another message popped up. Becca wanted more information. *Has she changed her travel plans?*

No.

Before Alex shoved his phone in his pocket, she messaged again: *Have you asked her to stay?*

With all that Kate had been through, he understood her desire to go home. He couldn't ask her not to. He answered Becca: *No.* And hoped she didn't push the conversation any further. He wasn't looking forward to saying goodbye to Kate. Returning to the way things were, to his quiet, isolated existence, held no appeal. He tried to focus on the fact that she planned to move back to San Antonio, but it did little to lift his spirits.

April 20, 2015

Dearest Claire,

There won't be a birthday letter from your mom this year. I buried her today. She fought so hard. She so desperately wanted to see you again. Forgive the water drops and smeared ink. They can't be helped. I promised Emma I would find you, that I would give you Betty's letter and all the birthday letters your mom wrote over the years. I want to find you, but, Claire, I don't know how.

Wherever you are, I need your help. Help me find you. All the times I held you and bounced you around the room, I thought you were the cutest niece in the world. When I learned that you, the brightest spark in Emma's life, were my little girl, I determined to search forever to find you. I want to see my little girl.

I loved Emma, long before she married Scott. But I was busy with my plan, and I thought Scott was smitten. I stuffed my emotions and stepped aside. But when he scared her that night and broke her knick-knacks, the pain in her eyes brought all the feelings I buried up to the surface. I wanted to be there for her, to comfort her, and assure her she was not alone. We made a mess of things, but we made you. For that, I will not apologize. Emma forgave Scott before she passed away, I'm not quite there, yet.

Please, Claire, find me. I made a promise I don't know how to keep.

Love Always,

Daddy

CHAPTER TWENTY-FIVE

January 18, 2016 – 8:27am

Alex was nowhere to be found while I packed my bags. I hadn't looked in his office, but that door was closed, which was unusual. I folded the clothes that Becca bought me that first day and stuffed them into the floral bag she'd loaned me. I'd check my suitcase and use hers as a carry-on. If I had room in my suitcase for his grandmother's quilt, I would've begged him to let me take it. I turned when I heard Alex in the doorway.

His eyes were red.

"I'm almost ready."

He focused on invisible lint on the rug and kicked at it with the tip of his boot. Because his hands were buried deep in his pockets, it was hard to tell if his shoulders were tight. "What time is your flight?" He'd asked the same question earlier.

"3pm. I need to be at the airport no later than 2pm. I can call a shuttle from the restaurant if that's easier."

"No, I want to drive you." He glanced at his phone. "We need to leave here soon."

"I'm packed." I stroked Bureau as he sniffed the suitcase.

Alex slung the carry-on over his shoulder and pulled up the handle on the wheeled suitcase. I climbed into the passenger seat while he loaded both bags into the backseat. As Alex pulled away from the cabin, I hugged my purse, trying not to cry.

Travis was waiting for us when we arrived at the restaurant. He looked like he hadn't slept.

Alex extended his hand. "Good morning."

The three of us followed the hostess to a private dining room. All the other tables in the room were empty. While Travis conferred with the hostess, I whispered in Alex's ear, "I'm not sure what to say."

Travis joined us at the table, and Alex patted my hand.

"I wanted us to be able to talk privately. Order whatever you'd like. Brunch is on me." Travis unbuttoned his jacket but waited to sit down.

"You don't have to do that." Alex pulled out the chair across from Travis for me to sit down.

"I insist. It's the least I can do after all that Lorraine did." Travis pushed his menu to the side.

"I'm sorry we haven't been able to locate Claire for you." It was hard to look Travis in the eye. I wanted so much to be able to help him.

"Anyone would believe you were Claire. You're the spitting image of Emma." Sadness hung in his eyes.

"I'm sorry. I grew up in Denver with my parents, Judy and Gavin Westfall, and my sister, Meg." I felt I had to prove I was not his Claire, both to him and to myself.

The waitress ambled up to the table and asked for our orders. Once she'd written them all down and collected the menus, Travis sighed. "I know you learned Claire's story from Gram. News from Schatzenburg still reaches me. What was it you wanted to tell me about Claire?"

I clenched a napkin in my fist. "I wanted to warn you that someone was trying to trick you by finding a Claire look-a-like. But you know that now." I blinked repeatedly trying to hold myself together. "I'm not sure why I came today."

"Kate is a talented genealogist. Perhaps if you told her about what leads you've found, she could research and uncover something the others missed."

"They always told us the best leads were photos of her, but they weren't enough to bring her home." Travis's grim face relaxed a bit. "But I'm out of options and willing to let Kate try." He pulled photos out of his pocket and slid them across the table one at a time. "This is a photo of Claire with Emma."

"We saw a similar photo," Alex answered Travis, but glanced at me.

"This is a photo of Scott, Emma, and Claire taken the same day, not long before Scott left." Travis slid the photo across the table without looking up.

As soon as I saw the photo, I froze. I blinked, thinking my mind was playing tricks on me. Tears spilled down my cheeks. "Cuddle Bunny." All my determination not to even consider the idea I was Claire melted away. Growing up I'd whispered so many secrets to my treasured friend, and now he whispered to me.

Alex reached for me, and I clung to his hand. He tapped the photo. "I think you found Claire."

Hope and confusion danced in Travis's eyes. He wanted to believe it was true. I let go of Alex's hand and reached into my purse. Grabbing my phone, I opened Facebook and navigated to the family photo. I slid my phone across the table toward Travis. He instantly recognized my dad as his brother, Scott. "What about the rabbit?"

"His name was Cuddle Bunny. His initials were monogrammed on his paw." My chest heaved as I choked out the words.

"Claire Bentley? It's really you. I bought you that floppy rabbit and had your initials embroidered on it."

"He's on my bed in Denver." The levees opened. Instead of shedding a few pretty tears, I tried not to wail. Everything was upside down. "There were no pictures … of the day … I was born." Sobs interrupted my words. "Dad always said that they were so excited they forgot the camera." I soaked up my tears with the napkin in my fist.

"I snapped more than a hundred photos the day you were born."

Travis pulled two more photos from his stack and placed them on the table. "Emma was never happier than the day you were born." He laid down a photo of Emma holding a pink bundle. "And you were as beautiful then as you are now." He handed me a photo of a newborn with big, dark eyes staring into the camera.

I tried to hold back my sobs as I stared at my baby photo. My shoulders shook as I fought back the ugly cry. Alex caressed the back of my neck with his thumb.

The hostess led a courier into the room. "Mr. Bentley your delivery has arrived."

The courier handed Travis an envelope, then stuck out a clipboard for him to sign.

"Thanks." Travis set the envelope in front of him. "Kate, I hope you won't be upset with me."

I didn't respond.

"I sent your water glass to the lab and had them compare it to my cheek swab. They put a rush on it." He tapped the package. "These are the results. If you don't want to see them, I'll respect that."

Alex hugged me tighter.

"Open it." I knew what the paper would say.

Travis's hand shook as he slid out the single sheet of paper. It confirmed what I knew in my heart. Travis was my dad.

"I assume the kidnapping case is still open? What happens now?" Alex looked from me to Travis.

"I'll make some calls in a bit. I'm sure an agent will want to speak with her, but it can wait until she's ready." Travis smiled, his lashes wet from tears, and turned his gaze to me. "I have something for you." He picked up other envelopes that had been laying on the table during our meeting.

"Before Emma died, I promised her that I would find you, but I was afraid I wasn't going to be able to follow through on my promise." He handed me a large manila envelope and a small white envelope. Both had "Claire" written across the front. "My mom wrote you a letter before she died. We found it the day Scott took you. Emma kept it tucked in your baby book." He pointed at the white envelope. "And to help deal with her grief, Emma wrote to you every year on your birthday. The larger envelope has all of those letters." He wiped his eyes. "I thought today might never happen."

I hugged the envelopes to my chest. "I wish I could've met her, even just once."

Alex rubbed my back, pressing his fingertips into my shoulder blades.

"Alex said you're leaving today?"

"Yes. I have to be at the airport in a bit."

Alex's hand stopped moving at the mention of leaving. I wished I could read his thoughts. I didn't even know what I wanted to do anymore. This morning, I mostly wanted to go home to Denver, but now that wasn't home. I wanted to get to know Travis, now that I knew he was my dad, but I needed time to process all of this crazy mess.

"Can I come to Denver to see you? When will you be back? I'm don't want to push, but…" He took a deep breath. "You're my little girl, my Claire. I've searched almost thirty years."

The room started to spin as I tried to figure out what to say. I glanced up at Alex.

"How did you hear that Kate was in Schatzenburg?" Alex kept his arm around me, but wiped his eyes.

"Apparently, you took her to lunch at The Drugstore. Maggie called me. Gram called a few days after that."

"I'll delay my flight," I mumbled, unsure about my decision.

Alex and Travis stared at me, disbelief plastered on their faces. "What?" I wasn't sure who asked the question.

"I said I'd delay my flight, a day or two. It'll give us some time to…." I swallowed back tears. My eyes hurt from crying. "…to talk more."

Travis wiped his face. "Thank you, Kate. You don't know what this means to me." He glanced at Alex. "My schedule is open. Nothing is more important."

I didn't dare look at Alex. Delaying the goodbye only made it more difficult. I felt his eyes on me, waiting for me to look at him. "I want to read the letters."

"Of course." Travis glanced at his phone. "We can go to my office. It's private. You can be alone and read."

"Thank you." I picked up my purse and the letters. When I braved a look at Alex, the sheer happiness in his eyes pounded at my heart.

"Travis, text me the address, and we'll head that way." Alex grasped my hand.

Alex helped me into the passenger seat. I wanted to burrow into him and feel his arms around me. I wanted his warm hands on my face wiping my tears as he listened to me confide my inner turmoil about what we'd just heard. Instead of doing what I wanted, I buckled in. I needed thought bubbles to show up over his head.

Alex and I rode along in silence. I ached to discuss how all the pieces fit and to ask Alex if I could go home to the cabin. But I couldn't. He still dreamt about Ellie. He was wonderful in his efforts to comfort me, but I needed a two-way street. Protection wasn't the same as love.

I opened the letter from my grandmother. My vision blurred as my eyes filled again. Swiping the back of my hand across my face, I wished for a reprieve from the tears. Alex handed me a tissue, and I dabbed my eyes. The words came into focus. I read what my Grandma Betty wrote to her 2-year-old granddaughter. If I wanted to stop crying, reading the letter was not the way to do that. I managed to control my sobs and the wails escaped only as snivels. Alex looked over at me and stroked my arm. More tears.

I needed to say something. "My grandma wrote out the recipe for kolaches at the bottom. It is an old family recipe just like Dad always said."

I wanted to talk to Alex about my new past, the roots that I never knew existed, and how I could now build a family tree. For the first time in my life, I had a grandmother with a name. But like water in a glass aquarium, my deluge of tears was only held back by my silence.

His phone rang, but he made no move to answer it. I didn't offer. DJ called again, and Alex nodded at me to answer it.

"Hey, DJ. What's up?" My voice cracked a bit.

"Where are y'all? I need to talk to Alex." DJ sounded all business, and it scared me a little.

"He's driving. Want me to put you on speaker?"

"No. I need to talk to him in person. It's important."

"What's wrong, DJ?"

"I need him to meet me. Becca and I are on our way toward San Antonio now."

"Uh, well, let me tell him." I looked at Alex. "DJ needs to see you. Can we meet them somewhere?"

"I'll drop you at the office and meet him while you read the letters." He reached for my hand.

"I can go with you..."

"No, Kate. Read the letters. I'll come back."

I nearly forgot DJ was waiting on the answer. "He said he would meet you."

"I'll meet him at the gas station at the corner of Huebner and Fredericksburg."

I conveyed the information to Alex.

"I know where it is." Alex turned into the parking lot.

Travis was waiting in front.

I squeezed Alex's hand before sliding out of the truck. "I'll see you later."

"Rainy," He didn't release my hand. "I'll try to be quick. You okay?"

I nodded, then closed the door and watched as the truck pulled away. I felt less and less okay.

Travis quietly waited next to me.

I turned toward the door and clutched the envelopes to my chest.

"We can wait until he returns." Travis held open the large glass door.

I shook my head. If I couldn't read letters without him next to me, getting on a plane would be impossible. "I think I need to read them now."

When we walked through the building, it wasn't the furnishings or décor I noticed. People smiled and stepped out of the way for Travis. I struggled to remember what I'd read about him. *A businessman.* Everyone that passed greeted him, either with a nod, or a cheery "Hello, Mr. Bentley."

We joined several others on an elevator, and I sensed the questions being batted around the small space. At each floor, the elevator stopped, and one or two people disembarked. When the doors closed at the fifth floor, Travis and I were alone.

I looked at the lit up button for the seventh floor, and it dawned on me that Travis wasn't a middle tier manager. He had an office on the top floor. As these thoughts spiraled in my head, I realized I'd been quiet too long. "I don't want you to think that my silence means—"

He put his hand up. "Kate, you don't need to explain anything to me."

The doors opened at the seventh floor. Immediately, a woman clicked up to Travis. "I've cancelled all your appointments as requested."

"Thanks, Mari." He pushed open a large wooden door. "Please hold my calls."

Travis's office wasn't on the top floor. It was the top floor. A reception area took up the small space near the elevator, but his office took up almost all the rest. Walls of windows offered views of the loop and nearby neighborhoods. I stepped close to the glass. "Wow."

He smiled. "Through that door is a conference room, private kitchen, and Mari's office. Over here…" He pointed to a door on his right. "is a small sitting area if you'd like to be alone."

"I think I would."

"Can I get you something to drink?"

I shook my head and opened the door. Sun pouring through the glass walls lit the cozy room. Two sofas and a table filled the small space. I dropped my purse onto one of the couches and set the envelopes on the table.

I stared at the big envelope but wondered about Alex. DJ sounded different when we'd talked. As I pondered what he'd said, I worried something was wrong. I dug around my purse looking for my phone. Panic gripped me when I couldn't find it. *Did I leave it at the restaurant?* I emptied the contents onto the table. Still no phone. Feeling disconnected, I walked in a circle around the sofas. I stuffed my hands in my pockets, careful not to scrape my still-healing wrists. My phone was in my pocket.

I texted Becca: *Is everything okay?*

Seconds ticked by without a response. After staring at the phone for more than two minutes, I opened the envelope. White envelopes with Claire's name and a birthday year written on the front of each one poured out. I picked up the one labeled *3rd birthday* and unfolded the wrinkled pages. Huddled in the corner of a sofa, I started reading the first letter. Water stains and smeared ink said as much as the words on the page. I didn't even make it through the first letter before I started crying.

After a soft knock, the door opened. Travis held out a box of tissues. "Just in case."

Nearly an hour passed as I read. Year by year, the letters painted a picture of Emma's grief but also the glimmer of hope that I'd someday return. As I aged, the letters changed. There was so much Gram didn't know, or chose not to say.

When I read Emma's last letter, I sobbed. Her words of advice bounced around in my head. I dropped the letters to the table. I feared Alex couldn't move on. That fear stopped me from telling him how I felt, from staying.

Then I noticed there was one last letter. I picked it up and read the words slowly, stopping to catch my breath between sobs. Nothing could have prepared me for Travis's letter.

When I opened the door, Travis sprang out of his office chair. Like a child, I ran and threw my arms around his neck. He hugged me, and I bawled into his jacket. The letters introduced me to a man who'd loved Emma immensely and spent years hunting for me. He didn't quite feel like a stranger anymore.

Tears that were no longer bitter slipped down his cheeks. "I wish Emma could have seen you. She would be so delighted with how you've turned out."

"I wish I could've met her."

"She'd have liked Alex, too."

I stared at him.

Travis continued, seemingly unfazed by my gaping expression. "Whenever you're ready, we'll meet with the attorney about the inheritance."

"You don't have to ..." I hadn't met him for the money, and it was downright weird even thinking about inheritance when I'd just learned Emma was my mom.

"It was what Emma wanted." He dried his tears with his jacket sleeve.

My phone beeped a text notification. "Let me check that. I'm concerned about Alex."

Becca texted: *He'll be okay, I think.*

What did that mean? I texted her back: *Call me.*

My phone rang almost immediately. "Hang on a second." I hugged Travis again before closing myself in the cozy room.

CHAPTER TWENTY-SIX

January 18, 2016 – 2:38pm

Alex parked next to Becca's car outside the gas station. He jumped out, irritated that DJ had pulled him away from Kate as she learned more about her new identity. "What's going on? Kate found Claire, by the way."

"Sorry to pull you away." DJ snapped his head around to look at Alex. "She found Claire?"

"She *is* Claire."

DJ ran his fingers through his hair. "I need to talk to you about Ellie. Want to talk in the truck?"

"That's why we're right by the cemetery."

"I thought maybe…"

"Tell Becca we'll be back." Alex climbed into the driver's seat. Whatever it was DJ had to tell him, he preferred to hear it in the cemetery rather than across the street.

DJ gave Becca a quick kiss, then got into the passenger seat. "We—"

"Not yet." Alex drove across the intersection and pulled into the tree-shaded cemetery. He slid out of the truck and stood with his hands in his pockets staring at the nearby gravestones. "Why now?" He looked back at DJ.

He couldn't imagine what DJ wanted to tell him, but being here fueled the guilt he thought he'd tamed. He filed along next to the markers until he reached Ellie's headstone. Crouched in front of it, he pulled weeds away from the base. "I miss you, Ellie. I'm sorry I wasn't there to protect you when you needed me."

Thoughts of Kate pulled at his heart. "Never in a million years did I think I could feel this way about anyone but you." He closed his eyes. "Please forgive me."

The truck door closed, but Alex stared at the epitaph. *Beloved Wife.*

DJ trudged toward him. "Alex?" his voice wavered.

Alex stood up and wiped his eyes. "What's so important?"

"We closed Ellie's case."

"What? How?" Alex stared at Ellie's headstone. "Who?"

"Jim Smitty. He had her rings and several others stashed in his closet. I'm guessing he didn't pawn them because of the engravings. I don't know why he kept them. Other physical evidence matched as well."

"Jim Smitty? Really?"

"Strange, isn't it? Kate shows up at your cabin, and that ends up solving Ellie's case."

"When did you find out?"

"I knew about the rings the day we searched his house in town, but I didn't want to risk saying anything until the results came back on the physical evidence. I got those today."

Alex knelt down and ran his finger along the engraving. "Ellie, they finally found out who killed you. It was the same man that tried to hurt Kate. He's dead now."

DJ walked toward the truck.

Alex wept. His guilt, like a plaster cast chiseled away, fell to the grass in chunks. "I thought my happiness died with you, but Kate helped me find it again." He stood up and paced by the headstone.

DJ strode back toward Alex. "You okay?"

He nodded. "I need Kate. I mean, I need to go get her." He took a few steps toward the truck, then stopped. "Can you give me a second?"

DJ climbed into the truck.

Alex knelt down again. "Goodbye, Ellie." He tapped the top of the headstone before striding away. He left the cemetery without the baggage of guilt he'd carried as penance.

In the truck, DJ checked his phone. "Can I ride with you? Becca had something come up."

Caught in traffic, Alex tapped the steering wheel waiting for the cars in front of him to inch forward. "At this rate, it'll take us an hour to get there."

"Highway construction. Lanes are closed."

"If you knew that, why did you insist I take the interstate?"

"I didn't think it would be this bad."

Alex shook his head and shot DJ an exasperated look.

Thirty-eight minutes later, Alex parked outside Travis's building. "You coming in?"

"I'll wait here. Weather's nice. No hurry." DJ lowered his window.

Alex hurried inside and walked directly to the reception desk. "I'm here to see Travis Bentley."

The woman behind the desk picked up the phone. "Mari, I have a gentleman here to see Mr. Bentley. ... Oh, I see. ... I'll tell him." She put down the receiver. "I'm sorry. He's not available."

"But—. Nevermind. I'll call him myself." Alex dialed Travis on his cell phone and paced near the elevators, waiting for him to answer.

"Alex?"

"Hey, I'm here. How's Kate?"

"She, uh—. Come up to the seventh floor."

Something in Travis's voice set off alarm bells. Alex stepped onto the open elevator and pushed the button for the seventh floor. No one else got on, which meant his trip to the top would be quick.

Travis met him at the elevator. "Let's talk in my office."

Alex followed him through the double doors and scanned the large office. "Where's Kate?"

Travis looked Alex in the eye. "I thought she was with you."

The doors shut behind them with a loud clunk, which sounded like Alex's heart landing near his feet. He breathed in deep, trying not to panic or lose his temper. "She's not." He walked to the window. "Tell me what happened."

"She texted, then someone called her. She took the call in the other room, then a short while later, she left." Travis rubbed his face. "I thought you picked her up."

"You didn't walk her down?" Alex caught himself before rubbing his chin.

Travis shook his head. "I was on the phone with the FBI. I started to hang up, but she told me not to." He laced his fingers behind his head and paced. "Alex, I'm sorry."

Alex nodded. The worry in Travis's face made it impossible to be angry with him, not that he'd done anything wrong. "I'm sure everything's fine." Alex wanted to believe that. "I'll let you know when I find her."

Alex climbed into the truck. "DJ, where's Becca?"

"Not sure. She said she had to do something."

"Kate's not here. Someone picked her up. I bet it was Becca."

Alex texted her: *Kate with you?*

He rubbed his chin. "What if she left?" He glanced into the backseat. "But I still have her luggage."

"I thought she was leaving today."

"She was, but changed her mind."

"She's staying?"

"Not like that. She was going to delay her flight a few days." He stared at his phone. "Why hasn't Becca responded?"

"Maybe she's driving."

Alex slammed his fist on the steering wheel. The phone beeped a notification. He stared at Becca's respose: *Not anymore. She wanted to go home.*

Alex's fingers flew across the screen: *Where is she?*

Becca replied: *Go home. She'll talk to you in a bit.*

Alex tossed his phone into the cup holder and, without a word, pulled on his seatbelt. He avoiding DJ's questioning look as he started the truck and backed out of the parking space. He drove toward the cabin.

DJ waited until they were past the town of Comfort before he spoke. "Claire, huh? How did she take the news?"

"Not now." Alex didn't feel like talking.

DJ glanced at his phone. "Want to come have a late lunch with Becca and me?"

"It'll be best for everyone if I'm not around Becca right now."

"She's Kate's friend. If Kate wanted to go home..."

Alex shook his head. "She wouldn't, not without saying good-bye."

"I don't know what to tell you." DJ looked out the passenger window.

As they approached the Kerrville exit, DJ texted furiously. "Mind dropping me by the house?"

"Fine." Alex sighed, then broke into a smile. "I'll go to Denver."

"What?"

"Will you watch Bureau?"

"Sure. When?"

"I'm going to pack a bag, then head to the airport."

"Today?"

"Am I crazy, DJ?"

"That's a hard question." DJ held up his hand. "Joking aside. I'm not sure I'm one to criticize."

"What happened to being worried about me?"

"Since Kate showed up, I've seen glimpses of the Alex I knew years ago. Hard to ignore that."

"I thought I'd be okay with her leaving, knowing she'd come back. But, I'm not."

"Tell her, not me."

Alex stopped in front of DJ's house. Becca's car was in the driveway. "Tell Becca not to say anything to Kate. I want to surprise her."

"Want to tell her yourself?"

"Still mad."

Alex parked in front of the cabin. Before getting out of the truck, he reached behind his seat and smiled when he felt the paper sack. He tucked it under his arm.

His keyring clattered to the ground as he tried to unlock the front door. Bureau jumped onto the window sill. Alex picked up the keys and, after two more tries, succeeded. He pushed open the door.

Dressed in his Aggie sweatshirt and yoga pants, Kate gave a little wave. Warm brown eyes smiled from under dark, wet lashes. Brown curls hung loose around her face. Her lips parted, but Alex didn't wait for her to speak.

He pulled her into his arms and kicked the door closed. "You didn't leave." He could've lit a small city with his smile. He was swimming in a happiness he hadn't felt in years.

"Leave?" She lifted her head off his chest and shot him a puzzled look.

"When Travis said you'd left…"

"I was worried about you. I didn't know where you were. Didn't you talk to Becca?"

"Not exactly. She— Wait! Becca knew where I was."

"She didn't tell you I was waiting for you at home?"

"I thought you were on a plane to Denver." He hugged her close and buried his face in her hair. "Why didn't you just wait for me?"

Kate rested her head against his chest. "I wanted to talk to you. Becca told me you'd meet me here." She wiped her face. "I never would've left without…"

He fumed at Becca's meddling but smiled down at Kate. "How did things go at Travis's office?"

"I read the letters from my mom. And that's why I wanted to talk to you." She looked up at him.

Alex kissed the spot just above her temple where little hairs refused to lay flat. "I'm listening."

Her eyes widened, and she looked at him, surprise and delight swirling in her brown eyes.

Since kisses distracted her, he restrained himself from planting them along her forehead and down her cheek. He waited.

She looked down at her hands. "Emma, *Mom*, included words of advice. The kinds of things she would have told me if … if I hadn't been taken away from her." Kate avoided eye contact as she spoke. She pushed back the cuticles on her thumbnail, her hands shaking.

Alex lifted her chin so she gazed into his eyes. "What was the advice?"

"Don't let fear stop you." Her eyes misted.

Still cradling her chin, he brushed his thumb across her lips. "What are you afraid of, Kate?"

"Afraid of saying what I really want and afraid it's something you can't give." Tears spilled out of her eyes as she blinked.

"What do you really want?" He tucked a strand of hair behind her ear.

She stared at the buttons on his Henley shirt. After a deep breath, she answered in barely a whisper. "I want you to *want* me to stay. But I'm afraid you can't let—"

He picked up the bag that'd fallen to the floor. "Open this." He pushed it toward her.

"But—"

"Kate, please. Just look at what I bought you."

She opened the crinkled sack and pulled out his gift. "You got me a tee shirt?" Disappointment and confusion registered on her face.

"Read it."

She unfolded the shirt and held it out in front of her. She could have read *Somebody in Texas loves me* twenty times in the time it took her to look up from the shirt. She ran her fingers over the large, red heart substituted for the word love. Tears puddled in her happy eyes. "Really?"

He wrapped his arms around her. "Don't sound so surprised. I wanted to say all this last night, but..." He kissed her on the top of the head. "...it wasn't the right time. Besides, I thought I sent clear signals. I mean, I don't go around hugging *every* woman that knocks at my door."

"I convinced myself you were only acting as my bodyguard."

He pulled her closer, nearly crushing her against him. "I want to do more than protect you."

"But your walls..."

"What walls?" He acted surprised. "Kate, I spent years stuffing emotions, avoiding feelings. But with you, I feel."

She ran her finger down the cleft in his chin.

"And you do things like that." He nuzzled her neck.

She draped the tee shirt over her shoulder and rested her forehead against his chin. "What else did you want to say last night?"

He whispered in her ear. "I hoped we'd spend some time not talking." He danced his eyebrows.

Her cheeks colored in a warm pink, but she grinned.

"I want you here, but if you need to go home to Denver, I'd like to go with you."

She gazed up at him, an inviting look playing in her eyes. "I did want to go…"

He leaned down and dropped kisses along the curve of her neck. She inhaled and snuggled her body closer.

"But…?" he breathed in her ear before nibbling on the lobe.

"But that's not home anymore." She tilted her head back as he danced his lips around to the other side. "You feel like home."

"I've wanted to do this for days." He brushed his lips along her jaw, making his way to her mouth. He pressed his lips to hers, and she relaxed into his arms just like she did the night at the restaurant.

She moaned softly and combed her fingers through his hair. His phone rang, vibrating in his pocket, but he ignored it.

When he let her catch her breath, she asked, her voice near a whisper, "Why did you wait?"

"I didn't." He grinned as he leaned in for another kiss.

She pulled back and stared at him with feigned irritation.

He chuckled, then folded her back into his arms.

When their cell phones rang in tandem for the third time, Kate laughed. "DJ and Becca, you think?"

"I don't want to talk to them." Alex winked and trailed his hands up and down her back. "I can't believe you thought I didn't want you to stay."

"I just assumed… Then Travis said that Emma would've liked you."

"Oh! Travis!" Alex pulled out his phone and texted: *I found her.*

ABOUT THE AUTHOR

Pamela Humphrey in the author of *Researching Ramirez: On the Trail of the Jesus Ramirez Family* and *The Blue Rebozo*. She is an amateur genealogist and researchers of family stories. When she is not searching records for traces of the past, she might be writing, reading, crafting, homeschooling, or practicing on her bass guitar. She lives in San Antonio, Texas, with her husband, sons, black cats, and leopard gecko.

CONNECT WITH ME ONLINE

Website www.phreypress.com
Facebook: http://www.facebook.com/phreypress
Twitter: @phreypress

Thank you for reading!
Would you like to read more about Alex and Kate? Subscribe
to my newsletter for updates about the next book in the series.
And if you'd like to read more about DJ and Becca, check out
The Wrong Path, a short story.

Made in the USA
Lexington, KY
12 December 2016